THE CRIME CLUB

STORIES OF CRIME BY

FRANK FROËST

AND

GEORGE DILNOT

WITH AN INTRODUCTION BY

DAVID BRAWN

COLLINS
CRIME
CLUB

COLLINS CRIME CLUB
An imprint of HarperCollins*Publishers*
1 London Bridge Street
London SE1 9GF
www.harpercollins.co.uk

This edition 2016

2

First published in Great Britain by Eveleigh Nash 1915
Published by The Detective Story Club Ltd
for Wm Collins Sons & Co. Ltd 1929

A catalogue record for this book is
available from the British Library

ISBN 978-0-00-813733-5

Typeset in Bulmer MT Std by Palimpsest Book Production Ltd,
Falkirk, Stirlingshire

Printed and bound in Great Britain by
Clays Ltd, St Ives plc

INTRODUCTION

When *The Crime Club* was first published by Eveleigh Nash in 1915, little did the authors—both of them ex-policemen—know that the book's title would become synonymous with detective publishing for the next 100 years.

Frank Froëst had risen through the ranks of the Metropolitan Police, attaining the position of Superintendent of the CID in 1906. He had become famous for his involvement in a number of high-profile international incidents, including the mass arrest in South Africa of more than 400 of the Jameson Raiders in 1896—the biggest mass arrest in British history—and for bringing high-profile villains such as society jewel-thief 'Harry the Valet' and the notorious Dr Crippen to justice. (More of Froëst's exploits are discussed in Tony Medawar's introduction to *The Grell Mystery*, also in this series.) Froëst retired in 1912, moving to Somerset where he joined the County Council and became a magistrate. Putting his 33-year experience in the police service to good use, he also turned to writing, and his detective novel *The Grell Mystery* (1913) proved popular with readers, who felt that its author was giving them an authentic insight into the detail of real police work—a genre that would become referred to as the 'police procedural'.

Speculation that Froëst had help from a professional writer to produce a debut novel as fine as *The Grell Mystery* is given some credence by his sharing the byline on his two subsequent books with writer George Dilnot. Turning to journalism after six years in the army and subsequent service in the police, Dilnot's first major book, *Scotland Yard: The Methods and Organisation of the Metropolitan Police* (1915), owed a great deal for its detailed content to the recently retired Froëst. The book was one of the earliest attempts to make public the inside workings of 'the finest police force in the world', which at that time employed 20,000, and must have been an invaluable resource for early detective writers. Froëst himself is name-checked numerous times, and comes across as the epitome of determination, organisation and innovation.

Whether or not Dilnot did ghost-write *The Grell Mystery* as a favour to his former boss, by the time Froëst's other detective novel was published, *The Rogues' Syndicate* (1916), they were sharing equal billing. First serialised in the US as *The Maelstrom* in the magazine *All-Story Weekly* over six weeks in March and April 1916, the book marked the end of Froëst's short writing career, although his name lived on in reprints and in silent movies of both *The Grell Mystery* and *The Rogues' Syndicate* in 1917, the latter film retaining its magazine title of *The Maelstrom*.

In between the two novels came *The Crime Club*, a collection of eleven detective stories (plus a prefatory chapter) that had originally appeared in the monthly *The Red Book Magazine* between December 1914 and November 1915. The stories were linked by the conceit of a secret London club located off the Strand where international crime fighters would go to help solve and also share tales of their most outlandish cases. Although the idea of a fictional detectives' club was not entirely new, previous instances—for example Carolyn Wells' five stories about the International Society of Infallible Detectives, starting with 'The Adventure of the Mona Lisa' in January 1912—brought together pastiches of well-known sleuths such as Sherlock Holmes and Arsène Lupin, whereas *The Crime Club* featured all-new creations, with the exception of Froëst's own Heldon Foyle from *The Grell Mystery*, who appeared in 'The String of Pearls'.

The stories were collected and published in book form as *The Crime Club* by Eveleigh Nash in 1915, apparently before their run in *The Red Book Magazine* had ended. In 1929, keen to have a book of short stories in the initial run of their new sixpenny Detective Story Club series, William Collins licensed the rights from Nash to print a cheap edition of the book, which was published in July 1929; *The Grell Mystery* and *The Rogues' Syndicate* would follow within a year. Like many of the other early books in that series, *The Crime Club* also appeared in Collins' 'Piccadilly Novels' imprint as an exclusive edition for Boots Pure Drug Co. Ltd (who also sold books), using the same typesetting and with the painting from the back of the Detective Story Club jacket transposed to the front.

Frank Froëst gave up writing in 1916 when his wife died, focusing on council work until the onset of blindness forced him into retirement and a convalescent home in Weston-super-Mare, where he died in 1930 at the age of 71. However, his association with George Dilnot continued, helping him to research his landmark book, *The Story of Scotland Yard* (1927), a completely new and expanded version of his first book. Dilnot continued to write about the police and true crime, including two volumes in Geoffrey Bles's *Famous Trials* series, on which he was Series Editor, and revisited the subject of the Yard again with *New Scotland Yard* in 1938. But he was much more prolific in fiction, writing another 16 novels under his own name, with series characters including Jim Strang, Horace Elver, Val Emery and Inspector Strickland, plus three books for the popular *Sexton Blake* series.

When the reissue of *The Crime Club* came out in 1929, George Dilnot was therefore still very active and by then better known to readers than Frank Froëst. The book enjoyed a new lease of life, and within a year there were 19 titles in the Detective Story Club series. One of the secrets of its success, like so many cheap editions being published at that time, was their availability in newsagents and tobacconists as well as traditional bookshops (many of whom frowned upon the concept of cheap editions and would not stock them). Their success convinced Collins to chase more sales from this market by launching its own monthly magazine, and in June 1930

'The Detective Story Club Limited' published a bold offshoot: *Hush Magazine.*

Like the book series that inspired it, *Hush* (the word *Magazine* being added to its title from issue No. 3) sold for just sixpence and sported brightly coloured covers, usually featuring the clichéd dame in distress, and contained in its 128 pages a mixture of fiction stories and non-fiction articles, some with new line drawings, and a small amount of advertising. The covers proudly proclaimed that the monthly magazine was 'Edited by Edgar Wallace', and indeed every issue began with a Wallace story—and usually a page advertising his new Collins book *The Terror* and/or *The Educated Man*. But like the more famous and longer-running *Edgar Wallace Mystery Magazine* that began in 1964, Wallace was not involved; the compilation and editing was by an uncredited George Dilnot. He adapted his own *The Story of Scotland Yard*, serialised every month from issue No. 3, and recycled some of his stories from *The Red Book Magazine*, interestingly dropping Frank Froëst's name from them.

Hush Magazine ceased publication after only a year with No. 13 dated June 1931. There was no indication inside that it would be the last, with two 'Next Month . . .' adverts appearing in its pages. Collins was not a magazine publisher, and either the effort of compiling a varied and illustrated monthly collection of stories had got too much for them, or the circulation figures simply dropped below a sustainable level. Over its run, however, George Dilnot and the team had assembled a respectable if increasingly predictable mix of content, with regular reprints of fiction stories by stalwarts including J. S. Fletcher, Arthur B. Reeve, Sydney Horler, H. de Vere Stacpoole, Maurice Leblanc, G. D. H. & M. Cole, Edgar Allan Poe and even H. G. Wells. The most notable inclusion was a run of five Miss Marple stories by Agatha Christie beginning in November 1930, the month following the character's very first book appearance in *The Murder at the Vicarage*, and which would not themselves appear in a book until *The Thirteen Problems* in June 1932. The publication of one-off detective stories by unknown authors in amongst these popular names provided some interesting reading, but this aspect of the magazine was soon curtailed as it was presumably the well-known names, emblazoned on the covers, who guaranteed sales.

Undaunted after a year on the magazine, George Dilnot returned to writing novels with *The Thousandth Case* (1932), averaging a book a year throughout the 1930s. His final novel was a Nazi war thriller, *Counter-Spy*, published by Geoffrey Bles in 1942. At almost 60 years old, Dilnot appears like Frank Froëst to have decided to stop writing ahead of retirement, and died nearly a decade later on 23 February 1951 in East Molesey in Surrey, aged 68.

Of all their books, *The Crime Club* is probably the least well remembered of any by Froëst or Dilnot, such is the fate of collections of short stories in most writers' careers. Largely typical of detective stories of their era, the most interesting now is 'The Red-Haired Pickpocket' (from *The Red Book Magazine*, February 1915) as a rare example of a plot being 'borrowed' by Sir Arthur Conan Doyle. The solution to 'The Problem of Thor Bridge', published in *The Strand Magazine* in two parts in February and March 1922, and collected in *The Case-Book of Sherlock Holmes*, is so similar, even down to the small mark on the side of the bridge, that it doesn't need Sherlock Holmes to deduce that Conan Doyle must have read the Froëst and Dilnot story.

In addition to the dozen stories that comprised *The Crime Club*, the pair collaborated to write three more in the same vein also for *The Red Book Magazine*: 'Crossed Trails', 'The Dagger' and 'Found—A Pearl' appeared in the February, August and September issues of 1916. One hundred years later, they are reprinted here for the first time in book form.

If the stories were forgotten, at least their collective title was to live on in another Collins publishing initiative even more ambitious than *Hush Magazine*—and one with decidedly more success. On 6 May 1930 Philip MacDonald's detective novel *The Noose* was the first of the monthly 'Recommended' titles to be published by a brand new imprint—the Crime Club. But that is another story.

David Brawn
March 2016

CONTENTS

I.	THE CRIME CLUB	1
II.	THE RED-HAIRED PICKPOCKET	3
III.	THE MAN WITH THE PALE-BLUE EYES	21
IV.	THE MAKER OF DIAMONDS	40
V.	CREEPING JIMMIE	57
VI.	THE MAYOR'S DAUGHTER	77
VII.	A MEETING OF GREEKS	94
VIII.	THE SEVEN OF HEARTS	115
IX.	THE GOAT	133
X.	PINK-EDGED NOTEPAPER	150
XI.	THE STRING OF PEARLS	168
XII.	THE 'CON' MAN	182
XIII.	CROSSED TRAILS	201
XIV.	THE DAGGER	216
XV.	FOUND—A PEARL	236

I

THE CRIME CLUB

You will seek in vain, in any book of reference, for the name of the Crime Club. Purists may find a reason in the fact that a club without subscriptions, officials, or headed notepaper is no club at all. The real explanation probably is that the club avoids advertisement. It is content to know that even in its obscurity it is the most exclusive club in the world.

No member is ever elected; no member ever resigns. Yet the wrong man is never admitted, the right man rarely excluded. Its members are confined not only to one profession but to the picked men even of that profession. Its headquarters is as unostentatious as its existence—a little hotel handy to the Strand wherein some years ago Forrester and Blake of the Criminal Investigation Department had discovered a discreet manager, a capable chef, and a back dining-room.

The progress of time, and the tact of the manager, had conceded a sitting-room with a dozen or so big and deep arm-chairs. From noon onwards, the two apartments had become sacred to the Crime Club.

Quiet, comfortable-looking men dropped in for luncheon or dinner and a chat that was as likely to cover gardening or politics as murder or burglary. Perhaps the only trait that they showed in common was some indefinable trick of humour that lurked in their faces. An experienced detective has seen too much to take himself too seriously.

The rank and file of the world's detective services have no entrée to the Crime Club. Only men whose repute is beyond suspicion are among its members. Strictly, it is an international club, for although its most determined frequenters are a dozen

Scotland Yard men, there is always a sprinkling of detectives from abroad to be found there. You may see perhaps a thin, hawk-faced Pinkerton man grimly chaffing an excitable, black-bearded little Italian, none other than the redoubtable Cipriano of the Italian Secret Service. In the group about the fire are Kuntze of Berlin—a stolid, bovine-faced man whose looks belie the subtlety of a tempered brain; Heldon Foyle, the tall, urbane superintendent of the Criminal Investigation Department; a jolly-faced, fat officer from the Central Office in New York; the slim-built, grey-moustached commissioner of a great overseas police force—himself an old Scotland Yard hand; a spruce-ly-dressed Frenchman from the Service de Sûreté; a provincial chief constable; a private inquiry agent so fastidious about the selection of his clients that he is making only a couple of thousand a year instead of the five thousand that could be his if he did not object to dirty hands; and a couple of chief inspectors from the Yard.

Search the newspaper files of the world and you will here and there get a hint of remarkable things done by these men—of supreme feats of organisation in pursuit, of subtleties in unveiling mysteries, of bulldog courage and tenacity, of quick-witted resource in emergencies. You will not find all the truth there because there are sometimes happenings of which it is not well all the truth should be known; but you will gather much from the manner of men they are.

Sometimes, over coffee and cigars, the talk may drift to some of the affairs of the profession. Some of these find a place in the present chronicles.

II

THE RED-HAIRED PICKPOCKET

JIMMIE ILES was 'some dip'. That was how he would have put it himself. In the archives of the New York Central Detective Bureau the description was less concise, but even more plain: 'James (Jimmie) Iles, *alias* Red Jimmie, *alias*, etc . . . expert pickpocket . . .'

And Red Jimmie, whose hair was flame coloured and whose indomitable smile flashed from ear to ear on the slightest provocation, would have been lacking in the vanity of the underworld if he had not been proud of his reputation at Mulberry Street. Nevertheless, fame has its disadvantages, and though he was on friendly terms with the headquarters staff individually, he hated the system that had of late prevented his applying his undoubted talents to full profit.

England beckoned him—England, where he could make a fresh start with the past all put behind him. Do not make a mistake: Jimmie had no intention of reform. But in England there were no records, and consequently the police would not be allowed points in the game. It would be hard, therefore, if an energetic, painstaking man could not pick up enough to keep him in bread and butter.

Behold Jimmie, therefore, a first-class passenger on the S.S. *Fortunia*—'Mr James Strickland' on the passenger list—a suit in the Renaissance style of architecture built about him, the skirts of his coat descending well towards his knees, his peg-top trousers roomy and with a cast-iron crease. Behold him explaining for the fiftieth time to one of his sometime 'stalls' the reason that had driven him from God's own country.

'I'm too good-natured. That's what's the matter with me.

The bulls are right on to me. If I carried a gun or hit one of 'em, like Dutch Fred, I might get away with it sometimes. But I can't do it. They're good boys, though they've got into a kind of habit of pulling me whenever they're feeling lonely. I can't go anywhere without a fourt' of July procession of sleuths taggin' after me— Holy Moses, there's one there now. How do you do, Mr Murray? Say, shall we find if there's a saloon?'

Detective-Sergeant Murray grinned affably. 'Not for mine, Jimmie old lad. I've got that kind of lonesome feeling. Won't you see me home?'

Jimmie thrilled with a tremor of familiar apprehension. 'Honest to Gawd, I ain't done a thing,' he declared earnestly. 'You're only jollying, Mr Murray?'

The officer laughed and vanished. Jimmie decided to make himself inconspicuous till the vessel sailed. Luckily for his peace of mind, he did not know that the Central Office was paying him the compliment of a special cable in order that he might receive proper attention when he landed.

Jimmie was 'good' on board, though more than once he was tempted. It was not till he was on the boat-train from Liverpool to London that he fell. There was only one fellow-passenger in the compartment with him—a burly, prosperous man of middle age whom Jimmie knew from ship-board gossip to be one Sweeney, partner in a Detroit firm of hardware merchants. There was a comfortable bulge in his right-hand breast pocket—a bulge that made Jimmie's mouth water. He had no fear but that he could reduce that swelling when he chose. The only trouble was 'the getaway'. He had no 'stalls' to whom to pass the booty. He would have to lift the pocket-book as they got out at Euston if he did it at all. It was too risky to chance it before.

Five minutes before the train drew in at Euston, Sweeney began to collect his hand baggage. He patted his breast pocket to make sure that the pocket-book was still there. Jimmie felt pleased that he had restrained himself. He brushed by Sweeney as the train drew up, and as he passed on to the platform he knew the exultation of the artist in a finished piece of work. The pocket-book was in his possession.

Not until he had reached his hotel, and was safe in the seclusion of his own room did he examine the prize—having first ordered a fire in view of eventualities. There was a bunch of greenbacks and English notes totalling up to forty pounds—not a bad haul. Also there were a score or so of letters. Jimmie dropped the pocket-book itself on the fire, and raked the coals round it. Then he settled himself to read the correspondence before consigning it to the flames. Waste not, want not; and although Jimmie held rigidly to the line of business in which he was so adept, he was not averse to profiting from the by-products. One never knew what information might be in a letter. Jimmie had more than once gained a hint which, passed on to the right quarters, had earned him a 'rake off' from a robbery that was decidedly acceptable.

There seemed, however, nothing of that kind here. The letters were merely ordinary business jargon on commonplaces of commerce, and half a dozen or so introductions which a business man visiting Europe might be expected to carry. One by one the flames consumed them. Then he came to the last one and hitched his shoulders as he read. It had been printed by pencil, evidently at some trouble.

> 'DEAR SWEENEY,—We are not going to be played with any longer. If you are in earnest you will come over and see us. The *Fortunia* sails on the seventeenth. The evening following her arrival, one of us will wait for you between ten and twelve at the Albert Suspension Bridge, Battersea. You will make up your mind to come if you are wise. We can then settle matters.—O. J.'

A man may be a pickpocket and retain a certain amount of human nature. A crook who is in business for profit rarely has opportunities to consider romance. If there is anything in the nature of a show, he usually plays the part of the foiled villain. So if he has a taste that way he indulges in fiction, the theatre, or the cinema, so that he can safely gratify his natural sympathies on the side of virtue. Jimmie was fond of the cinema. Often he had been so engrossed by the hair-raising exploits of a detective that he had totally neglected the natural facilities afforded by darkness and entertainment.

Now, however, he was suddenly plunged into an affair that promised real life melodrama. The printed characters, the mysterious appointment late at night, the ambiguous threat, were something for his imagination to gloat over. His fertile brain wove fancies of the Black Hand, the Mafia, and kindred blackmailing societies which the Sunday editions of the New York papers had painted crimson in his mind. He thrust the letter into the fire, and went out in search of one Four-fingered Foster, sometime an associate of his in New York, now established in a snug little business 'bunco steering' in London. Foster had been notified in advance of his coming.

He found his four-fingered friend established under the rôle of an insurance agent at a Brixton boarding-house, and Foster was willing and anxious to show the friend of his youth the town. So thoroughly indeed did they celebrate the reunion that ten o'clock had gone before Jimmie recalled the note. He swallowed the remnants of some poisonous decoction while they lounged before the tall counter of an American bar near Leicester Square.

'Say, Ted,' he remarked, his pronunciation extremely painstaking. 'Where's Albert Bridge?'

'Search me,' answered his friend. 'Who is he? What's your notion?'

'It's a place,' exclaimed Jimmie. 'I gotta get there. Got a—hic—'pointment.'

'We'll go get a cab,' said Foster, staggering away from the bar. 'Taxi driver sure to know.'

Jimmie grabbed him by the lapel of his coat. By this time he had made up his mind that the Black Hand had got its clutches on the prosperous Sweeney, and he had a fancy that he might play the part of hero in the melodrama. Friendship was all very well, but it could be stretched too far.

''Scuse me, Ted.' He rolled a little and steadied himself with one hand on the bar counter. 'Most particular—private—hic—'pointment.'

'Aw—if it's a skirt—' Foster was contemptuous.

Jimmie did not enlighten him. His wits never entirely deserted him. He moved uncertainly to the door, explained his need to the uniformed door-keeper, and soon was flying south-west in a neat green taxi.

The driver had to rouse him when he reached his destination. Jimmie paid him off and began to walk under the giant tentacles of the suspension bridge, his blue eyes roving restlessly about. It was very lonely. He passed a policeman, and then a stout man came sauntering aimlessly along. Sweeney did not seem to recognise Jimmie, and Jimmie did not wish to attract his attention yet. Apparently the Black Hand emissary—Jimmie was sure it was the Black Hand—had not yet turned up. Out of the corner of his eyes he saw Sweeney standing absently near the iron rail gazing down on the swirling, blackened waters beneath. The pickpocket passed on.

He had gone a dozen paces when a thud as of a heavy hammer falling upon wood brought him about with a jerk. He had recognised the unmistakable report of an automatic pistol. Into his line of sight came a vision of Sweeney, no longer on the pavement, but in the centre of the roadway. He was on his knees, and while Jimmie ran, he fell forward. There was no sign of an assailant.

Jimmie knelt and raised the fallen man till the body was supported by his knee. There was a thin trickle of blood from the temple—such a trickle as might be caused by a superficial surface cut. The American loosened the dead man's collar.

It had all happened in a few seconds, and even while he was trying to discover if there was life remaining in the limp body, the constable he had passed came running up. 'What's wrong here?' he demanded.

Jimmie, satisfied that the man was dead, laid the body back gently, and brushed the dust from his trouser-knees as he stood up. 'This guy's been shot,' he said. 'The sport that did it can't have got far. He must have been hiding behind one of the bridge supports.'

The constable placed a whistle to his mouth in swift summons. Then he in turn knelt and examined the dead man. Jimmie stood by, his hands thrust deep in his pockets, his eyes searching every shadow where an assassin might still be in hiding.

The deserted bridge had suddenly become alive. In the magical fashion in which a crowd springs up in places seemingly isolated, scores of people were concentrating on the spot. Among them were dotted the blue uniforms of half a dozen policemen.

Jimmie had given up any idea of being a hero, but he still saw the tragedy with the glamour of melodrama. He watched with interest the effective way in which the police handled the emergency. A sergeant exchanged a few swift words with the original constable, and then took charge. The crowd was swept back for fifty yards on each side of the murdered man. Jimmie would fain have been swept with it, but a heavy hand compressed his arm and detained him.

The sergeant gave swift orders to a cyclist policeman. 'Slip off to the station. We want the divisional surgeon and an ambulance. They'll let the Criminal Investigation people know.'

A murder, whatever the circumstances, is invariably dealt with by the Criminal Investigation Department. The uniformed police may be first engaged, but the detective force is always called in.

'Now, Sullivan, what do you know about this?'

The constable addressed straightened himself up. 'I was patrolling the bridge about five minutes ago,' he said. 'I passed him'—he nodded to the dead man. 'He was walking slowly to the south side. I didn't pay much attention. A little farther on I passed this chap'—he indicated Jimmie—'but I didn't pay any particular attention. I had just reached the other end when I heard a shot. I ran back, and found the first man being supported by the other, who was searching him. There were no other persons on the bridge to my knowledge.'

Jimmie's mouth opened wide. He was thunderstruck. 'Searching him!' he ejaculated. 'Say, Cap'—he was not quite sure of the sergeant's rank—'I never saw the guy in my life before. I was taking a look around when I heard a shot. I was just loosening his clothes when this man comes up.'

He was too paralysed to put all he wanted to say into coherent shape. He was sober enough now. A man confronted with a deadly peril can compress a great deal of thinking into one or two seconds. Jimmie could see any number of points that told against him, and he strove vainly to concoct some plausible explanation. The entire truth he rejected as seeming too wild for credit.

'Better keep anything you're going to say for Mr Whipple,' advised the sergeant. 'Two of you had better take him to the station.'

With his head buried in his hands, Jimmie sat disconsolate on a police cell bed. He was filled with apprehension, and the more he considered things, the more gloomy the outlook appeared. For an hour or more he waited, and at last he heard footsteps in the corridor. A face peered through the 'Judas hole' in the cell door, and then the lock clicked.

'Come on!' ordered a uniformed inspector. 'Mr Whipple wants to see you.'

'Who's Mr Whipple?' demanded Jimmie drearily.

'Divisional detective-inspector. Come, hurry up!'

There were places in the United States where Jimmie had been through the 'sweat-box' and though he had heard that methods of that kind were barred in England, he felt a trifle nervous. He preceded the inspector along the cell-lined corridor, through the charge-room, and up a flight of stairs to a well-lighted little office. Two or three broad-shouldered men in mufti were standing about. A youth seated at a table with some blank sheets of paper in front of him was sharpening a pencil. A slim, pleasant-faced man was standing near the fireplace with a bowler hat on his head and dangling a pair of gloves aimlessly to and fro. It was his eyes that Jimmie met. He knew without the necessity of words that the man was Whipple. He pulled himself together for the ordeal of bullying that he half expected.

'I don't know nothin' about it, chief,' he opened abruptly and with some anxiety. 'I'm a stranger here, and I never saw the guy before.'

'Take it easy, my lad,' said Whipple quietly. 'Nobody has said you killed him yet. I want to ask you one or two questions. You needn't answer unless you like, you know. If you can convince us that you were there only by accident, and had no hand in the murder, so much the better. But remember you're not forced to answer. Everything you say will be written down. Give him a drink, somebody. Now take it quietly, old chap. What's your name?'

His voice was soothing, almost sympathetic. It gave Jimmie the impression, as it was, intended to, that here was a man who would be scrupulously fair. He drank the brandy which someone passed to him, and for an instant his old, wide-mouthed smile flashed out. The spirit gave him a momentary touch of confidence.

'That's all right, boss. James Strickland's my name. I'm from New York. Come over in the *Fortunia* and landed this morning.'

'What are you?'

'Piano tuner.' The trade was the first one that occurred to

Jimmie. 'Over here to see if there's an opening,' he rattled glibly. 'Trade's slack the other side.' The shorthand writer's pencil scratched rapidly over the paper. Whipple's face was expressionless.

Question succeeded question, each one quietly put, each answer received without comment. Jimmie was becoming involved in an inextricable tangle of lies. Had not the horrible fear still loomed over him, he might have avoided contradictions, extraordinary improbabilities, and constructed a connected, if false, story. And he could see, not in his interlocutor's face, but in the faces of the others, a scepticism which they scarcely troubled to conceal.

The catechism finished, Whipple began drawing on his gloves.

'That will do. You will be detained till we have made some more inquiries.'

Jimmie shuddered. 'You don't really think I done this, boss? You aren't goin'—'

'You're not charged yet,' said Whipple. 'You're only detained till we know more about things.'

It was a poor consolation, but with it Jimmie had to be content. He was taken below, and Whipple turned an inquiring face on one of his sergeants. The man made a significant grimace. 'Guilty as blazes, sir,' he said emphatically. 'What did he want to tell that string of lies for?'

'I don't know,' said Whipple thoughtfully. 'You'd be thrown a little off your balance, Newton, if you were suddenly up against it. He's a liar, but he's not necessarily a murderer.'

Newton grunted, but ventured no open dissent till his superior had gone. He was a shrewd man in dealing with the commonplaces of crime, but he lacked subtlety, and accordingly despised it. 'The guvnor's too kid-glove,' he complained with asperity to the uniformed inspector. 'What's the use of mucking about? The bloke's a Yankee crook. He admits he came over in the *Fortunia*, and says he don't know Sweeney, who came over in the same boat. Why, he must have been laying for him. He must have shadowed him till he got a fair chance. Mark me, when we've traced those notes we took off Strickland, we shall find that they were originally paid out to Sweeney. Waste of time finicking about, I call it.'

Now some of this reasoning had been in Whipple's mind, but he liked to feel the ground secure under his feet before he took an irrevocable step. There was no hurry—at any rate for the twenty-four hours during which he was entitled to detain Jimmie on suspicion without making a charge. But there were certain points on which he was not entirely satisfied.

He was on hand at Scotland Yard early next morning. The report of the tragedy was in the morning papers, but they had given it little prominence. From their point of view it was of little news value—just a shooting affray, with a man detained. This was the view the superintendent of the Criminal Investigation Department, to whom Whipple had come to report, took of it.

'Straightforward case, isn't it, Whipple?'

'There are one or two queer points about it, sir. I must admit it looks rather bad for Strickland, but somehow I don't believe he did it. I can't say why, but that's my impression.'

'You must be careful of impressions, Whipple. They carry you away from the facts sometimes.'

'I know that. Well, the facts are these: Sweeney, the dead man, was the president of a hardware company at Detroit. I sent a cable off last night. He had come over partly on business, partly on pleasure, and was held in very good repute there. About five minutes ago I got this fresh cable.' He smoothed out a yellow strip with his hand and read: '"News Sweeney's death precipitated crash his firm. His business unsound for years. Insurance company informs us recently increased life premiums for half-million dollars. Suspect fraud. Request you will make stringent tests of identity, alternatively suspect suicide." That's signed by the Detroit Chief of Police.'

The superintendent stretched out a hand and took the cablegram. He read it through twice with puckered brows. 'That's a queer development,' he admitted. 'I don't see what they're getting at. If the murdered man is not Sweeney, that hypothesis assumes that Sweeney got someone else to impersonate him and that the second person knew he was to be killed. That's ridiculous.'

'So I think, sir. There's more to the suicide end. The divisional surgeon says that the dead man's temple was blackened by the explosion of the pistol. That shows that the weapon, when it was fired, was but a few inches from his face. Of course, when I saw the surgeon I didn't know what this cable tells us, but luckily I put the point to him. There was no weapon found. I asked him if, supposing that Sweeney had killed himself, he could have thrown the pistol into the water after pulling the trigger—it was a distance of several yards to the parapet of the bridge. He was emphatic that it was impossible.'

'Then it comes back to murder after all. Yes. it's certainly curious about the insurance. Who's the chap you've got in?'

Jimmie would have been interested in the reply even had he been less vitally concerned. It would have shown him how vain were his hopes of cutting away from his record. 'A little red-haired chap with a big mouth, who gave the name Strickland—a Yankee pickpocket, Jimmie Iles, or Red Jimmie. You'll remember, sir, New York cabled us he had sailed.'

'Yes, I remember. We ought to have something about him then.'

'We have. I spent part of last night picking it up. The Liverpool men spotted him in a compartment of the boat-train, alone with a man who fills the description of Sweeney. Sergeant Fuller, who was on duty at Euston, saw him when he arrived and took the number of his cab. He was not with Sweeney then. We found the cabman early this morning. He had driven him to a little hotel off the Strand. The hotel people remember him because he wanted a fire in his bedroom—a fire this weather! He went up there and stayed for over an hour. Then he went straight out.

'At nine o'clock Tamplin of the West End saw Four-fingered Foster in the Dewville Bar, Coventry Street, with a red-haired American whom he thought was being strung. The Grape Street people recalled this when the tape report of the murder came over to them. I sent a man to rake out Foster, and sure enough his red-haired pal was Jimmie. Foster said they had parted in the Strand about eleven o'clock. Jimmie said he had an appointment at the Albert Bridge—Foster thought with a girl . . .

'Those are pretty well all the facts, except this: when Jimmie was searched at the police station there were found on him three five-pound notes. These notes had been issued to Sweeney by a bank at Detroit before he left. I have the man's own statement here, sir, if you'd care to look at it. It's a string of lies.'

His chief waved aside the document and fiddled with his pince-nez as he considered the problem for a while. 'You're right to go easy, Whipple, but don't overdo it. There's almost enough evidence as it is to hang Red Jimmie. Intuition is good, but a jury won't be interested in your psychology. They'd sooner read a book.'

'Very good, sir.' The detective-inspector went away, still far from satisfied. In view of the evidence now accumulated, he would have been inclined to believe Jimmie guilty had it not been for the singular news of Sweeney's smash and the insurance. Coincidence is a factor in criminal investigation work, but this was straining it. If Sweeney had been murdered, the crime had come just right to provide for his family.

'There's some point that I've overlooked,' he murmured to himself. 'I can't quite place it.'

He went back over the Albert Bridge to the police station, but no inspiration came to him. There was a bundle of reports awaiting him in his office, but after a casual glance he flung them aside and went down to the cells. He wanted to see Jimmie alone.

Jimmie looked up with pitifully haggard face as the door clanged behind the detective. Whipple nodded cheerfully and sat down.

'Jimmie,' he said familiarly, 'wouldn't you like to give me the straight griffin? I've heard from New York. You'd better let me know exactly what happened. What passed between you and Sweeney in the train coming down from Liverpool?'

He spoke in a quiet, conversational tone, but Jimmie jerked his head back as though to avoid a blow. He had had plenty of time to reflect on the leading points of circumstantial evidence that told against him. It staggered him more than a little that the police had been so quickly able to follow his trail backwards. He was conscious of his innocence of the major crime, conscious also that there was nothing he could do or say which would get away from the deadly array of facts that pointed against him.

'Well, Jimmie?' said Whipple persuasively.

Jimmie ran a hand through his dishevelled red hair. Then he shook himself as though trying to throw off the thoughts that possessed him. 'See here, boss,' he cried in an impulsive burst, 'I'll put you wise to the whole shemozzle. You won't believe me anyway, but it's the solemn truth, so help me. The bulls, they wouldn't give me a rest in New York, so I chased myself over here where I've got one or two chums.'

'Four-fingered Foster?' queried Whipple absently. His thoughts were quite away from Jimmie, but he was nevertheless keenly following every word.

'Has he squealed? Never mind, it don't matter. Well, on the boat I got some chances, but I held myself in. There'd been a Central Office man to see me off, and I didn't know but what he might have passed the word. I cut out the funny business till I got ashore, but I marked out one or two likely guys, Sweeney amongst them. Of course I steered clear of them on the ship, didn't talk to 'em or nothing. I didn't want to be noticed too much—you understand? When we shifted over into the boat-train at Liverpool, I saw Sweeney on his lonesome and got into the carriage with him. I lifted his leather from him—I admit that, boss—just as we reached London.'

'You picked his pocket?'

'Yes, his pocket-book. Then I went on to my hotel and sorted out the stuff. Some of them notes they took off me when they brought me in was among them. Then there was a lot of letters.'

'What did you do with them?'

A flash of cunning crossed Jimmie's face. 'What do *you* think? Burnt 'em. Things like that don't talk when they're in the fire. There was one there, though, that I wish I'd saved now. It was written in print, if you understand what I mean, and told Sweeney to meet someone who had wrote it at Albert Bridge.'

'Wait a minute. Can't you remember exactly what it said?'

Jimmie wrinkled his brow in cogitation. Slowly he repeated the letter, which Whipple took down in shorthand on the back of an envelope. 'I thought,' said Jimmie, a little haltingly, 'that I might butt in and catch this Black Hand gang and do Sweeney a turn. You see, I never believed in this gun-play myself, and I thought if I could stop it I might put myself right with Sweeney and perhaps he'd put me on to something—'

'Take you into partnership,' said Whipple; 'saviour of his life and all that kind of thing.'

'That's it,' agreed Jimmie.

Whipple smiled inwardly, but his face was grave. 'And you want me to believe this yarn that you've been sitting thinking out, do you? Ah—don't be a fool.'

Jimmie was utterly unstrung, or he never would have allowed himself a resort to violence which, even if it were successful, must have been futile. He thought he saw that he was still disbelieved, and had leapt at the detective's throat with a mad idea of escape. Whipple side-stepped quickly, stooped, and the pickpocket felt himself lifted and flung to the other side of the cell.

'Don't be a fool, Jimmie,' repeated Whipple mildly. 'Even if you did knock me out, you couldn't do anything. The cell is locked on the outside, and even I can't get away till I ring. Sit down again quietly—that's right. Now tell me one other thing: Did you notice anything in particular when you got on to the bridge last night?'

The other rubbed himself tenderly. 'Nothing in particular,' he answered. 'There was a smell of paint—that's not much good.'

'Isn't it!' said Whipple, and pressed the bell that summoned the gaoler.

Two men sauntered on to the Albert Bridge. Whipple had got an idea, and though he had yet to test it, he was convinced that he was on the right track at last. He nodded as he saw the fresh green paint on the rails, and kept his eye fixed on them till he had passed a dozen yards by the spot where the murder had been committed. Then the two crossed to the other side of the bridge. The inspection of not more than three yards of the rail had taken place when Whipple halted and gave a satisfied chuckle. 'We're on it, Newton,' he declared. 'Look here.'

He pointed to some marks on the fresh paint-work. Across the top of the upper part of the rail, and continued downwards on the outer side, the paint had been scraped away. On the river side there were a couple of irregular bruises on the paint.

'Kids been playing about,' said the sergeant with decision. 'I remember in the flat murder case we got mucked about by a lot of marks on a doorway. Some bright soul thought they were Arabic characters. It turned out they were boy scout marks.'

The detective-inspector laughed. 'All right. Seeing's believing with you. I'll have a shot at this my own way, though. You might go and phone through to the river division. Ask 'em to send a couple of boats up here with drags.'

Newton spat over the rail into the tide. 'You'll not find

anything with drags,' he said, and with this Parthian shot, went to obey his instructions. Whipple remained in thought. Once, when there was a lull in the traffic, he paced out the distance between the marks on the rail and the place where Sweeney had been killed.

'I'm right,' he declared to himself; 'I'd bet on it.'

Within twenty minutes two motor-launches were off the bridge and Newton had returned. Leaving him to mark the spot where the paint had been rubbed on the rail, Whipple went down to be picked up off a convenient wharf. A short discussion with the officer in charge as to the effect of the tide-drift, and they were in mid-stream again.

Then the drags splashed overboard and they began methodically to search the bed of the river. When half an hour had gone, Whipple was beginning to bite his lip. A drag came to the surface with whipcord about its lines. A constable began to unwind it. The detective leaned forward eagerly. 'Steady, man, don't let it break, whatever you do.'

They pulled the thing attached to the string on board and steered for the bank, Whipple in the glow of satisfaction that comes to every man who sees the end of his work in sight. He went straight to the police station telegraph room.

'Whipple to Superintendent C.I.,' he dictated. 'Inform Detroit police Sweeney's insurance void. Absolute proof committed suicide. Details to follow.'

Later, in his own office, his stenographer took down to be typed for record:

> 'Sir,—I respectfully submit the following facts in regard to the supposed murder of the man Sweeney—
>
> 'I first gained the impression that it was suicide from the doctor's report that the explosion of a pistol had scorched the dead man's face, showing that it had been held very closely to his head. This impression was strengthened by the fact that Iles, the American who was found by

the body and at first suspected of the murder, could, if his motive was robbery, have attained this end more simply without violence. He is known to the New York police as an expert pickpocket. I need scarcely add that the knowledge that Sweeney was practically a bankrupt before he left the United States and had insured himself very heavily disposed me still more to the theory of suicide. If Sweeney had it in his mind to kill himself, it was indispensable to his purpose (since practically all life insurances are void in the event of suicide) to make the act appear (1) as an accident; (2) as a murder. He chose the latter.

'Unfortunately for himself, Iles picked Sweeney's pocket on the journey to London. Whether the latter discovered his loss before his death it is impossible to say with certainty. I believe not. Among the documents which Iles found was a letter in printed characters (which with others he burnt) demanding an appointment on the Albert Bridge, and conveying indirect threats. It is my belief that this letter was written by Sweeney himself with the idea that it would be found on his body and confirm the appearance of murder. I considered very fully the various means by which Sweeney might dispose of a pistol after he had shot himself. Only one practicable way occurred to me, and this was confirmed by an examination of the bridge rail, which had been newly painted. There were the paint stains on the dead man's clothes, and Iles had said he noticed him looking over the rails.

'It seemed to me that if the butt of a pistol were secured to a cord, and a heavy weight attached to the other end of the cord and dropped over the rail of the bridge before the fatal shot was fired, the grip on the pistol would relax and it would be automatically dragged into the water. The river was dragged at my request, and the discovery of an automatic pistol tied by a length of whipcord to a heavy leaden weight proved my theory right . . . With regard to

Iles, I shall charge him with pocket-picking on his own confession, and ask that he shall be recommended for deportation as an undesirable alien . . . I have the honour to be your humble servant,

'LIONEL WHIPPLE,
'Divisional Detective-Inspector.'

'All the same, sir,' commented Detective-Sergeant Newton, 'it looked like being that tough. He's in luck that you tumbled to the gag.'

'That's right,' agreed Whipple smilingly. 'It's luck—just luck.'

III

THE MAN WITH THE PALE-BLUE EYES

A BLUE haze of smoke which even the electric fans could not entirely dispel overhung the smoking saloon of the S.S. *Columbia*. With the procrastination of confirmed poker players, they had lingered at the game till well after midnight. Silvervale cut off a remark to glance at his cards. He yawned as he flung them down.

'She can call herself Eleanor de Reszke or anything else she likes on the passenger list,' he declared languidly, 'but she's Madeline Fulford all right, all right. She's come on a bit in the last two years, though she always was a bit of a high stepper. Wonder if de Reszke knows anything about Crake?'

Across the table a sallow-faced man, whose play had hitherto evinced no lack of nerve, threw in a full hand, aces up, on a moderate rise. No one save himself knew that he had wasted one of the best of average poker hands. His fingers, lean and tremulous, drummed mechanically on the table. For a second a pair of lustreless, frowning blue eyes rested on Silvervale's face.

'So that's the woman who was in the Crake case? It was her evidence that got the poor devil seven years, wasn't it? As I remember the newspaper reports, she was a kind of devil incarnate.'

'I wouldn't go as far as that,' observed Silvervale dryly, 'and I'm a newspaper man myself. I didn't hear the trial, but I saw her afterwards. It never came out why she gave him away. There must have been some mighty strong motive, for he had spent thousands on her. I guess there was another woman at the bottom of it. Anyway, her reasons don't matter. She cleared an unpleasant trickster out of the way and put him where he belongs. But for her he might have been carrying on that swindling bank of his now. I'll take three cards.'

The man with the pale-blue eyes jerked his head abruptly. 'Yes, he's where he belongs,' he asserted, 'and she—why, she's Mrs de Reszke and a deuced pretty woman . . . Hello!' He broke off short, staring with fascinated eyes beyond Silvervale. The journalist swerved round in his chair, to meet a livid face and furious eyes within a foot of his own.

It was Richard de Reszke himself. He had not made himself popular on ship-board—indeed, it is doubtful if he could ever have been popular in any society. A New Yorker who had made himself a millionaire in the boot trade, he was ungracious both in manner and speech. He had entered the saloon unperceived, and now his tall, usually shambling figure was unwontedly erect. His left hand—big and gnarled it was—fell with an ape-like clutch on Silvervale's shoulder.

'You scandal-mongering little ape,' he snarled, with a vicious tightening of the lips under his grey moustache. 'By God, you'll admit you're a liar, or I'll shake the life out of you.'

The chair fell with a crash as he pulled the journalist forward. Men sprang to intervene between the two. Cursing and struggling, de Reszke was forced back, but it took four men to do it. Suddenly his resistance relaxed.

'That's all right,' he said quietly. 'We'll let it go for now.' A fresh access of passion shook him, and he shot out a malignant oath. 'I'll make you a sorry man yet for this, Mr Silvervale.'

The journalist had picked up the fallen chair. His face was flushed, but he answered coolly. 'I apologise,' he said quietly. 'I had no business to talk of your wife.'

'Then in front of these gentlemen you'll admit you're a liar.'

'I guess not. I am sorry I said anything, but what I did say was the truth. Mrs de Reszke was Madeline Fulford, and she it was who gave evidence against Crake.'

The little group between the men stiffened in expectation

of a new outburst. But none came. The stoop had come back to de Reszke's shoulders, and he lifted one hand wearily to tug at his moustache. Then without another word he turned and shambled from the room.

There was a momentary silence, broken at last by the scratch of a match as someone lit a cigarette. The embarrassment was broken, and three or four men spoke at once.

'Look out, Silvervale,' said Bowen, a young New York banker. 'Lucky for you we touch Southampton tomorrow. The old man is a-gunning for you, sure. His face meant murder.'

'Thanks. I'll look after my own corpse,' drawled the journalist. He spoke with an ease he did not entirely feel. 'I suppose the game's broken up now. I've had enough excitement for one night. I'm going to turn in.'

The short remainder of the voyage, in spite of de Reszke's threat and the prophecy of Bowen, passed without incident. It was not till he was back in London that the episode was recalled to Silvervale's mind. The boat train had reached Waterloo in the early afternoon, and at six o'clock, Silvervale, for all that his two months' vacation had yet three days to run, had been drawn into the stir and stress of Fleet Street.

The harrassed news editor of the *Morning Wire* was working at speed through a basket of accumulated copy. He paused long enough to shake hands and exchange a remark or two, and then resumed his labours with redoubled ardour, for he was eager to hand over the reins to his night assistant.

He snatched irritably at a piece of tape that was handed to him by a boy, and then, adjusting his pince-nez, glanced at Silvervale.

'Here's a funny thing, Silver. Didn't you come back on the *Columbia*? Read that.'

Silvervale took the thin strip and slowly read it through:

'5.40: Mrs Eleanor de Reszke, the wife of an American millionaire, was this afternoon found shot dead in her sitting-room at the Palatial Hotel. She had been at the hotel only an hour or two, having arrived by the *Columbia* from New York this morning.'

Hardened journalist though he was, with a close acquaintance with many of the bizarre aspects of tragedy, Silvervale could not repress a little shudder. Here was a grim sequel for which he was in a degree responsible. He traced the sequence of events clearly in his imagination from the moment when de Reszke first heard that his wife had been the associate and betrayer of a swindler, to the ultimate gust of passion that must have led to the tragedy when it was borne upon him that the statement was the truth.

'Yes. It's—it's queer, Danvers,' he said unsteadily, 'deuced queer.' Then with a realisation that the news editor was regarding him with curiosity: 'I'm sorry, old man; you mustn't ask me to handle the story. You'd better put Blackwood on it. It should be a good yarn, but I'm rather mixed up in it. I may be called as a witness.'

Few things are calculated to startle the news editor of a great morning newspaper, but this time Silvervale had certainly succeeded. To tell the truth, the young man was astonished at his own scruples. He made haste to escape before he could be questioned.

Out in Fleet Street he hailed a taxi and was driven straight to the Palatial Hotel. A couple of men were in the big hall, smilingly parrying the questions of half a dozen journalists. One of them shook his head as Silvervale pushed his way to the front.

'Good Lord! Here's another vulture. It's no good, Mr Silvervale. We've just been telling your friends here that we don't know anything. The doctors have not finished their examination yet.'

'But it looks like suicide, Mr Forrester,' interposed one of the crowd. 'You've found a pistol.'

A knowing smile extended on Detective-Inspector Forrester's genial countenance. 'That won't work, boys,' he remonstrated with a reproving shake of his head. 'You don't draw me.'

Silvervale managed to get the detective aside. 'You must give me five minutes,' he whispered hastily. 'I know who killed her. I came over in the same boat.'

Forrester thrust his hands deep in his trousers' pockets. His brow puckered a little, and he studied the journalist's face thoughtfully. For all his casual unworried air, his instinct rather than anything definite in the preliminary investigations had warned him that the case was likely to prove a difficult one. A detective—the real detective—is quite as willing to take short cuts in his work as any other business man.

'The deuce you do,' he said. 'Come, let's get out of this. Half a moment, Roker.'

His assistant disengaged himself from the other newspaper men, and Forrester led the way to the lift. At the third floor they emerged. Very quietly the door of the lift closed behind them, and half-unconsciously Silvervale found himself tiptoeing along the corridor, although in any event the soft carpet would have deadened all sound. A man standing stiffly against a white door flung it open as they approached. Within, a couple of men were bending over something on a couch, and two more were busy near the window overlooking the river. No one looked up. Forrester passed straight through to another and smaller room, and fitted his burly form to a basket arm-chair. He waved Silvervale to another one.

'And now fire away, sonny,' he said.

Concisely, in quick, succinct sentences, Silvervale told his story. As he concluded, Forrester drew a worn briar pipe from his pocket and packed it with a meditative forefinger.

'Are you writing anything about this?'

'Not a word. I know I may be wanted as a witness.'

'That's true.' The inspector puffed contemplatively for a moment. 'Then there's this, I don't mind telling you: That chap downstairs was right. There was a pistol—a five-chambered revolver—found clutched in that woman's hand. But de Reszke is missing. He never came with her to the hotel.'

'Then you think it is suicide after all?'

The detective leaned forward and levelled a heavy forefinger at his questioner. 'You've earned a right to know something of this business, Mr Silvervale. It's no suicide. The body was discovered by the maid just after five o'clock. No one had heard a shot, but that's nothing—these walls are pretty well soundproof. The dead woman was lying on a couch with the revolver in her hand—so the girl's story runs. She thought her mistress was asleep, and it was only when she touched her and the weapon fell to the floor that she discovered she was dead. She was shot through the left eye.'

'I see. You mean a woman wouldn't kill herself that way. She'd poison or drown herself—some bloodless death.'

'There is something in that, but it proves little by itself. But there are not many people who'd shoot themselves deliberately in the eye. It's curious, but there—But to my mind the conclusive thing is the pistol. Any student of medical jurisprudence will tell you that usually it needs considerable force to relax the grip of a corpse from anything it is clutching at the moment of death. No, Mr Silvervale, this is a carefully calculated murder, if ever there was one. And I think your information will help us to fix the man. Roker'—he addressed his companion—'you might get hold of the maid again. Get a full description of de Reszke, and there's bound to be a photograph somewhere. Take 'em along to the Yard and have 'em circulated. We merely want to question him, mind. Now, Mr Silvervale, we'll see what the doctors say.'

The two doctors, the police divisional surgeon and the medical man who had been first called on the discovery of the murder, had finished their examination as Forrester passed into the next room. He spoke a few words in an undertone to the surgeon, who nodded assentingly.

The two men by the window were still busy. Now Silvervale had an opportunity to see what occupied them. They were busy with scale plans of the room whereon were shown the relative positions of everything in the room, marked out even to inches. Photographs, he surmised, must already have been taken.

Forrester seemed to have forgotten Silvervale's existence. As soon as the doctors had gone, the inspector had extracted a small bottle of black powder from his pocket and sprinkled it delicately over the open pages of a book resting on a table a couple of yards from the couch. Presently he blew the stuff away. The finger-prints had developed in relief on the white margin.

'There's a blotting-pad over there on the writing-table, Mr Silvervale,' he said; 'would you mind helping me for a moment?'

Forrester was cool and business-like, yet it was very gently that he lifted the dead white hands and impressed the finger-tips on a sheet of paper on top of the pad. Silently he compared the impressions with those on the book.

'I'm only an amateur at this finger-print game,' he said at last. 'Grant ought to have been here. See if you make these prints agree, Mr Silvervale.'

Silvervale carried the book to the window and bent his brows over it. He found it slow work, but at last he raised his head. 'These are her thumb-prints on the outer margin,' he said. 'The one at the bottom of the book is not hers.'

'That's how I make it. Now we can get a fair theory of how the thing was done: Mrs de Reszke was on the couch reading. The murderer entered softly from the corridor, closing the door behind him. She looked up and placed the book beside her. He must have fired point-blank. Then to work out his idea of suicide he placed the pistol in her hand, and, picking up the book, put it on the table. Here's where we start from—a piece of indisputable proof when we catch the murderer.'

A little contempt at the apparent deliberation of the detective—at the finesse wasted on what seemed an obvious case—had come to Silvervale's mind. He hazarded a suggestion; Forrester grinned.

'I'll bet a dollar I know what you're thinking. I'm wasting my time meddling with details while the murderer's escaping. Do you know I had five men here besides these'—he nodded towards the draughtsmen—'questioning every one who might know anything about the case? Mrs de Reszke has received no one; no one resembling her husband has been seen in the hotel. Do you know that there is not one railway station in London, not one hotel that is not even now being searched for a trace of de Reszke? We are not so slow as our critics think. If de Reszke did this murder he won't get away, you can take it from me. There's plenty of people trying to catch him—I've seen to that.'

He checked himself suddenly as if he realised that he had for a while lost his wonted imperturbability. 'I thought you knew better than to run away with the delusion that all we've got to do is to arrest a man we've fixed our suspicions on. In point of fact it is often more difficult to get material evidence of a moral certainty than to start without any facts at all.'

He moved heavily to the door. 'I'm going on to the Yard,' he said. 'Care to come?'

As they turned under the big wrought-iron arch that spanned the entrance to New Scotland Yard, Silvervale noted that they avoided the little back door that leads to the Criminal Investigation Department and went up by the broad main entrance to those rooms on one of the topmost floors devoted to the Finger-print Department.

Grant, the chief of the department, a black-moustached giant with lined forehead and shrewd, penetrative eyes, was seated at a low table pushing a magnifying-glass across a sheet of paper. Forrester had clapped him heavily on the shoulder, and he wheeled around frowningly.

'It's you, is it?' he growled. 'One of these days you'll play that trick too often, my lad. Of course, you come when every one's gone home. What do you want?'

'Don't be peevish, old man,' smiled Forrester, and seated himself on the table. 'You'll be sorry you weren't more kind to me when the daisies are growing over my grave.'

'Fungi, you mean,' retorted Grant acidly. 'What's the bother?'

'This.' Forrester produced the book he had found at the hotel and the scrap of paper on which he had taken the murdered woman's finger-prints. 'It's the Palatial Hotel business. The prints on the paper are those of Mrs de Reszke. They agree with those on the sides of the book. The one at the bottom of the book is that of the murderer.'

'H'm.' Grant glanced at the prints and gave a corroborative nod. 'You'll want photographs of these, I suppose?'

'Yes—as soon as I can get them. I suppose you'll have to have a search to make sure that the other print isn't on the records. It's unlikely, though.'

'That will have to wait. I'll have the photographs taken and sent down to you as soon as they're ready. Now go away.'

He dismissed them abruptly, and they could hear his deep voice thundering into the telephone receiver as they made their exit. He was ordering a wire to be sent recalling one of the staff photographers. As in any other big business firm, the ordinary staff of Scotland Yard goes off duty at six.

Downstairs in his own room, Forrester found three or four subordinates and a handful of reports and messages awaiting him. His leisurely manner dropped from him. He became brisk, official, brusque. A shorthand clerk with open notebook was waiting, and to him the chief inspector poured out the bulk of his instructions to be forwarded by telegraph or telephone. Silvervale realised how vast and complex were the resources that were being handled to solve the mystery.

Forrester dismissed the clerk at last and turned abruptly on the waiting men. There was no waste of words on either side. As the final subordinate left the room, Forrester yawned and stretched himself wearily.

'That's all right,' he said. 'I guess we can't do anything more for an hour or two. It may interest you, Mr Silvervale, to know that de Reszke has booked a passage back to New York in his own name, by the boat that leaves Liverpool the day after tomorrow. He called at the White Star offices at five o'clock. It's a bluff, I guess, and pretty obvious at that. He thinks we'll concentrate attention on that scent while he slips some other way. Yes—what is it?'

Someone had torn the door open hurriedly. A young man, tall and sparse, whispered a few words into Forrester's ear. The chief inspector sat up as though galvanised. His hand searched for the telephone.

'Get him put through here . . . You have a taxi-cab ready, Bolt. You may have to come with me.' The young man vanished and Forrester spoke into the telephone. 'Hello, that you, Gould? . . . Yes, this is Forrester . . . At the Metz, you say . . . How many men have you? All right, I'll be along straight away. Good-bye.'

'Located him?' ventured Silvervale.

'Yes.' Forrester's brow was puckered. 'He's at the Metz under his own name. Hanged if I can make it out. He's either mad or he's got the nerve of the very devil. Come on!'

Bolt was awaiting them in a taxi-cab outside, which whirled them swiftly away as they took their seats. They drew up in Piccadilly, a hundred yards or so from the severe arches of the great hotel, and walked forward till they were met by a bronzed, well-dressed man of middle age who nodded affably and fell into step with them.

'Well, Gould?' queried Forrester.

'Everything serene, sir. He's gone in to dinner. There's two of our men dining at the next table.'

'That's all right then. I'll see the manager and fix things.'

A commissionaire pushed back the revolving door and the four walked in.

Five minutes later a waiter crossed the softly-lighted dining-room with a card. It did not contain Forrester's name—nor indeed that of anyone he knew. Nor did de Reszke seem to know it, for he frowned as the waiter presented it to him.

'I don't know any Mr Grahame Johnston,' he said. 'This isn't for me.'

The waiter was deferential. 'The gentleman said, "Mr John de Reszke," sir. He says it's very urgent, and wants you to spare him a minute in the smoking-room.'

The millionaire slowly divested himself of the serviette, and rising, shambled after the waiter. Curiously enough, one of the diners at the adjoining table seemed simultaneously to have occasion to leave the room by the same exit.

Forrester and his companions were waiting in a small room which had been placed at their disposal. As de Reszke was ushered in, the first face he caught sight of was that of Silvervale. His face lowered and he paused on the threshold.

Quickly and deftly Gould shouldered by him as though to pass out. De Reszke gave way, and the detective closed the door and leaned nonchalantly against it.

'Mr de Reszke,' said Forrester quickly, 'I am a police officer. Your wife has been murdered since her arrival in London. If you wish to make any statement as to your movements you may do so, though I must warn you that unless you can definitely convince me that you had no hand in the murder I may have to arrest you.'

Blankly, uncomprehendingly, de Reszke stared in front of him as though he had not heard. His lean fingers clenched and unclenched, and his eyes had become dull. The police officers, although neither their attitudes nor their faces showed it, had braced themselves to overcome him at the first hint of resistance. But this man had no appearance of being the madman that

Silvervale had pictured. The life seemed to have gone out of him.

'You heard me?' questioned Forrester sharply.

'I heard you,' said de Reszke dully. 'You say Nell's dead—no, not Nell—her name's not Eleanor; it's Madeline—Madeline Fulford; that's it—she's been murdered? I heard—ha! ha! ha!' He broke into shrill uncanny laughter, and then pressing both hands to his temples pitched forward heavily to the floor.

'A doctor, someone,' ordered Forrester, and Gould vanished. Unconscious, de Reszke was lifted to a couch by the other three. Forrester shrugged his shoulders. 'Looks like a bad job,' he muttered.

The doctor summoned by Gould confirmed the suspicion. 'It's a paralytic stroke,' he explained. 'I doubt if he'll ever get over it. You gentlemen are friends of his?'

Forrester inserted a couple of fingers in his waistcoat pocket. 'Not exactly,' he said. 'We are police officials. There is my card.'

'Ah!' The doctor's eyebrows jerked up. 'Well, it's no business of mine. Of course, it's obvious that he's had a shock.'

'Of course,' agreed Forrester.

The inevitable search of de Reszke's room and baggage had been conducted with thoroughness, but it yielded nothing that seemed of importance to the investigation. Forrester voiced his misgivings as he walked back to Scotland Yard with Silvervale.

'This business is running too smoothly. I don't like it. I feel there's a smack in the eye coming from somewhere. There's several little odds and ends to be cleared up. It would have been easier if he hadn't had that stroke.'

'There's the finger-print on the book,' ventured Silvervale.

'Yes. I took de Reszke's and sent Bolt with them to the Yard. Grant will have fixed all that up by the time we get there.'

Grant was waiting for them when they arrived. On his table he had spread out a series of enlargements of finger-prints. He shook his head gravely at Forrester. 'It's no good, old chap,' he said. 'These things you sent me up by Bolt don't tally.'

Forrester, suddenly arrested with his overcoat half off, felt his jaw drop. For a second he frowned upon Grant. Then he writhed himself free of the garment. 'Don't tally?' he repeated. 'You're joking, Grant. They must.'

'Well, they don't.'

The chief detective-inspector brought his fist down with a bang on the table. He laid no claim to the superhuman intelligence of the story-book detectives. Therefore he was considerably annoyed at this abrupt discovery of a vital flaw in the chain of evidence that connected de Reszke with the murder. He had no personal feeling in the matter. It was merely the discontent of the business man at finding that work had been wasted. He brought his fist down with a bang on the table.

'It beats me,' he declared viciously. 'It fairly beats me. Who else could have done it? Who else had a motive?'

Grant stole out of the room, and Silvervale rested his elbows on the table and his chin in his cupped hands, striving to recall some avenue of investigation that he might have overlooked.

Suddenly his face lightened and he jerked himself from his chair with a swift movement of his whole body. Ignoring the journalist, he rushed from the room. It was long before he returned. When he did he was accompanied by Grant.

'Tell me'—he addressed Silvervale—'did you ever see Crake?'

The other shook his head. 'I was out of town when he was tried. It was after the case was over that I interviewed Madeline Fulford.'

Grant was frowning. 'If I hadn't seen the records, Forrester, I'd say you were mad. It's the most unheard-of thing . . .'

'We'll see whether I'm mad or not,' said the chief inspector grimly. He placed a photograph, the official side and full-face, before Silvervale. 'Did you ever see that man before?'

'No.'

'Nor that?' The second photograph was a studio portrait with the name of a Strand firm at the bottom. It awoke some vague reminiscence in Silvervale. He held it closer to the light.

'Wait a minute.' Grant placed a sheet of paper over the bottom of the face, hiding the moustache and chin. Recollection came to Silvervale in a flash. It was Norman, the man with the lustreless blue eyes who had commented on Madeline Fulford in the smoking-room of the *Columbia*.

He explained. 'The hair's done differently,' he added, 'but I can recognise the upper part of the face, though he's older now than when this photograph was taken. Do you think he's mixed up in this?'

'Maybe,' answered Forrester enigmatically. 'I'll have a man motor down to the prison now'—he was speaking to Grant—'and we'll go on to the Palatial. If I'm any judge he'll still be there. His room was No. 472, almost opposite her suite. I had him questioned, of course, but I never dreamed—'

Silvervale lit a cigarette resignedly. 'It's all Greek to me,' he complained. 'Still, I have no right to ask questions.'

'You'll understand in an hour or two,' said Forrester. 'It would take too long to explain now. Come on and you'll see what you'll see.'

It was back to the Palatial Hotel that he took the journalist and a couple of subordinates. There he remained closeted with the manager for five minutes. He reappeared with that functionary, a master-key dangling on his finger.

'Our bird's at home,' he said. 'Gone to roost, probably.'

Nothing more was said till they reached the third floor. The manager led the way until they came opposite a door facing the suite which Mrs de Reszke had occupied. 'This is No. 472,' he said in a low voice. 'Shall I knock?'

Forrester made a gesture of dissent and his hand fell coaxingly on the door. He made no sound as he pushed a key in the lock and turned it. With a sharp push the door flew open, and a quick, angry question was succeeded by confused sounds of a struggle. The next Silvervale saw was a pyjama-clad man being held on the bed with Forrester and a colleague at either wrist.

'I don't know who you are or the meaning of this outrage,' he protested angrily. 'Someone will have to pay for this.'

'Hold on to his hand a minute, Roker,' said Forrester, and one of the other detectives seized the wrist he had been grasping.

The chief inspector thrust his hand beneath the pillow and produced a small automatic pistol. 'I just grabbed him in time,' he said a little breathlessly.

'I want to know—' persisted the prisoner.

Forrester turned sternly upon him. 'I am a police officer,' he said. 'I am arresting you as an escaped convict, one John Crake.'

Something approaching a gleam of interest shot into Crake's lifeless eyes. 'So that's it, is it?' he said quietly. 'I wonder how you got on to it. According to official reckoning, John Crake has still got five years to serve.'

It was impossible to doubt that the man knew the real reason of his arrest, but his manner gave no hint of perturbation. He smiled sardonically as a shiver swept over his slight frame. 'I suppose you aren't going to take me to the police station in my sleeping-suit? Will these gentlemen allow me to dress?'

At an order from Forrester his clothes were searched and passed to him. He was adjusting his tie with a steady hand when he next shot out a question: 'You have something else to say?'

'That can wait,' returned Forrester. 'Remember that anything you say—'

'I know,' interrupted Crake; 'you're bound to give that warning. What's the good of all this finesse, Mr—er—er—Forrester—thank you? I know you want me for murder, and if you want me to say anything you'd better listen now while I'm in the mood. First of all, though, how did you get on to me?'

'There was a finger-print, and we had yours in the records taken when you were on trial for the other thing.'

'Look here.' Crake spoke as though he were merely an interested observer with no personal concern in the affair. 'You'd better tell me the full story, and if there are any gaps I'll fill them in for you. Is that a bargain?'

Forrester reflected a moment. 'All right,' he agreed, with a glance at Silvervale. 'There can be no harm in that if you want to know. In the first place, when the woman was found it was easy to penetrate the idea of a clumsy attempt to simulate suicide. We had little to guide us beyond the fact that she was a Mrs de Reszke who had come over from the States in the *Columbia*. Then Mr Silvervale, here, turned up with the story of the bother on board, and some of our men picked up the same story from other passengers we traced out. Of course, with de Reszke missing, we went off full cry on a false trail. There were scores of circumstances that pointed against him, and but for the accident of the finger-print it might have looked very ugly.'

'I don't understand about that finger-print,' remarked Crake.

'It was left on the book the woman had been reading when you placed it on the table. Well, anyway, we got de Reszke, and when I found that his finger-print did not agree with that on the book, I was at a dead loss. Of course, I had had your record looked up when Mr Silvervale identified the dead woman as Madeline Fulford, and I found you were supposed to be still in prison. Naturally, we had not considered you after that. But when I found myself right up against it I took a forlorn chance and compared the prints from the book with those we had of yours. Then Mr Silvervale identified a portrait of you as that of a passenger named Norman who came over on the *Columbia*. I remembered that a Mr Norman had been questioned here by our people, and we came on. That's all.'

Crake's thin lips curved into a sneer. 'It was just the off-chance of your comparing the prints that did it,' he said.

Forrester made a disclaiming gesture. 'The records would have been searched sooner or later in any event, and we'd have hit on you. It would have taken a day or two though, and you'd have got a start.'

'And you don't know how it is I'm still not in prison, and no one knows I've been at large for a year?'

'No, not altogether,' admitted the chief detective carelessly. 'There's been a change of identity and big bribery somewhere. That's for the prison people to explain.' He was careful not to ask any questions.

'Well,' said Crake slowly, 'I can help you out on that. This is what happened: When that Jezebel there'—he jerked his thumb towards the door—'sold me at the trial, I swore I'd get quits with her, if I swung for it.' He spat out the words in an even voice that made them ten times more venomous. 'Mark you, in the time that I knew her she had bled me for thousands. Then when the other man turned up, she had to get rid of me—and the Old Bailey was the method she chose. I don't know if any of you gentlemen know what hate is—real, white-hot, flaming hatred that eats a man's vitals out,'—he choked a little—'but never mind that. My first idea was to work an escape, for I knew my sentence would not be a light one. I had plenty of money—never mind how I kept it out of other people's clutches.

'There was a man sentenced the same day as myself to two years. There was a certain similarity between us in height and build and physical characteristics—I don't mean that we were in any way doubles, but it was enough to give me an idea when I learned that, after the rising of the Court, we were to be taken to a fresh prison. In the van I got my chance. I offered him a thousand a year to exchange sentences and identities with me—seven thousand pounds in all. He fell in with the idea, and when we descended in the prison yard he was John Crake and I—I was Isaac Wells. That was his name.

'I had forgotten one thing. When my term—or rather Wells's term—was drawing to a close, my finger-prints were to be taken as a matter of ordinary routine to be sent to Scotland Yard for comparison. That staggered me at first, but I was not done. My prison record had been good—and that and the fact that I was well-educated caused me now and again to be chosen for work in the office. I watched and waited, and pure accident helped me at last. I managed to lay my hands for a few seconds on the prints the day they were to be sent to London. And the prints that went up were those of the real Wells.

'I wanted to be free—partly for the sake of freedom, mainly to get even with Madeline Fulford. Prison had altered my appearance in some respects, and I did what I could myself. I won't trouble you with my adventures in tracking her down. I found the man for whom I had been sacrificed had committed suicide in Paris, and from there I followed her all over the world, sometimes going on a blind, sometimes getting a hint here and there that satisfied me I should get her sooner or later. I heard at last that she had married de Reszke, and I reached New York a day before they sailed for England.

'There was a vacant berth on the *Columbia*, and I took it. I kept out of her sight, but I watched for my chance like a cat. She never seemed to be alone, and it was not my purpose to take any risk of involving myself if it could be avoided. Then there was the row in the smoking-room. That frightened me for a while, but when I saw that Mr Silvervale did not recognise me, I did not mind.

'I was in the next carriage to her in the boat-train from Southampton to London, and my taxi-cab was close behind hers when she arrived at the Palatial. I took this room on the same floor as her suite—and you know the rest.'

The scratching of a pencil as a detective who had followed Crake's statement in shorthand put the finishing touches to his notes was the only sound for a few seconds after Crake had finished. The manager fished in his pocket and produced a letter which he handed to Forrester.

'I forgot to give you this,' he said. 'It was left in the office early this morning. It is addressed to Mrs de Reszke.'

Forrester broke the seal and read the letter, silently at first and then aloud:

'MADAM,—You have no moral claim upon me since your admission yesterday that you are the infamous woman formerly known as Madeline Fulford. I then told you as plainly as possible that you need look to me no longer for support. I have now, however, thought the question over, and will allow you three thousand dollars per annum, paid quarterly, on condition, first, that you assume some other name than mine; secondly, that you make no attempt in future to molest or communicate with me either in person or by letter.

'I shall instruct my lawyer that the foregoing payment is to be made to you. I sail for New York in two days' time.

'R. DE RESZKE.'

IV

THE MAKER OF DIAMONDS

Fleeting twisted his watch-chain absently around his fingers till it cut the flesh.

'They're diamonds all right, all right,' he said. 'That's the blazes of it.'

Heldway smiled genially at the jeweller. 'Where do I come in then? I don't see what you've to complain about. You admit, yourself, there's a fortune in it.'

He spoke quietly, yet there was a subtle inflection of irony in his tone that caused the jeweller to scrutinise his face with suspicion. Somehow Heldway made him feel a fool, and Fleeting knew he was not a fool. He recognised himself—more, other men recognised him—as one of the keenest jewellers in Hatton Garden.

Being a jeweller, he was one of the least credulous of men. It spoke for itself that he had called in Heldway. There were those at Scotland Yard who held Heldway in high esteem.

'There's a screw loose somewhere,' he protested, releasing his chain and pushing out a pair of delicate hands. 'I feel it. The thing's too good to be true. Why, if I hadn't seen it myself, I'd have sworn those diamonds came from Kimberley.'

The detective-inspector shrugged his shoulders listlessly. 'Ah, of course, an expert can always tell which mine a stone has come from.'

Fleeting seethed inwardly. He was in a burning excitement, and the placidity of the other annoyed him. He did not consider that while his own agitation was to be attributed to the possibility of making a fortune beyond his wildest dreams, or losing a sum that would long cripple him, the detective had nothing to gain or lose.

'What do you make of it?' Fleeting demanded bluntly.

Heldway slowly changed his position till his elbow rested on the mantelpiece. He seemed to be weighing the question. At last he spoke. 'What it comes to is this: This man Vernet says he can make diamonds, and offers to sell a half-interest in his secret to you for a hundred thousand pounds. He gives a demonstration under the most stringent tests, and you fail to find out any fake. The diamonds are genuine. Now it seems to me one of two things—either Vernet can do what he says, or your precautions against trickery have not been effective.'

'Hang it all!' retorted Fleeting impatiently. 'What more could I do? The room in which he works is here in my office. It was fitted up by firms whom I specified, according to his ideas, with a little charcoal furnace and certain chemical preparations. I did all the buying. Everything passed through my hands. It is impossible that he should have had any confederate among the workmen. When he has gone in to supervise the construction of the furnace, I have been with him, watching every movement. That he could have hid anything in the room is quite impossible.'

'Have you seen him actually make these gems?'

'No,' admitted Fleeting. 'I can't very well expect him to lay his hand down till I have paid cash. It's too big a thing to take chances on. Mind you, Vernet's perfectly reasonable. He invited me to take precautions against trickery, and I have. Each time he goes into the laboratory he changes every stitch of clothing for a suit I have provided. I have engaged an expert searcher, who used to be at the diamond fields, to examine his hair, his mouth, his ears, and so on. I have stood guard over the door while he's been inside. And always he has come out with perhaps one, perhaps two, perhaps three, rough stones, well up to the average size and quality.'

Heldway had been softly whistling a bar of ragtime. He broke off to press home the logical fact. 'Well, if they're not already in the room, and he doesn't take 'em in, he must manufacture them.'

'I wish I could be sure,' said Fleeting. 'It seems all right, and yet—one does not like to sink a hatful of money . . . I want to be dead sure. That's why I'd like you to look into the business.'

The detective-inspector settled himself in a chair. 'The long and short of it is, that you're in for a gamble and want to be sure you'll win before you risk your money. I guess you know if I take it up, and it is a swindle, you'll have to take it into court. Let's be clear about that.'

The jeweller reddened. 'Look here, Mr Heldway, I don't mind so much myself; but there's another thing—my daughter—'

'Oh, there's a lady in the case?' The corners of Heldway's eyes wrinkled. 'Suppose you tell me all you know about Vernet.'

'We ran across him while we were in Chamonix last summer,' replied Fleeting. 'You know how one falls into these holiday acquaintanceships. Don't run away with the idea that I've got any fixed suspicions of him, Mr Heldway. I believe in him—but I want to be sure. He's certainly a gentleman, and he was in touch with some very nice people. He made himself agreeable to Elsie—that's my daughter—and he and I fell rather together. I'm not impressionable, but I must say I like him. Apart from the money, I should be sorry if there were any fake in this. I should put him about thirty. His mother was English and his father French. He's got a little estate in France, but for these last ten years has been knocking about the world. He speaks English as well as you or I . . .

'Of course my business leaked out. I'm a pretty well-known man. I don't remember precisely how the matter arose, but one day Vernet asked me for a private interview. I thought he wished to see me about something else—'

'Miss Fleeting?' interjected Heldway.

'Yes . . .' Fleeting hesitated. 'I didn't intend to tell you this, Mr Heldway, but you may as well know it. It makes the situation rather more delicate. He *did* see me about Elsie, but he introduced the other affair, and that matter remains in abeyance for the time being. He told me he had stumbled on the discovery while making certain chemical experiments, and offered to submit to any test I might propose short of showing me the actual process. I, of course, accepted, and invited him over to my little country-place till inquiries were completed.'

The detective's whistling stopped. 'Made any inquiries about the chap?' he demanded.

'Naturally. His estate is near Danville in the Department of Eure. I pleaded business in London, and put a couple of days in there myself as a tourist. I corroborated all that he told me about his affairs. His income, translated into English, would be about seven hundred a year. Nothing tremendous, but quite enough.'

A superficial insight might hold that a lifetime of detective work would make a man a cynic. Heldway had his share of cynicism, but, like all successful men of his profession, he had sympathy. He could appreciate something of the diverse feelings by which the jeweller was torn—his care for his daughter, his pocket, his vanity. He rose and dropped his hand lightly on the other's shoulder.

'When does the next demonstration take place?'

'On Monday.'

'Good. Now, can you invite me down to your place for the weekend as a friend? I'd like to see Vernet. Meanwhile, if you've got a photograph of him, any writing, any scrap of material concerning him, you let me have it. And by the way, I'd like a description of Vernet—hair, eyes, height, and so on. Good-bye for the present. I'll be down some time Saturday afternoon.'

Ten minutes later Heldway sauntered out of the office, whistling softly. He did not wonder that Fleeting, canny man, felt uneasy. The making of diamonds—profitably—was a big thing, and a man who could prove his good faith would easily obtain more than one hundred thousand pounds for a half-share. True, there was Elsie Fleeting—but, not having seen her, Heldway did not know exactly how far she might weigh in the transaction.

The spade work of detection is a laborious business, but very necessary to every detective outside the story-books. Juries do not convict on theories, however brilliant and plausible. They want facts—facts that can be sworn to. And so far Heldway had no facts—only a statement by Fleeting.

For half an hour or more Heldway laboured diligently. The Criminal Record Office put him in possession of facts relating to every one of the adventurers of this type known to be in England. Big Grant, the head of the department, who knew the science and practice of identification backwards, assisted in a close comparison of the portraits available with the amateur photograph of Vernet in the midst of a group which Fleeting had supplied. But they drew blank.

The finger-prints of Vernet might have simplified the search to a matter of minutes. As they were not available, the Record Office staff was set to work to trace through the old system of indexes, a tedious, lengthy job, by the light of the description Vernet had offered. They looked not under the letter 'V', but in that section of the records devoted to men of five feet nine in height with brown hair and hazel eyes.

This phase of the search Heldway left to the department, though at times he brought in a colleague to examine the photograph on the chance that Vernet might be recognised. At intervals he despatched cryptic cables to Paris and New York. Possibly Roger Vernet would have been flattered had he known how many people were being stirred to an interest in his career.

A neat little motor-car was waiting for Heldway at Haslemere station, and a run of a couple of miles brought him to a pine-shaded villa in which Fleeting had his country retreat. The detective nodded approval at the trim gables, the rose-bordered lawn, and the well-rolled gravel paths.

Fleeting, a little nervous and ill at ease, welcomed him with effusion, and with a wave of his hand introduced the couple who were standing in the shade of the veranda.

'Mr Heldway—my daughter. Vernet, a friend of mine—Mr Heldway.'

The detective found himself gripping a slender, almost effeminate hand, and Vernet's eyes did not drop under his scrutiny. Indeed, they were scrutinising him with a languorous ease that was almost insolent. The maker of diamonds had no appearance of the scientific student. He had been dressed by an artist in tailoring. His boots, his meticulously creased trousers, the sloping waist of his jacket, were all beyond criticism. He had a little toothbrush moustache, which he stroked from time to time with a delicate forefinger. His handkerchief was tinged with scent. Heldway, who was not self-conscious, felt uncouth in his presence.

'Delighted to know you,' said the young man, but his face had the abstract look of one wrestling with an abstruse mental problem. Heldway wondered if he had any suspicion of his identity. He murmured some commonplace, and his gaze wandered momentarily to the girl—a picture in grey and white. Erect and slender, with sparkling blue eyes and cheeks tanned to a wholesome clearness by fresh air and exercise, she did not conform at all to his mental impression of her. This was not the sort of woman to become infatuated with an adventurer. And yet—

They went in to lunch. Heldway was a good talker when he was in the vein, and conversation moved swiftly. He set himself to draw Vernet out, and the other was nothing loath. He had apparently been everywhere and seen everything.

'If this man's playing with a cold deck, he's got a nerve,' meditated the detective.

Once, during a lull in the conversation, he again surprised the bland hazel eyes surveying him with abstract calculation. Vernet pulled himself together.

'Come, Mr Heldway, a man of your profession is always running against experiences. I appeal to Miss Fleeting. Here's a real live detective, and he hasn't told us one of his adventures.'

The shot was sudden, and for the moment Heldway was thrown off his balance. A flicker of astonishment passed across his features. Then he smiled. Vernet was evidently determined to drag him boldly into the open.

'Are you a detective?' inquired the girl. 'How exciting! Dad only told us you were a friend of his.'

Heldway went imperturbably on with his sweet. 'Yes, I am a detective, Miss Fleeting. I'm afraid it is not so exciting as the novelists would have you believe. How did you know?' He addressed Vernet.

The other shrugged his shoulders. 'I didn't recall your face till this moment,' he answered indifferently. 'I saw you give evidence at the Old Bailey in a murder case last year. Are you down here on business?'

It was difficult for Heldway to repress a laugh. Whether Vernet was a rogue or not, he was not so simple as not to put a construction on the circumstances. 'An official of police is always more or less on business,' he parried. 'But I'm here, through Mr Fleeting's kindness, only for fresh air.'

'So you haven't brought your handcuffs?' Vernet was smiling inwardly. The official wondered if he meant a challenge.

'I don't anticipate any occasion to use them down here,' he laughed.

Fleeting, who had been fidgeting uneasily in his chair, broke in: 'Here's coffee. Have a cigar, Heldway. My daughter doesn't mind. I never ask Vernet. He's got his own particular brand of poisonous cigarettes. I believe he smokes them in his sleep.'

'It's a bad habit,' said Vernet. 'If I had any strength of will I should give them up. But I'm lost without a cigarette.' He extracted a fat one from a gold case, and lighting it, blew a circle of smoke into the air. 'If I were a criminal, now, there would be a clue for you, Mr Heldway. You'd only have to look for an insatiable consumer of cigarettes, like *Raffles*, eh?'

He held the white tube up to the light. 'I have them specially made, with my initials on the paper.'

'The perfect criminal—and thank Heaven there is none—would have no fixed habits,' commented Heldway.

It was late in the evening before he got the chance of a word alone with his host. Miss Fleeting had accepted the diamond-maker's challenge to billiards, and the two elder men were contemplating the moonlight from the veranda. Fleeting was anxious to make it clear that he had given no hint of the detective's identity. Heldway brushed away his explanation.

'Never mind about that. You haven't shown me over the house yet. Suppose we take the opportunity now.'

'I didn't suppose you'd be interested. It's entirely modern. However, come along.'

So it was that, when he retired, the detective had in his mind a very complete plan of the sleeping apartments of the house, especially the relation of his own bedroom to that occupied by Vernet. Beyond taking off his boots and collar, he had made no attempt to undress, He stretched himself out in an arm-chair with a novel, and composed himself to read until such a time as the household should be asleep. At two o'clock he laid aside his book and rummaged in his kit bag. A small electric torch about the size of an ordinary match-box, a dozen master-keys, and a red silk handkerchief with a couple of holes cut in it rewarded his search. The handkerchief he adjusted on his face, the holes serving as eye-slits. The keys and the torch he carried in his hands.

There are moments when a police officer steps out of the limits of strict legality. He knows how great a risk he runs, for if he fails of his purpose he can expect no countenance from his superiors. There was no possible excuse for Heldway in what was, in effect, an act of burglary. He had deliberately refrained from saying anything to Fleeting of his intention, partly, it must be admitted, because he was afraid that the jeweller might exercise a veto.

Softly he stepped into the corridor, his stockinged feet making no sound on the soft carpet. A thin thread of light cut through the darkness, affording just enough light to prevent his blundering into any furniture. More than once he switched off the light and stood stock still as his ear caught those indefinite sounds that are always audible in a sleeping household.

He reached Vernet's door and softly turned the handle. As he expected, it was locked.

Very stealthily he tried his keys one after the other.

His muscles contracted involuntarily as a slight *click* told that the bolt had shot back. He stood stiffly, listening intently.

Five minutes elapsed before he ventured to thrust open the door and cautiously edge his way inside. He waited for a matter of seconds till the deep regular breathing from the bed reassured him. Then he flashed the bead of light on the wardrobe, and all his movements quickened. Whatever he sought he had guessed the diamond-maker would carry on him during the day—otherwise Heldway would not have waited till now to ransack the room.

Presently he gave an almost unconscious ejaculation of triumph, as he dragged out of a pocket a little wash-leather bag. With hasty fingers he opened it and directed the rays of his lamp on twenty or thirty uncut diamonds. And then, even while he chuckled to himself, the room was suddenly flooded with light. He wheeled abruptly. Vernet was sitting up in bed, one hand on the electric light switch, the other holding a revolver, its muzzle steadily directed towards Heldway.

'Stand still, my friend.' Vernet's voice was cold and menacing. 'Perhaps it would be as well if you put your hands above your head.' His own hand had deserted the switch and began groping for the bell. 'I see you have masked your face—a wise precaution.'

Heldway lowered his head, swerved sideways, and plunged forward so swiftly that it seemed as if all his movements were simultaneous. A quick report rang out, and a bullet shattered the glass of the wardrobe. Before Vernet's finger could compress on the trigger again, Heldway was upon him. His full weight was behind his left as he swung it to Vernet's jaw, and the man dropped limply back on his pillow.

The detective fled. It was a matter of seconds from the time Vernet had fired till he reached his own room and closed and locked the door. He could hear people rushing about and sleepy voices raised in inquiry. Hastily he tore off his clothes and tumbled into his pyjamas. A thunderous knock interrupted him before he had finished. He continued an audible yawn the while he ruffled his bed noiselessly to give it the appearance of having been slept in, and in his voice as he put a question was the querulous tone of a man just aroused.

'It's me—Fleeting. Wake up. There's been burglars. They've murdered Vernet.'

'Good heavens!' There was a fervour that was unfeigned in the detective's voice. He had had no time to calculate his blow with nicety, and trusted that he had not struck harder than he meant. A moment later he flung open the door, and while Fleeting waited, put on his slippers and dressing-gown. His alibi was convincing.

They went together to the diamond-maker's room. He was relieved to find that Vernet was very far from dead, though still unconscious. 'Somebody has knocked him out, that's all,' he diagnosed. 'He'll be all right in a little while.' He turned on the group of servants who had gathered in the room. 'Some of you men get out into the grounds. The burglar can't have got far.'

'Hadn't someone better go for the police?' said the jeweller.

'Not worth while. They can do nothing tonight that we can't do without them. If we don't catch the man ourselves, I'll run out to put the case in their hands myself.'

No one disputed his authority. He calculated that the flustered men-servants would make enough confusion in the garden to keep up the illusion of a burglar, and he did not want to have to cause the local police useless trouble. Nevertheless, after seeing Vernet comfortably disposed, he went to direct the search. He it was, curiously enough, who discovered a broken pane of glass in an unfastened scullery window—proof of the means by which the burglar had effected an entrance.

Nothing resulted from a search of the grounds. One man at least had scarcely expected there would. He was undecided whether to take Fleeting into his confidence. If all had gone well he would have done so—indeed, it would have been necessary to his plan.

'I reckon that if Vernet was on the ramp he would have a stock of diamonds to draw on,' he explained to a colleague later. 'I wanted to lay my hands on them, and to get Fielding to weigh and measure and examine them, so that he could tell them again. Then I was going to replace them. If Vernet played any of them during his manufacturing stunt, then we would have had him.'

Heldway was a man who rarely did a thing without an object, and there was now no object in telling Fleeting. He might safely be allowed to nurse the delusion of a burglar if he would. The diamonds he resolved to keep, for the time being. Unless Vernet had a reserve store, which was unlikely, he would be forced to procure more or postpone Monday's demonstration. There was, of course, the possibility that he really could make diamonds. But the detective had little fear of that.

'Nothing gone,' repeated Fleeting, who had been stocktaking with the butler. 'That is, unless Vernet's lost anything.'

'Let's hope he hasn't,' said Heldway cheerfully. 'The chap's got away, whoever he was. Perhaps Vernet will give us something to work on when he comes around.'

As a fact, Vernet a quarter of an hour later was able to throw little light on the situation. He was still a little dazed and unable to think or express himself clearly. 'Woke up . . . masked man . . . going through my clothes . . . came for me . . . fired . . . missed him. Then he hit me.' He lay back wearily and, at Heldway's suggestion, was permitted to sleep.

But it was a different man who appeared at breakfast. Spruce and debonair, he seemed little affected by his adventure, as in well-chosen phrases he told of his encounter with the burglar. 'He was confoundedly quick,' he admitted. 'I didn't think I could have missed at that distance. As it was, all he got was a bag of twenty-five rough diamonds—the result of some of my experiments.' He smiled brightly at Heldway.

'Experiments?' repeated the detective blankly.

'Ah! I forgot, It's a little secret between Fleeting and myself. By the way, Fleeting, can the chauffeur run me into Haslemere after breakfast? I want to send a wire.'

'I'll go with you if you don't mind,' interposed Heldway. 'We may as well see the local police. This burglary is really their affair.' He had his own ideas as to what Vernet's wire might contain.

No one who beheld the two side by side in the car would have considered them as the hunter and the hunted, the attacker and the defender. Heldway had risen to Vernet's flow of spirits, and accepted the light chaff of the other without resentment.

'Now, if I didn't know you were above suspicion,' remarked the diamond-maker once, 'I should be inclined to think you were the burglar all the fuss was about last night. He was just about your build.'

It was deftly conveyed intimation that Vernet had guessed something of the object of the midnight raid. Heldway laughed. 'Oh, there's no need for me to turn burglar yet.'

'One never knows,' retorted Vernet.

Vernet went on to the post office, but Heldway got out of the car at the police station. As a matter of detail he reported the burglary, and the facts were solemnly written down on an official form by the officer in charge. Looking up for a fresh dip of ink, the officer saw a wink flicker on Heldway's grim face.

'I shouldn't waste too much trouble over the case if I were you,' said Heldway. 'Of course, it's none of my business, but if I might suggest a policy of masterly inactivity—you understand?'

The other was a man of quick perception. He grinned. 'Not altogether. I'm not going to cross-examine you. If you like, I'll go back with you. You just want me to look wise?'

'Exactly,' assented Heldway. 'Now can I use your phone for a moment? I want to talk to the Yard.'

When he put down the receiver he was whistling softly to himself.

The three men—Vernet, Heldway, and Fleeting—had travelled to Waterloo together, and there separated, the last named to Hatton Gardon, Heldway to Scotland Yard, and Vernet to keep an appointment. The demonstration was fixed to take place at noon.

Heldway's business with the department did not keep him long, and when he left it was in a taxi-cab straight for Fleeting's place of business. A couple of men were loitering in conversation outside the door, but as Heldway brushed by them they might have been perfect strangers to him instead of two of his most acute subordinates.

Fleeting was in a pessimistic mood.

'I've got to make a decision today, one way or the other, Heldway. Unless you can prove something definite after Vernet's experiment, I shall close the deal. He threatens to go to Burnett's. You've not found out anything?'

'Only that he's a smart man,' parried the detective evasively.

'I'll make a report to you after the demonstration. Meanwhile, I'd like to get up to the laboratory. Is there any place there where I can hide?'

'Not room for a mouse,' declared Fleeting. 'I had it cleared specially.'

'Then the outer room will have to do. Is there a cupboard or a curtain in that outer room anywhere, where I can be out of sight?'

'There are heavy, long plush curtains to the windows. But why out of sight? I am sure Vernet would not object—in fact, I am certain he has guessed you are watching him in my interests.'

'So am I,' answered Heldway grimly. 'But even if he guesses I am concealed, he will say nothing.'

'I like that, you know. It shows he isn't afraid of investigation.'

'H'm!' grunted Heldway.

Twelve o'clock was striking when Vernet entered, accompanied by Fleeting and a third man, whom the detective, watching from behind the curtain, guessed to be the expert searcher. Little time was wasted in preliminaries. The diamond-maker at once began to strip. The inevitable cigarette was still between his lips. The searcher made a slow, painstaking examination, and Vernet put on the suit which had been arranged for him.

He puffed out a cloud of blue smoke and stepped to the laboratory door.

Heldway flung back the curtain. 'One moment, Mr Vernet,' he said.

Vernet stood with one hand on the door, the other holding his cigarette. His eyebrows went up in well-bred surprise, and he made a little gesture of annoyance. 'This isn't quite fair, Fleeting. I asked you to take every precaution you wished, but I did think you'd be open and above-board—not set this man to spy—Oh!'

The detective had gripped his wrist. There was a second's

struggle, and then he staggered back from a quick push by the detective. Heldway had in his hand the broken fragments of the cigarette Vernet had been smoking. The diamond-maker had gone white. His fists clenched and his lips moved without speaking.

'Look at that!' exclaimed Heldway.

He had crumbled the cigarette into shreds. In the tobacco in the palm of his hand lay three rough diamonds.

It was then Vernet saw his opportunity. With a rapid movement he was at the door and, flinging it open, vanished before anyone could lift a finger to intercept him. 'Never mind,' said Heldway quietly, and lifting the window, he gave a long, low whistle.

He could see his two men arrange themselves one on each side of the door. One calmly stuck out a foot as Vernet emerged. The other caught him as he tripped. He was as helpless as a child in their hands. Not a word was spoken as he was marched with business-like haste back into the office.

'Vernet,' said Heldway, as he again confronted the trickster, 'you will be charged with attempting to obtain money by means of a trick. You may volunteer any statement, but, remember, anything you say may be used against you. One of you two fetch a cab.'

Returning from the police station, Heldway accepted one of Fleeting's choice cigars, and explained.

'There are a lot of people,' he said, 'who believe that when you know a man's guilty, all you've got to do is to arrest him. Those same people would raise Cain, of course, if one really did so. I believe Vernet was a wrong 'un from the start, but when you told me of your inquiries, I was not quite certain. He wasn't in our records, nor could I find any of our men who recognised him. Of course I cabled to France and had a little investigation made there. The French police got hold of Vernet's bankers, who assured them that he had last been in touch with their agents at Cairo. That was only five weeks ago.'

'But,' remonstrated Fleeting, 'Vernet was—'

'Wait a minute, please. It was clear there were two Vernets. I asked the French people to procure me a photograph or a description of their Vernet, and at the same time posted them a copy of the portrait of ours. You see, it didn't matter very much whether the man was an impostor or not until I could prove that our man was trying to defraud you. I came down to Haslemere pretty positive in my own mind. Vernet—our Vernet—showed pretty clearly that he knew I was gunning for him, and that worried me a little, for it showed he was confident of getting away with his game in spite of me. Bear in mind that I had nothing against him that was definite. I wanted to get hold of the reserve diamonds that he was planting on you. I put up the burglary hoping to get them, take a record of them and put them back. However, that fell through.

'This morning, when we came up, I had arranged for a couple of men to pick up Vernet at Waterloo. They shadowed him to the bar of a public-house in Shaftesbury Avenue. There he met a crook well known to us—a man called Wiggins. They had a drink together, and then Vernet took out his cigarette-case. It was empty. Wiggins at once produced his. "Take two or three," he said; "you'll like them. They're a special brand."

'I had waited at the Yard, and one of my men reported this over the 'phone. Things began to take shape and I took a chance. I ordered them to detain Wiggins on suspicion the moment the two separated. Meanwhile, there was a batch of correspondence from France for me. They had identified the photograph I sent over as that of a young Englishman named Meldrum who had once been a sort of companion to Vernet. They had broken off association over some card-cheating business. You see, you had made the mistake of confining your attention to Vernet's standing, and as the man you were dealing with was not Vernet, you were deceived by Vernet's good reputation.

'When I came on here I knew what I had to look for. It was now merely a question of catching Meldrum in the act. I waited until the last moment, took the cigarette from him, and—there we were. Of course, Wiggins and he had concocted the idea together, and Meldrum was laying for you at Chamonix.'

Fleeting looked rueful. 'I must seem rather a fool,' he said.

'Not at all,' said Heldway politely.

V

CREEPING JIMMIE

Creeping Jimmie had invested one shilling on a cigar and nine shillings on a first-class ticket to Townsford. Both of these events advertised an exceptional occasion, for he was a careful man. Besides, he did not like cigars. He preferred cigarettes.

Nevertheless, one must keep up appearances. What was a shilling cigar—what, for the matter of that, was a nine-shilling fare—with the rosy prospect of £5000 or its equivalent in diamonds in the imminent distance?

So Jimmie, ponderous and prosperous, strode the platform at Waterloo, his little beady eyes alert and a comfortable glow of anticipation beneath his well-cut lounge jacket. For many long weeks he had been an habitué of Hatton Garden cafés, and the fruits of that vigil were ripening at last.

Mr Lawrence Sheet and Mr R. K. Adhurst stepped into the picture at the same moment. But Sheet was then the only person who interested Jimmie. He breathed out a thankful cloud of smoke and picked up his suit-case.

Now the senior partner of a Hatton Garden firm of diamond merchants who travels third class is a mean man. He is not only mean but cautious, since the publicity of the more democratic carriage is a safeguard usually as effective to the bearer of a precious burden as steel bars. Jimmie was too old a hand to swear aloud, but he was chagrined. It was at least a clean loss of four-and-sixpence, and, as if with deliberate perversity, Mr Sheet had selected a non-smoker.

Jimmie dropped ninepennyworth of cigar on the asphalt, and with a sigh followed an athletic young parson into Sheet's carriage. But R. K. Adhurst, sauntering slowly by, came to a dead halt. Jimmie's luck was dead out.

'Why, Jimmie, lad. Fancy meeting you.' There was a joyousness in Mr Adhurst's voice that aroused no response in Jimmie's face.

He stared blankly at the detective. Beneath that round mask of a face he was swiftly considering the best way to meet the situation. He met Adhurst's greeting blankly, with a stony stare of non-recognition.

'I beg your pardon,' he said frigidly. 'I think you've made a mistake.'

Adhurst grinned confidently. 'Not on your life, Jimmie. Never mind. There's nothing doing.' And he sauntered away.

There is coincidence sometimes in the affairs of the Criminal Investigation Department, but it is coincidence born of organisation. Jimmie mentally cursed the luck that had brought about the conjunction of Sheet and Adhurst. Casting his mind back he could see no flaw in the arrangements he had made for the relieving of Sheet of the small tissue-paper parcel stowed away somewhere on the person of the dapper diamond merchant. He had spent much time and patience in selecting a man who lived out of town, and who followed a not unusual custom among the jewel firms of carrying his stock about with him instead of entrusting it to a safe. By methods all his own he had found out the day when Sheet's cargo was likely to be more valuable than usual—and now everything looked like being spoilt. Sheet—whom he knew held a first-class season—was perversely travelling third, and to crown it all Adhurst had butted in.

Shrewd as he was he did not connect the two events. How should he have known that his discreet inquiries had reached the ears of the destined victim, and that Sheet was travelling third-class on the advice of Adhurst?—that, in fact, the divisional detective-inspector was there by request, merely to see Sheet off and, incidentally, to observe who were his fellow passengers. The engine gave a preliminary snort and the train drew smoothly out. Two hours later a white-lipped porter at Townsford was babbling incoherently to the station-master that Mr Lawrence Sheet, of the Red House, was dead in a third-class compartment with a bullet through his heart.

If you had scooped twenty or thirty men haphazard out of the street you would not have found a more mixed lot. There was not a pair of handcuffs among them. At the risk of discrediting an estimable body of men it must in candour be added that there was probably nothing more efficacious for purposes of disguise than a pocket comb.

As they lounged about the lofty room, distempered in two shades of green which Scotland Yard affects, you—if you are an astute reader of detective fiction—would readily have diagnosed them as butchers, bakers, barristers, stockbrokers, actors, or millionaires—anything you chose except the hawk-eyed sleuth.

In the mass they looked eminently commonplace respectable men—fathers of families who lived in trim suburban villas and played golf, motored, or rolled the lawn on Sundays, according to their means.

Yet this was a big council of crime—the fortnightly meeting of divisional heads of the detective force of London—at which any newspaper man would have given his ears to be present. They were placid business men everyone, and their business happened to be matters of crime. In every respect they were very much human beings with, outside of business, diverse tastes and interests. Only in office hours were they enthusiasts. One does not become even a divisional detective-inspector without enthusiasm and many years of experience.

Experience—and the qualities begot of experience—were there in plenty. There was not a corner of the world, however remote, which someone in that room had not visited, not a civilised language which was not understood. But first of all there was not a man who did not know where to go for information on any point that was ever likely to concern him. The super-detective who knows everything is a rarity in the Criminal Investigation Department.

Now and again Foyle, the spruce blue-eyed superintendent who presided, would join in some discussion, and the talk ranged widely from the recent release of Banjo Pete, to the suspicion that, somewhere in London, Russian paper currency was being forged and to the possibilities underlying the recent epidemic of burglaries at Brixton. This informal comparison of notes had more than once had deadly effect on the promising operations of some ingenious scoundrel.

It was on this gathering that Adhurst entered—a lank, stoop-shouldered man, with greying moustache and untidy brown hair. He moved straight to the superintendent with a sheet of paper in one hand, a yellow A.B.C. in the other. Even among his colleagues a long-cultivated habit of caution prevailed and he lowered his voice.

'Home Office message,' he said laconically. 'Job for someone. It looks like Creeping Jimmie.'

Foyle wrinkled his brows as he read: 'Chief Constable Blankshire requests assistance Scotland Yard officer in connection with murder of Lawrence Sheet found shot in train today. Wire time arrival Blake Townsford.'

'There's a train from Waterloo in quarter of an hour, sir,' said Adhurst. 'I've ordered a taxi.'

The superintendent wasted no unnecessary words. 'You'd better catch it yourself, old man,' he said crisply. 'You'll want some money. Let's go and raid the war-chest.'

They moved out together. In the big safe in Foyle's room there was always sufficient money to take a man to the ends of the earth if need be, and there was a musical tinkle as the inspector slipped twenty sovereigns in his pocket.

Foyle paused long enough to write a message with the mystic letters 'A. S.' in the corner. That message told a great deal of Creeping Jimmie. In five or ten minutes the tickers in the two hundred police stations of London would be insistently calling twenty thousand men to find him if he was anywhere within the seven hundred square miles of the metropolis. The superintendent strolled back to the conference.

'Bad case of murder broken loose at Townsford.' he observed calmly. 'Anyone running across Creeping Jimmie had better detain him on suspicion. Adhurst has gone down. You'd better handle the thing from this end, Grenfell.'

In the ordinary way a murder in the provinces has no more to do with Scotland Yard than a burglary in Timbuctoo. Only by request of the local police through the Home Office does a metropolitan detective investigate a criminal case that has occurred outside London. Even then, technically, he is only an adviser to the local police.

Adhurst, as he took his seat in a second-class smoker, was not enamoured of his job. Human nature being what it is—even in police circles—it was a toss-up whether the executive officers of the county constabulary would resent his intrusion or work loyally in co-operation with him. Luckily the case looked simple. Although pre-conceived opinions are apt to be dangerous to a police officer he had little doubt that Jimmie was the murderer, and equally little doubt that he would almost instantly be hunted down.

It was five o'clock on a blazing summer's day when he reached Townsford, and a little group of men moved forward as he descended to the platform. He held out his hand to an erect soldierly looking man he diagnosed as the chief constable.

'Major Borden, I presume. My name's Adhurst. My people wired you I was coming.'

The chief constable shook hands. 'Yes. I've just been speaking to Foyle on the phone. I'm afraid you've had rather a wasted journey.'

'Oh?' Adhurst's tone was interrogative.

'That man you saw—er—Creeping Jimmie, was arrested as

he returned to Waterloo. You must have actually passed him on the line on your way down.'

Adhurst sucked in his under-lip thoughtfully. 'That's not like Jimmie,' he said, 'unless he absolutely lost his head. I can't imagine him rushing back to London by the next train and putting his head straight away in the lion's jaws. Were the diamonds found on him—or a weapon?'

'Nothing; but he'd hardly keep them about him in the circumstances. By the way, I was forgetting. Mr Adhurst—Superintendent Trelway, Inspector Penn. This is Mr Livrey, Mr Sheet's brother-in-law.'

The detective gravely acknowledged the introductions. As he gripped Livrey's hand it lay for a second very cold in his own, and he surprised a keen flicker of surmise in the other's eyes.

'This is a terrible business, Mr Adhurst. Fortunately I was staying here on a short visit. My sister is naturally much distressed.'

'Naturally,' agreed Adhurst.

'She asked me to say that, should you care to stay at the Red House during your investigations here, she would be most pleased.'

'That is very kind of her. If it is not inconvenient I shall gratefully take advantage of the offer. It is unlikely, however, that I shall be here long. The case seems very straightforward.' He turned to the chief constable. 'And now, sir, it might save time if I had a look at the railway carriage in which the body was found.'

'Shall I be in the way if I come?' asked Livrey deprecatingly. 'I have a motor here, and we might go back together.'

'By all means,' agreed Adhurst. 'I don't expect to be free for some little time, though. We'—he spoke significantly in the plural, so that it should not be assumed that he was running the affair—'must fix up one or two matters before I can take it easy. I'll get you to take my bag back, though, if you will.'

The carriage had been detached from the train and lay in a siding. Headed by the stationmaster the group of men moved down across the metals towards it. Once again Adhurst, apparently languidly indifferent, caught Livrey surveying him with a certain quality of speculation in his gaze.

The chief constable and Adhurst climbed aboard. 'Nothing much to be learned here,' said Borden perfunctorily. 'Sheet was sitting in that corner. The murderer must have been sitting in that farther corner on the opposite side when he fired. The bullet passed clean through Sheet's head and then through the window. There's the bullet-hole in the glass.'

'H'm,' grunted Adhurst. His forehead corrugated into a frown, and, thrusting his hands into his trousers pockets, he dropped lazily into the corner that had been occupied by the murdered man. He turned his eyes wearily to the window and stood up again with a yawn.

'You're right. This doesn't seem to carry us far. I think, though, it might be locked for a while and a man put here to see that it isn't interfered with till after the inquest. Now, if you don't mind, we'll see the doctor, and perhaps we can hunt up one or two passengers who came by this train.'

For an hour or more Adhurst kept those officers of the local police who were available hard at work, though he was very careful to pass all orders through the superintendent. He knew that a little loss of tact might result in blunders and difficulties which would be hard to counter. They were able, intelligent men, but a provincial force gets small practice in detective work, and their perspective had to be continually adjusted. He sighed for the trained men who would have been available in London or any other big city. Only the fashionable amateur detective of the romances can work effectively single-handed.

In a dozen or twenty towns along the line the telephone stirred police inquiries, for Creeping Jimmie had not been seen to alight at Townsford. Also there was the young clergyman he had seen in the carriage with the two of them to be found. So far as London was concerned Adhurst was easy. Grenfell could be relied on to pick up every fact there—from Sheet's office, his solicitors, his bank, and any by-line that might suggest itself.

Once a wire interrupted him. It came from Grenfell. 'Bringing our man down 7.40 train,' it said. Adhurst passed it across to the chief constable without comment.

Borden raised his eyebrows. 'Kind of him to take that trouble,' he said. 'Why couldn't they have held him till we sent an escort?'

'I reckon,' said Adhurst slowly, 'that Dicky Grenfell has stumbled across something and wants to put us wise. There's no other reason why he should want to bring the prisoner down. And now, sir, about the doctor? It seems to me that a great deal is going to turn on the medical evidence.'

'Eh? What's that? I thought everything was plain enough. You got a statement from the doctor, didn't you, Trelway?'

Instantly Adhurst saw his mistake. By no means had he intended to hint that any routine matter had been insufficiently covered. The grizzled superintendent could not repress a sneer. 'Perhaps I'm not quite up to Scotland Yard mark, sir. I saw him myself when he examined the body. Mr Adhurst has seen the statement I took.'

Behind his untidy moustache the detective hid a smile. He dropped a friendly hand on the provincial man's shoulder. 'We're old hands, both of us, Mr Trelway,' he said genially. 'You know how it is. They might ask me up there'—he jerked a thumb vaguely over his shoulder to indicate superior authority—'why I didn't see the doctor person myself. Just a matter of form, that's all. Well, I can't help you any more just now, can I? I'll see the doctor and cut along to the Red House for an hour or two. I'll be back in time to meet Grenfell.'

He went out. The chief constable turned an inquiring eye on his subordinate. 'Now what the devil does he mean?' he demanded.

Trelway shrugged his shoulders. He was too wise to express an opinion.

A genial country practitioner, to whom murders were rare, had received the Scotland Yard man with cordiality and importance. Adhurst mingled half a dozen crisp questions with a flood of generalities, and went his way with his brain working at high tension, though his face did not betray that he had a care in the world.

He walked the one and a half miles to the Red House with deliberation. He wanted to get the bearings of his problems, for, since his arrival at Townsford, it had not seemed so simple. He was a sociable soul, and more than once he stopped to lean over the railings of a cottager's garden and admire the sweet peas. He went so far once as to buy a bunch of flowers, which he dropped into a ditch when he was out of sight. Nevertheless, by the time he passed up the gravel drive of the Red House he had assimilated a large amount of local gossip.

Livrey met him on the veranda. 'My dear man!' he exclaimed, 'you don't mean that you have walked out? If I'd have known I'd have sent the car—'

Adhurst flashed a disarming smile at him. 'I've thoroughly enjoyed the walk, thanks. This is a beautiful district.'

'Very. Well, come along in. You won't trouble to dress for dinner. You are just in time.'

It was at the dinner-table that the detective caught his first glimpse of Mrs Sheet. Somehow she was different to the type his imagination had conjured up. She was beautiful—there was no gainsaying that—but it was with a vivacious Southern beauty, now marred by the dark rings that encircled the dulled eyes. She could not have been more than twenty-five, and her voice was low and musical as she spoke to the detective.

'I can't realise it,' she said. 'I can't realise that he is gone—that I am—'

A crash interrupted her, and Livrey, with an apology, rang

for a servant to pick up the knives which he had accidentally swept off the table.

'They say that you have got the man who did it?' She went on with a quick catch of her breath, 'You think you will be able to prove that he did it? It is dreadful of me, I know, Mr Adhurst, but'—for the moment her face flamed and she clenched her fist passionately—'I could kill him myself . . . For the sake of a few paltry jewels . . .'

She rose abruptly and left the table.

Livrey seemed little affected either by her emotion or her abrupt departure. 'Sad, very sad,' he observed perfunctorily, and applied himself to the soup. Adhurst followed his example without comment. There were one or two things he would have liked to have asked Mrs Sheet, but they could wait.

This *tête-à-tête* meal with Livrey had a certain piquancy for him, for he had begun to conceive that the place he occupied in the family affairs of the dead man might be worth considering.

There are always possibilities of surprise in even the most ordinary case of murder, and Adhurst had had too much experience ever to feel sure. Creeping Jimmie—though things on the face of it were against him—might be able to prove definitely his innocence. And if Jimmie was not guilty it was advisable to find out what other person might have a motive for wishing Sheet out of the way. The bunch of flowers that the detective had bought on his way outwards had gained for him the local gossip that there had been talk of a separation between Mr and Mrs Sheet, and that his brother-in-law was an infrequent and unwelcome visitor to the Red House. Still, it might all be country scandal without foundation.

Yet here he was, with the body of Lawrence Sheet scarcely cold, assuming all the airs of a host in the house, and reposing within the detective's breast-pocket was a cipher wire to Scotland Yard requesting inquiries might be made into his career. It was all very hazy and indefinite, and Adhurst knew that he had to walk warily.

'What I can't understand,' said Livrey, 'is where the diamonds have gone. It is possible, I suppose, that this man you have arrested has passed them to a confederate or hidden them?'

'Easily possible,' agreed Adhurst. 'We can't say till inquiries have got a bit closer.'

Livrey glanced at him sharply. 'You have no doubt you have got the right man?'

'Not the least in the world,' lied the detective glibly. 'It is only a matter of collecting evidence now. We don't often make mistakes.' That last touch of brag was unusual with Adhurst. In the ordinary way he would no more have spoken of his efficiency than of his honesty.

He believed he saw the least trace of relief in Livrey's face. Yet it might have been the passing of a shadow.

'I shall be glad, for my sister's sake, to get it all over,' said the other. 'By the way, I must run up to town tomorrow to see about his affairs—that is, unless you are likely to need me down here for anything.'

'Not at all likely. You'll be required for evidence at the inquest, of course, but that isn't till the day after tomorrow.'

'Oh, I shall be back before then. You will make your headquarters here, I hope, while you remain—eh? My sister would wish you to do absolutely as you please. If the car will be of any use to you in getting to and fro I will leave orders that it is to be at your disposal.'

'That is very good of you.' Adhurst had been wondering how he should lead up to the proposal that had been volunteered. 'In point of fact it would be most useful. I have to meet a colleague tonight, and if I might venture—'

'Certainly. I will tell Cody—that's the chauffeur—to have it ready.'

Creeping Jimmie, very chastened and with handcuffs spanning his broad wrists, cast a reproachful glance on Adhurst as he was assisted to alight on Townsford platform.

'I thought you would ha' known better than this, Mr Adhurst,' he said dolefully. 'I had no more to do with croaking that guy than the babe unborn.'

'So you say, Jimmie,' assented the inspector. 'Hullo, Grenfell. Shake hands with Mr Trelway. There's a couple of men and a cab waiting to take Jimmie to the station. Suppose we go and have a pow-wow at the hotel.'

He had foreseen the necessity of a conference and arranged for a private room at the hotel adjoining the station. Grenfell caught him by the arm as they entered. 'Adhurst, old son,' he said quietly, 'this is a mess-up.'

'Meaning?'

'Meaning that Jimmie isn't the man.'

Adhurst kicked the door to. 'My bright young friend,' he said blithely. 'You're a day behind the fair. We knew that an hour ago, didn't we, Mr Trelway. I've got Jimmie's alibi in my pocket.'

Grenfell's grip tightened. 'I don't stand for any mystification stunt,' he declared. 'Now cough it up. Have you got the right man?'

'I don't know. I've got hopes. Sit down and I'll order drinks and we'll get to the agenda.

'Well,' he went on, when the waiter had answered the ring and gone out, 'Mr Trelway and I have been busy for quite a while. We know that Jimmie got out thirty miles up the line—at Gillington—and that Sheet was alive then, and that Jimmie couldn't have gone back to the compartment. The Gillington police have cleared all that up.'

'That's what's brought me down,' interrupted Grenfell. 'Jimmie's story is that there was a clergyman in with him and Sheet, and that the jewel merchant seemed a bit uneasy when the parson began to get out. He whispered something to the parson through the window, who stared at Jimmie hard. Taking that in conjunction with your turning up at Waterloo, Jimmie decided that it was not his day and got out, took a stroll round the town, had some food and returned—to find us waiting for him.'

'That's so. The Gillington people have found the parson—a local curate. Sheet had asked him to take a good look at Jimmie, as he was carrying valuables and believed the other to be a crook. The parson saw Jimmie get out, and later noticed him in the town, so he couldn't have committed the murder. All the same, we'll hold him for a while. What do you think, Mr Trelway?'

'That's best,' agreed the superintendent sagely. 'Better not let Livrey have an idea we've got the slightest suspicion that we've got the wrong man.'

Grenfell held up his hands. 'You people are forgetting I don't know anything of this side of the case. Suppose we be a bit clearer.'

Adhurst began to unstrap a small attaché case which he carried. Like all Scotland Yard men he relied largely on method, and he had systematised the various reports gathered by the local men and sent in by telegraph and telephone, so that he could instantly lay his hands on anyone.

'My dear Watson,' he quoted, 'it's very simple—or will be, I hope. Listen!'

For an hour the three talked. Then Adhurst flung up his arms and gave a prodigious yawn.

'Heigho,' he sighed, 'I'm tired. I think that clears us up. You'll keep an eye on Livrey, Grenfell, and you'll arrange about another man meeting you at Waterloo. Mr Trelway will swear out a search warrant, and I'll arrange with the stationmaster, if possible, about a dummy train.'

Punctually at twenty minutes past nine next morning Livrey leaned from the window of a first-class compartment to say good-bye to Adhurst, who had come to see him off. Three compartments behind Grenfell was immersed in a daily paper, but no sign of recognition had passed between his colleague and himself. He had sauntered once or twice along the platform, and he knew he could make no mistake about the suspect, who henceforth would never be out of sight until he was arrested or cleared. No bloodhound could hold more tightly to a trail than Grenfell.

As the engine gave a preliminary cough Trelway and the chief constable sauntered up. 'Everything going smooth, I hope?' said the latter.

'Quite, thanks,' said Adhurst. 'Well, good-bye, Mr Livrey. See you tomorrow.' The train glided out and he turned to the chief constable. 'I have a car waiting outside, sir. You've got the map?'

Major Borden pulled an ordnance survey chart from his pocket and unfolded it. 'This is the thing.' His forefinger traced the course of a line in red ink that had been run along one of the roads and stopped at a cross. 'There we are, I think. It won't be long before we're able to test your theory. What time's this special?'

Adhurst looked at his watch. 'A matter of ten minutes now. I think I'll be moving. We don't want to hold up traffic more than we can help.'

With a nod he strode away to where Cody the chauffeur, an alert little Cockney, was waiting with Livrey's, or rather Sheet's, car. To the chauffeur he produced a map marked in similar fashion to that which the chief constable had possessed.

'There, Cody,' he said, pointing to the cross. 'That's where we've got to make for. How long is it going to take us?'

'Stoner's Cray. That's twelve miles. It's a bad road, sir, and the tires on this old jigger are none too good. Mr Livrey has cut 'em about something awful this last day or two. 'E don't know 'ow to treat a decent car, 'an that's a fact, if I may say so, sir.'

'Well, do your best and take the last mile or two easy.'

It was a picturesque drive, but the detective had no eye for scenery. Just at that time his mind was on hard business. He had achieved that perilous thing in detective work, a theory, and he had pinned himself to work it out.

They stopped at last at a point where the road for a matter

of a couple of hundred yards ran side by side with a railway line. Clumps of bushes and gorse grew on the open strip of waste land between the roadway and the line, and over this strip Adhurst quested to and fro like a hound at fault. Presently he called Cody to desert the car and aid him.

The keen little Cockney, though he had no idea of the ultimate object at the back of the detective's brain, joined enthusiastically, and in a little gave a yelp of triumph and pointed to a tangle of brambles and furze.

'Good boy,' said Adhurst, and his eyes roved swiftly over the ground in the neighbourhood. He gave a subdued chuckle as he observed a footprint in the sandy soil. 'Cody,' he remarked, 'be virtuous, and Providence will always be good to you. Neither you nor I made that footprint.'

'Is it a cloo, sir?' asked Cody breathlessly. This adventure with a real live detective was thrilling him.

'Something of the sort. Now we passed a house a mile or two back. You dodge along there with the car and ask if they can lend you a box or something to put over it till we're able to take a plaster cast.'

A puff of smoke warned Adhurst that the special which held the local police was coming. It advanced very slowly and Adhurst waved a handkerchief. The signal was answered, and he dropped behind a clump of bushes and sighted along his stick as though it were a rifle. Then he rose and, taking a ball of twine from his pocket, fastened one end to the bush, and, carrying it forward, tossed the ball to Major Borden through the open window of one of the compartments.

The train halted. Borden cut his end of the string and threaded it through a bullet hole in one of the side windows. Adhurst leapt on the foot-board and the train crawled in until he held up his hand. 'How's that, sir?' he demanded.

At the other end of the compartment Trelway was holding the string above his head. The chief constable jumped on a seat and, closing one eye, squinted along the line.

'Correct!' he ejaculated. 'That explains why there was only one bullet mark.'

'Tie a knot in the string and we can work out the distance afterwards. Now, sir, if you like to get out, I'll show you something else I have found.'

He took the chief constable and the superintendent back to the clump of bushes, winding up the string as he proceeded. Then he pointed out the footprint. 'I don't know whether we really need it,' he observed, 'but it may be calculated to help. Whoever killed Sheet lay under those bushes. You'll observe he could not be seen from the line or the road.'

'What's worrying me,' said Trelway, 'is why no one heard a shot.'

'That doesn't greatly worry me. When we raid the Red House that may be cleared up. We've got everything in broad outline now, and by tomorrow we ought to be close enough up to decide. Suppose we finish here. Will you have a talk with the nearest signalman, Mr Trelway?'

Well after midnight it was before Adhurst returned to the Red House, accompanied by his colleagues and four uniformed constables. There had been a hundred things to do, and they had been content to leave matters at the Red House till the last. There was no particular hurry, and Adhurst had wanted many details filled in.

The house was in darkness, save for a thin glimmer of light in the hall, and a sleepy-eyed servant answered the detective's ring. His face betrayed his astonishment as he saw Adhurst's companions. Adhurst, however, deigned no explanations.

'Your mistress has retired, I suppose? Will you tell her maid to let her know that we wish to see her at once? Hurry up, my man, and don't stand there like a dummy. We'll wait in the dining-room. Come in, gentlemen. Will you post your men, Mr Trelway? It may be advisable that no one should leave the house till we are finished.'

Mrs Sheet came to them in a few minutes, her dark hair

tumbling about the scarlet dressing-gown she had hastily donned. She stood at the door for a second looking from one to the other of the men. Adhurst bowed gravely.

'Sorry to have disturbed you. There are one or two points of importance on which it is essential to see you.'

She advanced into the room and mechanically sat in the chair which he offered. There was an involuntary tightening of her brows, and she put one hand to her heart.

'Well?' she said.

It was Trelway who answered. 'You are aware that we are police officers. We want to inform you that we hold a warrant to search this house.'

'I do not understand what you mean. Why should you search the house?' Her lips were white, and Adhurst judged that it was only by a great effort at self-control that she did not faint.

'Madam,' he said, 'you must understand your position. We suspect you of being concerned in the murder of your husband. You will be arrested. You need say nothing unless you choose, but anything you do say may be used as evidence. I should advise you to consult a solicitor—later.'

The deliberate warning, which at least had the effect of putting an end to any suspense she may have suffered, seemed to act on her like a tonic.

'This is absurd,' she said in a strained whisper. 'I did not kill him.'

'You will dress at once,' said Trelway.

'In this room,' said Adhurst quickly. 'We shall leave it at the disposal of your maid and yourself, but'—his tone was significant, for he had the possibility of poison in mind—'everything that is brought in to you will be searched.'

Her head dropped on to her arms on the table.

'Oh, my God!' she moaned. The police officers passed out.

The systematic search of a house for evidence in a matter of crime is not a thing airily undertaken, and daylight had long dawned ere the officers had finished. An urgent message brought in by a cycle constable had taken the chief local officers back into town about nine o'clock, carrying with them a man's shoe, a powerful air-rifle, and a bundle of letters.

Adhurst, who saw no sense in wearing himself out unnecessarily, stretched himself on a couch and seized the opportunity for a nap. To him there entered, a couple of hours later, Grenfell, who woke him by the simple process of inclining the sofa at an angle, so that its occupant rolled with a thud to the floor.

'That's a tom-fool trick,' said Adhurst irritably, dusting himself. 'What did you want to do that for?'

'Do you know what the time is?' asked his colleague. 'Livrey was arrested an hour ago.'

'I know. There was a brass band and a procession to welcome him at the station, of course.' Adhurst had not quite recovered his good humour.

'Something of the sort. The whole village seemed to know about the arrest. Your pal Trelway is in his glory. He told me how he had elucidated the case, though he was good enough to say that you had been of some trifling assistance. And now, since I've been your errand-boy in this affair, you might tell me something about it. I see they've let Jimmie go. He's made back to London in a cloud of dust. How'd you get on to Livrey anyway?'

'Oh, blazes! How'd you find out anything? Gun-play didn't quite agree with Jimmie's record, but it seemed a smashing case against him till I had a look at the compartment in which the murder took place. The local people here had taken the chief's wire, that Sheet had been seen travelling with a notorious crook, too much at its face value. If Jimmie hadn't complicated matters, the possibility of the murder having been committed by someone who was not travelling on the train might have occurred to them. There was only one bullet hole in the window, and I suppose a natural conclusion would be, that if a bullet passed through a man's head from the outside of the train it would have left a hole somewhere else. But that hole in the window seemed suspiciously low down, and when I came to look at it, there were tiny shreds of glass *inwards*.

'Well, it seems that they had carried the body to the doctor instead of bringing the doctor to the body. If he had known which way the man had been sitting he could have told them at once that it was no one inside the compartment who fired the shot, for the bullet had entered from the right and not from the left.

'That cleared Jimmie in my mind. That left two possibilities. One was that it was an accidental shot fired by some fool near the line; the other, that someone had an interest in removing Sheet. It was worth looking into. So I made some inquiries both through our people in town and down here. I found that Sheet had married a girl much younger than himself about whom very little was known, and that they did not get on well together. You know your own inquiries about Sheet in town showed that both Livrey and his sister had none too savoury a reputation before they entrapped Sheet into marriage. That confirmed local gossip about quarrels.

'Then I heard that Mrs Sheet and Livrey were out on a motor drive by themselves and did not return till after the murder had been discovered. I bought a shilling ordnance map and studied it out. Where the line ran by a lonely road some miles out seemed a likely spot, and when I heard that the down train was sometimes held up there, I gathered I was on a scent.

'The further I went the more it fitted in. There were people along that road who had seen the two in a car—and others who had seen Mrs Sheet waiting in the car a mile away from the stretch where the murder took place.

'We searched the place and found a clump of bushes where someone had been recently lying. A yard or two away was a footprint, of which we took a plaster cast. It corresponded with Livrey's boot. We ran out a train, as you know, and with a little juggling with a line found that from the spot where the murderer lay to the approximate position in which the train would have stopped, a bullet would have travelled through one window and out through the open window on the other side.

'When we reached this place we found a powerful air-rifle in the gun-room, and some letters from Livrey to Mrs Sheet which more than hint at the scheme of the whole tragedy.'

'But,' objected Grenfell, 'where are the diamonds that Sheet was carrying?'

'In a secret pocket in the waistband of his trousers. That's all there is to it.'

'Well,' said Grenfell, 'I'll reckon you'll have to stay down here to give evidence.'

Adhurst winked. 'Not me, sonny. The official arrests were made by Trelway. All the other facts are proved by different experts and witnesses. Little old London is good enough for me. I should fall a victim to mental paralysis if I had to stay in Townsford a week.'

VI

THE MAYOR'S DAUGHTER

It was all done very nicely and politely, but the Brigade de Sûreté left no doubt of its opinion of Mulberry Street, and Mulberry Street, justly hurt, neatly paraphrased into smooth official terms the retort that the whole of the French detective service was not worth a hill of beans.

Now this regrettable interchange of amenities between two great criminal investigation bureaux could not have arisen had they not both been a little strained by outside influences. It was a little matter of forgery. There had been an import of forged French notes of exquisite workmanship, and the Brigade de Sûreté had convinced themselves that the point of origination was in the United States. Mulberry Street was approached in form to 'see to it.'

It so happened that Mulberry Street was very busy. It pointed out to its French confrère that New York was a big place, and the United States a bigger. Wouldn't it be as well for the Brigade de Sûreté to catch the swindlers who were actually passing the notes? The Brigade de Sûreté replied that this had been attempted—vainly. 'The matter shall have our attention,' said Mulberry Street, and detailed two men who, for a time, made things extremely uncomfortable for persons who might reasonably be supposed to have leanings towards syndicated crime.

The Chef de Sûreté, stirred thereto by reports that notes were still being negotiated and longing for someone to kick, dictated the note already referred to, and the Assistant Commissioner of New York's police, also pleased to kick, made his reply. So a stimulant to efforts on both sides of the Atlantic was afforded.

Then it was that Grenfell of New Scotland Yard, London, who had been sent over to arrange the extradition of an embezzler, happened into Mulberry Street, and to him as an unprejudiced and sympathetic outsider many people opened their souls.

The kick administered by the Brigade de Sûreté had been passed on after due reflection to Detective-Sergeant McFall, who, pining for a kind word, met Grenfell as he was coming down the steps from the Assistant Commissioner's office.

'Hello, you?' he exclaimed, thrusting out a heavy fist. 'How'd you find the boss? Did y' mention forgery to him?'

'No. He did all the mentioning,' said Grenfell.

McFall fell into step with him and spat viciously. 'Hell's an ice-box to the chief when he gets going,' he said, with a touch of admiration. 'He had Gann and me up this morning, and you may have noticed the scorch marks on the carpet where he frizzled us. Yes, we were burnt-offerings all right by the time he was through. He told you that someone was handing out bad paper in France, I suppose?'

Grenfell slapped him on the back. 'Come and have a tonic,' he said.

They had a tonic. They had two. And on the second McFall spoke more freely. He was feeling bitter because he had been unjustly blamed. He was an able man, and it was because of his ability that he had been one of the two selected to unearth the forgers. ''Tisn't as if we had anything to work on,' he declared. 'We've had a line on every crook in little old New York, and we've pulled down a dozen if we've pulled one. The stuff goes over by mail, but we've kept our eye on the letters sent out by every likely bird. None of the boys is in it—that I'll swear.'

'How do you know they go out by mail?' asked Grenfell.

McFall lifted his shoulders. 'Same way as the French people know the stuff comes from here. There was a package at Rennes—R. J. Tupper, Poste Restante—New York postmark—

typewritten address—fifty one-hundred franc notes inside and nothing else. No one ever called for them, and they were handed over to the police. That's how. Now'—he smashed a fist down on the counter—'the chief, he says, "I want you to find out who's marketing the dope, and to find out quick." And because I can't work miracles I get it in the neck—some,' he concluded bitterly.

The Central Detective Bureau of New York is a wonderfully efficient body, and it expects its men to be efficient. It does not like excuses. Like all police bodies it has a keen esprit de corps. It considers itself without peer in the wide, wide world—again like every detective organisation that ever existed. Grenfell could understand. If it had been merely a matter of internal crime, McFall's failure would not have mattered. No detective outside fiction can work miracles. This, however, was an international matter—a question, in a sense, of rivalry.

'Hard lines, old son,' condoled Grenfell. 'Cheer up, there's worse troubles at sea. Get a week's leave and come with me fishing somewhere. I've got to hang about for that time before my extradition case comes on again.'

'I wish I could,' said McFall dolefully. 'I wish I could. I can see the boss's face if I asked for leave just now. No, I've got to keep busy.'

Detective-Inspector Grenfell made his fishing excursion alone. The place he selected was a flourishing little seaside town, which as yet had scarcely realised that it had the making of a 'resort'. He gave his holiday feeling full bent. London was many hundred miles away; the whole of it might be blown up, the Crown jewels stolen, the Cabinet assassinated—and he could not be recalled. His mission was almost automatic. There was nothing on earth that could prevent him throwing off the cares of his profession and forgetting that such a place as Scotland Yard existed.

It is at such self-congratulatory moments as this that fate loves to interfere—fate in this instance in the shape of a sportive puppy dog, of no particular pedigree, and a woman's handbag.

Grenfell had noticed the young woman, an oval-featured, fair-haired girl in white, as he strolled on the beach. She was reclining in a deck-chair, sunning herself, the hand with the bag listlessly dangling. The puppy arrived at a gallop, and in the next few moments was a hundred yards along the shore, growling ferociously as he strove to tear his loot to pieces.

The detective and the dog's owner raced to the rescue, but it was the latter who retrieved the handbag, now chewed to almost unrecognisable pulp, and returned it to its owner. Grenfell slackened his pace and the breeze blew a scrap of paper to his feet—a relic of the ruin the puppy had wrought. He stooped, picked it up, and mechanically crumpled it in his hand to throw away again. Then something about the pellet he had fashioned caught his attention. He straightened it out and examined it and looked round for the girl. She had vanished.

'May I be dodgasted!' exclaimed Grenfell, and with long, quick strides, returned to his hotel and wrote a short letter, in which he enclosed the scrap of paper.

Thus far he was only acting with the courtesy of the man who, having stumbled across a piece of information, passes it on to the one more immediately concerned. But morning brought with it a wire from McFall which might have seemed incoherent to any but a student of Kipling.

> 'The bleating of the lamb excites the tiger. Ten thousand dollars reward now offered. Coming first train.—McFall.'

By eleven o'clock the burly Central Office man had reached the English detective. He was chuckling with glee. The despondency of the previous meeting was all gone. 'We're on to it, old fellow!' he cried. 'You lucky dog! That was the corner of a five-thousand franc note that you got hold of, and it's turned out by a workman. Some folks are born lucky. I've been sweltering for weeks to get a line on the case, and you, without any interest in it, come over, and an end falls in your lap. Where's the lady?'

The Englishman shook his head. 'Never saw the going of her, Mac. To tell the truth, I haven't worried much about it. I thought I'd give you a tip. Now it's your funeral.'

McFall's lower jaw dropped and he whirled furiously on his friend. 'None of that,' he snarled. 'I ain't expecting no presents, and don't you forget it. There's ten thousand dollars that the French banks are offering hanging to this case, my son, and you'll dip your fingers in it, or I'll know why. You can't shunt out of it. Now, will you be good?'

'I'll be good,' smiled Grenfell. 'Where do we stand?'

McFall became serious. He unlocked his suitcase and took out a dozen photographs. 'I brought these on the off-chance,' he explained. 'There's no one in the gallery that answers your description, but I guess these are all the young women likely to be in a big job.'

Although he had only a few moments' view of the girl on the beach, Grenfell was a trained observer, and what he remembered of her features he remembered accurately. He shook his head over the photographs. 'She's not here.'

'May be a raw hand,' he reflected.

'She may be,' agreed McFall; 'but it's no beginner who is turning out the dope. See here, Grenfell, this show isn't being run single-handed. It needs appliances and skill to run a show like this. A pickpocket or a burglar can shift around as he wants to. A forger wants definite headquarters. He's got to be fixed somewhere. Now I don't admire this town for a residence, but if I were turning out phony paper I wouldn't ask for a better place. It's out of the way, and it's handy to New York—what?'

'That's so,' agreed Grenfell. 'How do you propose to locate them? I'm in your hands.'

McFall wiped the perspiration from his broad forehead. 'We'll get them,' he declared. 'We'll get them if we have to go through the State with a fine-tooth comb. Gann and Wills are coming this afternoon. Meanwhile we might go and have a chat with the chief of police here. We might want his help yet.'

If Grenfell had not had some knowledge of the free-and-easy ways of the American police he might have been a little astonished to meet an important functionary on duty in his shirt-sleeves, with his chair tilted back, his heels on his desk, and a cigar between his teeth. The chief paid them the compliment of bringing his feet to the floor and passing the cigar box.

He readily promised his assistance in searching the district, but scratched his head with a pen-holder as Grenfell described the girl. She could, he declared, be duplicated fifty times in the town. 'Might be anyone,' he added, a fact which the two detectives had reached for themselves long before. And then the door opened wide enough to admit a head and shoulders and Grenfell found himself looking into the face of a girl—*the* girl.

He half rose from his seat and then sank back again.

'I beg your pardon,' she said hastily. 'I am looking for father, Mr Burchnall. I thought he might be with you.' She withdrew her head, and the door closed with a click.

'Our mayor's daughter,' said the chief. 'Isn't she a peach?'

Grenfell was doing some quick thinking. A more impulsive or less ready man might have blurted out something. But it had flashed across him that the mayor of an American city holds a considerable influence in police matters—extending to the appointment of even chiefs of police—and he had no wish to be laughed at. Even in a land where politics is a profession, the daughter of a high municipal official is unlikely to be concerned in a syndicated crime.

The point, however, was gained that the girl was known. That, nevertheless, was far from simplifying the problem. In view of her position it was extremely unlikely that she had anything to do with a gang of forgers. On the other hand, why on earth should she have been carrying a French bank-note of high denomination?

'Mac,' he said, when they got outside, 'the local police can't help us.'

'Never expected much,' agreed McFall. 'Still, it's as well to get 'em interested.'

'I don't mean that. I've found the woman.'

McFall was quick on the uptake. 'The Mayor's daughter?' he inquired. And as Grenfell nodded, he gave a long, low whistle.

Now that a scent had been defined, McFall took the lead. He was a busy man for a couple of hours, though his labours were more real than apparent. He lounged through the little town, visited the barber, and chatted as an inquisitive stranger on local affairs while he was being shaved. He also displayed the little shield under the lapel of his jacket to a big policeman, swinging his stick by the loop on a side-walk, and the policeman, flattered by the attention of the sleuth from New York, also talked.

So did the editor of the local newspaper to whom McFall introduced hinself. None of these persons was aware that he was affording anything more than idle conversation.

Yet McFall, when he returned to his friend at the hotel, had a budget of information. He dropped into a lounge wearily. 'That kid's name's Prudence Fastlet,' he said. 'Playing the popularity game with a big "P" for her old man. He's been here for seven years, and mayor three, and I guess wants to keep on the Dick Whittington act. Retired theatre manager from Columbus, Ohio. The villagers swear by him. Can't see any fun in being mayor of a show like this myself.'

Grenfell mentioned a word. The other man rubbed a shiny cheek with his knuckles. 'Nope. He ain't grafting, and that's the funny part of it. He's straight. Working the popularity racket for all he's worth—father of the city, and all that sort of thing. Where *does* he come in?'

'Girl engaged?'

'No. Say, Gann and Wills are about due. I'll have a quick lunch and get a smart boy to slip 'em a note at the depot. We don't want to know 'em if we see 'em.' The eyelid nearest to Grenfell closed and opened again quickly. 'The police chief here is sweet on the kid—see?'

'I see,' said Grenfell. He had gathered McFall's idea. Burchnall would probably mention their visit either to the girl or her father, and the news of their presence in the town would certainly spread. It might be as well that any attention should be concentrated on them.

Within an hour, two drummers had arrived in town and registered themselves at an hotel. The two detectives, lounging in deck-chairs on the veranda, paid them not the slightest attention. In about half an hour they emerged again, and Grenfell rose lazily. 'Think I'll go for a stroll,' he said, and McFall grunted an indifferent assent.

Grenfell's sauntering took him by the mayor's house on the front, and curiously enough, the two commercial travellers strolled at much about the same pace in the same direction, but fifty yards behind. The Scotland Yard man dropped on a patch of grass, and extracting a magazine from his pocket began to read. His face was in the direction of the house. Fifty yards away the commercial travellers also sat down. One of them found a piece of rock which he stuck up on end, and the pair amused themselves by shying pebbles at it.

Half an hour or more elapsed. Then from the house there emerged a figure in white. Grenfell took off his hat and fanned himself. A glance sideways showed him one of the commercial travellers fumbling with a boot lace. He finished, and the pair strode away in the direction taken by the girl.

'That's all right,' muttered Grenfell to himself. 'They'll hang on to her now till all's blue.' He knew the competence of the Central Office men, and renewed his story with an eye on the white-painted house. He registered in his mind all the comings and goings of visitors during the afternoon, but that may have been merely a matter of habit. He had not intended to watch the house after he had pointed out Miss Fastlet to her shadowers. Indeed, though McFall insisted that he should share the reward if the forgers were run to earth, the case was no concern of his. He had no official standing in the United States, and he doubted if he could even legally effect an arrest.

But he hated the feeling of being a spectator, and presently he closed his magazine. There was no one in sight—no sign of life about the white house. The temptation overcame him. Rapidly he took a survey, decided the servants' quarters were probably located in the east wing, opened the gate, and moved into the shrubbery. It was indiscreet. It was probably criminal. But the lust of a chase was in his blood, and he coolly took his risk. He wanted to know more about the inside of the house, and this seemed an opportunity.

Fortune favoured him, for he found an open window on the ground floor which led into a small sitting-room. He moved quietly and quickly across it and into the passage. He wanted to waste no time in his investigation.

The ground-floor rooms were of a perfectly innocent character, though Grenfell raised his eyebrows at what he recognised must be expensive furnishings. For a retired theatrical manager and a mayor who did no grafting, Fastlet certainly had ideas of comfort.

Once Grenfell slipped behind a *portière*, and a servant brushed past him almost within an inch. He waited perfectly still for five minutes and then resumed his survey. If there had been nothing suspicious downstairs there was still less upstairs. He pushed his head in bedroom after bedroom, and the feeling that he was making a fool of himself became more convincing every moment.

There was one room, entered through a sort of sitting-room. The door refused to give as he twisted the handle. He swore softly to himself. 'I might have known!' he exclaimed. 'Bound to be locked.'

He remained standing in thought for a moment or so and then tried to peer through the keyhole. A flap on the other side defeated him. He sniffed inquiringly. Then he straightened himself up and found himself looking down the muzzles of a 12-bore shot-gun.

'Make yourself at home,' invited the man at the other end of the gun. 'Don't mind me.' He was a tall, awkward man of fifty or thereabouts, square-faced, clean-shaven, with thin grey hair, and a mouth like a rat-trap. He wore a light lounge suit, and the noiselessness of his approach was accounted for by the fact that he was in woollen slippers.

Grenfell stood stock-still. He knew that it would be very difficult to miss with a shot-gun at three yards. Had the weapon been a pistol he might have chanced a dash. He was wise enough to recognise that that was out of the question.

'Mr Fastlet, I presume,' he said politely. He was in a tight place, and he knew it. There was nothing to be gained by losing his head.

'That's me,' agreed the other grimly. 'Don't you be too fresh, Mr Man, and keep your hands away from your pockets. That's better.' He walked across the room, selected an arm-chair, and sat down, the gun still trained on Grenfell. It ran swiftly across the mind of the detective that an ordinary householder who had surprised a burglar would have summoned help. 'You can sit down if you like,' said Fastlet. 'Only move smoothly, because my nerves are rather out of order. I'd just hate to have a corpse on my hands.'

Grenfell leaned against the wall. 'I'd rather stand, thanks,' he said languidly.

'That's all right,' agreed the other, 'so long as you don't try any monkey tricks. Well, what do you think you're going to do about it?'

'It's up to you,' pointed out Grenfell. He was philosopher enough to accept things as they happened, and he judged that if he was in a dilemma his captor was no less so.

Fastlet studied him silently for a minute or so.

'So it's up to me,' he repeated slowly. 'You know that a man is justified in shooting a burglar whom he finds searching his house. Any jury would call that justifiable homicide.' He raised the gun and glanced along the barrels. Grenfell read murder in his eyes.

He shrugged his shoulders.

'I don't think you'll do that, Mr Fastlet,' he said. 'I wouldn't, if I were you. You see, there is a Central Office man staying in the town, and he knows where I am. If I'm any judge he'll stir around pretty soon, and a dead body won't be easy for you to explain away.'

The mayor's face was expressionless as he lowered the gun. 'And who in Hades are you?' he demanded doubtfully.

'My name is Grenfell, detective-inspector of the Criminal Investigation Department, New Scotland Yard.'

Fastlet dropped the gun and, standing up, broke into a thunderous roar of laughter as he extended a hand. 'Well, I'm jiggered. The joke's on you this time. Burchnall told me that you and McFall were here, but I didn't expect to catch you burgling my house. D'you think I'm a forger? Ha, ha! That's good. What the dickens are you doing, anyway?'

It was a question that was difficult to answer. Grenfell had no excuse, no explanation to offer. If he had held any authority he might possibly have taken action. He really believed that Fastlet would have murdered him had he not bluffed about McFall. There was only one course for him to adopt. He smiled blandly into the mayor's face.

'Come and have dinner with me tonight,' he said, 'and I'll put you wise to the whole thing. As you say, the joke's on me. Now let me hurry away, there's a good man, or McFall will be making trouble. See you later.'

Grenfell had run his hardest for ten minutes before he found a very fat and very dignified policeman. He seized that official's sleeve and dragged him along for a dozen yards in his headlong career. 'Get on to the fire-brigade,' he said breathlessly. 'Turn 'em out to the mayor's house. Don't ask questions. Get busy.'

The intelligent officer gave a guttural and indistinct sound which Grenfell took for assent, and his sleeve now released, plodded at a slower but no less breathless pace in the wake of the detective.

Grenfell raced into the hotel, threw an inquiry and an order at the clerk in the hall in the same breath, and found McFall at the telephone with Wills at his elbow. His hand fell on the sergeant's shoulder, and he tore him away in the middle of a sentence.

'Come on,' he urged. 'There's no time to waste. I've ordered a car.'

A bell clanged noisily and a motor fire-engine raced by in the street below. Grenfell was too out of breath for lengthy explanations, but luckily the Central Office men were people of action.

'Garage end of first block on the right,' said the clerk as they dashed once more into the hall. 'I've phoned 'em to get their best car ready.'

Nevertheless there was a wait of a few moments at the garage. Grenfell in short staccato sentences jerked out some of the conclusions he had arrived at. 'Yes. We've got to be quick if that's the case,' said McFall. 'We'll drop Wills at the house.' The car was ready by this time, and they jumped aboard. 'Now cut loose for all she's worth,' ordered McFall.

It had taken Grenfell a quarter of an hour to get from the mayor's house to the hotel. It took the car barely three minutes to cover the distance. A small crowd was gathered about the gates, and a thin, almost undiscernible wreath of vapour was circling from a window. The firemen had a hose out, and even in the roadway they could hear the smashing of axes on woodwork.

Wills jumped to the ground as the car slackened pace, and ran forward. They could see him making eager inquiries, and presently he came running back. 'Been gone ten minutes!' he shouted. 'Car a little old-fashioned, green-painted two-seater. You'll pick him up easy.'

The chauffeur pressed over a lever and the car slid smoothly forward. McFall took from his pocket a 44-automatic, took out a clip of cartridges, and pushed it back again. 'You got a gun?' he asked.

Grenfell shook his head.

'You never know,' said McFall, dropping the weapon in his jacket pocket and fixing his eyes ahead on the blinding white road as it whirled towards them. Twice they slackened speed to make inquiries. It was on the second occasion that they learned the green-painted car was but a mile ahead of them, and a few minutes later a little cloud of dust in front showed that they were rapidly overhauling their quarry.

'Keep straight on,' McFall advised the chauffeur. 'We'll run ahead of them and hold them up.'

In a little they were near enough to see a face peering over the back of the leading car. 'Look out,' cried Grenfell, and dropped without shame into the bottom of the car. The glass wind-screen shattered, and they could hear the shriek of a bullet as it tore overhead.

McFall was holding the barrel of his automatic balanced on the palm of his left hand. The thud of his answering shot was almost simultaneous. But a fragment of glass from the broken wind-screen had caught their chauffeur on the cheek. The car swerved, righted again, and then the brakes were on.

'I'm done,' said the chauffeur; 'he's got me.'

McFall swore. Grenfell was making a hasty examination of the man. 'You're all right,' he told him. 'That's only a bit of glass. That won't hurt you.'

The chauffeur looked relieved. 'Get on,' ordered McFall. 'Let her loose.'

'Not me,' said the man doggedly. 'This car isn't hired for gun-play. Count me out.'

It was no moment to waste time in argument. McFall stuck the muzzle of his weapon against the back of the chauffeur's neck. 'Get on with it,' he ordered curtly.

Sullenly the chauffeur started up again. It was a choice of evils, but the man in front might miss if he started shooting again, the detective certainly would not. In a matter of five minutes they were again within fifty yards of the green car. McFall commenced to fire. He was taking no chances. Once only was a shot returned, and as they drew nearer Grenfell, who was peering over the top of the seat, perceived the reason. Fastlet's chauffeur had also needed persuading with a pistol. He laughed as the situation became clear to him.

'Make him slack up as we come alongside the other car,' he told McFall. 'I'm going to jump for it.'

McFall nodded. The Scotland Yard man braced himself for a leap. Inch by inch they drew near the other car, and Fastlet, facing around, fired twice. Both shots went wide.

Then Grenfell jumped. He heard the wooden thud of McFall's automatic again, and as he landed, his face was scorched by the explosion of the mayor's pistol. Then his strong, wiry arms were around Fastlet, and he dragged him down backwards. Both cars slid to a halt just as the two struggling men fell heavily to the ground.

The mayor was a powerful man, but he had been taken at a disadvantage. Moreover, Grenfell was as physically fit as it is possible for a man of forty to be. By the time McFall had come running to his assistance he had the mayor pinned. The Central Office man put away his weapon and dragged out a shiny pair of self-adjusting, nickel-plated handcuffs, which he clipped round the prisoner's wrists.

'Now we're all hunky,' he said, and they assisted the prisoner to rise.

'This is you,' said Fastlet, glaring menacingly at Grenfell. 'If you hadn't been so darned quick—' He checked himself. 'What's the charge, anyway? You've got nothing you can bring against me. This means an action for damages.'

'Cut out the bluff,' said McFall sharply. 'You'll be held for forgery, and that's all there is to it. Let's get aboard.'

Far away, back in the Central Office records, long before the days of finger-prints, McFall came across the portrait of a young man. He pointed it out to Grenfell. 'That finishes it. Here he is 'way back in the nineties. Soapy Smith he is—he was in the green goods trade at one time—but he's an expert forger. Got ten years in ninety-two and has dropped out of sight since.'

'Let it alone,' growled Wills. 'Grenfell's going to tell us how he got on to the old man—not but what we've got him anyway,' he added, with a touch of esprit de corps. 'Once we nailed the girl it was plain enough.'

'I was lucky,' admitted Grenfell modestly. 'You people have been too long in the game not to know that luck counts a lot. But I'd have been nowhere without your backing. I couldn't have told for sure on my own that that piece of paper I picked up on the beach was from a forged note without your experts behind me. Still, that was luck to start with. Then when McFall here found out that the mayor was no grafter, we both got to thinking on the same lines.'

'That's right,' agreed McFall. 'A man who's all for purity in municipal affairs and lives in the way he did has got a reason, you bet.'

'Yes. Soapy must have had it all worked out when he went into politics. If the French police hadn't tumbled that the stuff was drifting in from the States he might have kept on for ever. Who was going to get suspicious of the high-souled mayor of a seaside town? Besides, he had the local police in his pocket, though I suppose they knew nothing of what he was doing. He kept clear of political graft because he didn't want Pinkertons or any outside people called in by a purity committee. Then he was handy to New York.

'I figured this out while I was waiting to put you on to the girl. I gave McFall credit for having the same line. But I wanted to get the thing done with quickly, and it didn't seem to me likely to work out in a hurry on soft lines. That was how it came into my head to break into the house on the off-chance of picking up something. I'd have waited to put you boys up to it, but after all, only one man could go in. There wasn't anything to be gained by sharing the risk among four.

'I'll own freely it looked as if I was on a dead end till I got upstairs. There was a room there—a sort of study—with another room leading out of it. The door of the second room was locked, but I got a kind of mixed smell of chemicals. I knew then that I was right, and that I had happened on the private laboratory. It was then that the old man happened on me with a shotgun.

'He knew who I was—he'd been talking to Burchnall—and at first I looked like qualifying for a funeral. I bluffed that McFall was lying in wait, and we called a truce. We shook hands and I came away.

'It was pretty obvious he wasn't going to sit around once he'd got me out of the house, and if he made a get-away he wouldn't want to leave any evidence behind him either. That was how I came to think of a fire-call.'

'Lucky you did,' observed Wills. 'The firemen had just broken into the laboratory when I got there. He'd simply piled the place with junk, emptied a can of kerosene over it, chucked in a match, and locked the door again. We saved enough out of the ruins to get hold of the whereabouts of their crooks in France. We've cabled the address over. He was supplying them with phony paper at 50 per cent discount.'

'You haven't told me about the girl,' said Grenfell. 'What's happened to her?'

'She's safe enough,' said Gann. 'The old man seems to have got somewhat disturbed when he heard that McFall and you were on the warpath. He is a wary bird, and had no dealings direct with those who were handling the paper. He had a little cigar store in the Bronx under the name of George James, with a manager in charge. The manager had no knowledge of anything wrong—he didn't even know where his employer lived. Soapy never came to the town himself. He always sent the girl, and she collected letters off the manager, and posted every mail that was to go out. Well, as I say, he smelt something and sent her off to New York to destroy any mail she found there, I pulled her actually in the store. She's his daughter, but I think she'll clear herself. He didn't trust even her. She never knew what was in the letters coming or going. By the way, she had in her bag the rest of the fragments of the note. It was a sample included in a letter to a crook named Wilson.'

McFall yawned and stretched himself. 'The chief's so pleased he'll eat out of your hand. Say, it's getting near hungry-time. I put it to the meeting that it's on to us to show Grenfell what little old New York can do in the way of dinners. As many as are in favour of the resolution will—'

'Ay,' interrupted Gann and Wills together.

'Carried unanimously,' said McFall.

VII

A MEETING OF GREEKS

HOLDRON tapped his desk peremptorily with a lean forefinger. He was a hard-eyed man with prominent cheek-bones, and his voice rasped.

'That's nothing to do with you,' he said brusquely. 'I only want you to recover the papers or to indicate the man who stole them, and I will do the rest. That's why I'm paying you a big fee instead of calling in the official police.'

Weir Menzies shrugged his shoulders. 'It's asking me to work in the dark,' he grumbled. 'If you were ill you'd expect to tell your doctor all your symptoms. You'd confide in your lawyer if you had any legal business.'

'I'm not going to argue about it,' said Holdron sharply. 'I hire you on my terms or not at all.'

There was an atmosphere of ponderous placidity about Weir Menzies which was apt to deceive those who were not familiar with him. Portly, prosperous looking, with a heavy black moustache and a ruddy genial face, he was obviously of the middle classes. One might have considered him a tradesman of moderate business astuteness—certainly not a man of specially subtle brain or resource. Yet Menzies, senior partner in the private inquiry firm of Menzies & Spink, had a reputation as well earned as the pension he enjoyed as chief inspector of the Criminal Investigation Department. A hard man and a tenacious man, in spite of the fact that he was a churchwarden at Tooting and spoken of in municipal circles as a coming borough councillor.

'I'd take it easy if I were you,' he warned icily. 'I'm not that kind of private inquiry agent. If you want to rush me into something blindfold, I've got to be careful. I'm not dirtying my fingers. And remember, Mr Man, I'm not a junior clerk in your city offices.'

The other abruptly twisted round his padded chair, and his harsh, astonished gaze met the level eyes of the detective.

Suddenly he gave a short laugh. 'You're right, Mr Menzies. I apologise. I forgot you were in a way my guest. I am rather worried over this business and it's got on my nerves,'

The detective nodded imperturbably. 'I only want to be treated right,' he went on mildly. 'You've dragged me fifty miles down here by motor-car leaving me to name my own fee, so that whatever you've got on is pretty urgent. I know now that your safe'—he jerked his head to a big steel vault built into the wall—'was opened between ten and midnight by someone who had evidently got the combination. I know that some papers have been taken, and you say it's not necessary that I should know what they are. Now you suppose burglary, because there are footprints leading from beneath this window to and from the stables, where there was a ladder. I don't say you're not right, but if you don't give me a hint of what was taken, how can I guess at any motive?'

Holdron stroked one eyebrow with a penholder. 'There's the footprints,' he suggested. 'There's a start.'

A flicker of irritability passed across the detective's face. 'I don't keep a pocket-register of footprints,' he retorted. 'You've a dozen guests in your house-party and a score of servants in the house besides outsiders. Do you want me to collect all their boots? Give me a reason why someone should want those papers, and I'll be that much nearer to saying who it was.'

He was getting annoyed at the way the point was continually parried. He knew nothing about Alfred Holdron save that he had some kind of financial and export business in the City, and was apparently a wealthy man, to judge by the style in which he was entertaining at his country house. But even wealthy City men have skeletons in cupboards, and Menzies was wary. Private inquiry agents have more than once been engaged to find out exactly what their employers have arranged they should find out.

'How did you know that I suspect someone in the house?' demanded Holdron.

'Since the combination was used you could hardly avoid it,' said Menzies dryly. 'Perhaps it would be as well if we went into the question of these papers.'

His client let his gaze wander thoughtfully through the broad windows on to the trim grounds. He had completely dropped his arrogant, curt air.

'No outsider knew I had those documents,' he said at last, 'and to the ordinary person they would be a meaningless string of letters and figures. They were in cipher, and I had intended to decode them this morning.' His eyes narrowed. 'They were of supreme importance in certain business negotiations in which I am concerned.'

He rose and paced the room uneasily, his feet making no sound on the thick carpet.

'There was a number of bank-notes in that safe laying with the papers. That must have been the real object of the theft. As you say, there was obvious collusion.'

'Let's be clear about this, then,' said Menzies speaking with precision. 'I can't act in leading-strings. You must give me a free hand.'

'Certainly. So long as you point out the thief to me and keep your mouth shut I don't care how you do it.'

Weir Menzies wore a frown when he emerged from the library. Somehow he distrusted Holdron, and yet beyond his first lack of candour about the contents of the missing ciphers there was no tangible reason why he should do so. That suspicion that he was being used as a tool for a crooked purpose would persist at the back of his mind. Yet, after all, if he were to refuse lucrative commissions on instinctive prejudice he might as well give up his profession.

For the time being Holdron was his employer and he had to earn his pay. He resolutely bent his thoughts on the definite problem. All that Holdron could tell, or would tell, about his guests or servants had been reduced to a few Greek notes on the back of an envelope. It was a long-standing habit with Menzies to make his notes in Greek. In case of loss, the odds were against the finder being able to understand them.

He had refused Holdron's company while he inspected the footprints and he stood for a while looking thoughtfully down on the flower border in which the first two or three were embedded—heavy, obviously men's tracks showing as distinctly in the soft earth as though picked out in plaster of Paris. Slowly he followed their course round to the stables—a matter of twenty yards—and then again he came to a halt, tilting his bowler hat and scratching his head with the brim.

Then a slow grin overspread his face. He knelt and took some measurements, and was entering them on his inevitable envelope when he became conscious of an onlooker.

A woman—she might fairly have been described as a girl—was watching him with frank curiosity. He saw a slim grey figure with smiling, ingenuous eyes and a glory of fair hair. He raised his hat, and he caught a flash of white teeth.

'You are the detective from London, are you not?' she said. 'Mr Holdron told me you had arrived. I am Lady Malchester. Have I caught you in the act of detecting something? Have you'—she breathed the words with an expression of mock awe—'got a clue?'

Now Weir Menzies was a business man and he liked his business taken seriously. Not that he had no sense of humour. He could stand ridicule as a part of the game, but he was thin-skinned with outsiders. He bowed stiffly.

'I am pleased if my antics afford you any entertainment, madam,' he said with frigidity.

Her big grey eyes opened widely in hurt astonishment, like those of a child who has been sternly checked in an innocent amusement. Then the sunshine flashed into her face again.

'I beg your pardon,' she said. 'It was silly of me to question you, wasn't it?—only, you see, I'm so frightfully fascinated. I've read a lot about detectives, but I've never seen one at work before. Mr Holdron was telling us at breakfast that he had sent for a man with a most tremendous reputation and I guessed it was you directly I saw you looking at those footprints. You are Mr Weir Menzies, aren't you?'

He had stood moodily with downcast gaze while she spoke, as though constrained only by politeness to listen to irrevelant chatter. Now he looked up and laughed.

'That's me,' he agreed. 'It's rather a disillusionment, eh? I not in disguise, and I'm afraid I don't carry either a microscope or a revolver. In fact, Lady Malchester, practically the only tool I carry around with me is plain horse sense.'

An idea had come to him that this ingenuous young lady was not quite so verdant as she seemed. He knew that Holdron had told his guests that the safe had been robbed—there had been no particular reason for keeping the disappearance of the bank-notes secret—and that he had sent for Menzies. He had mentioned Lady Malchester's name to the detective in describing his guests—a society beauty, a young widow of a baronet with plenty of money, who spent a good deal of her time looking for new amusements.

'Not even handcuffs?' she said wistfully.

He shook his head. 'Not even handcuffs. They'd be a frightful nuisance.'

'But the footprints,' she persisted. 'Don't tell me the footprints aren't a clue. You'll destroy my faith in fiction for ever and ever if you say that.'

His face was solemn. 'I'll let you into a secret,' he said portentously. 'They are a clue. Men's boots, size 9, according to the tracks. You'll observe that the quality of the earth round this side of the house is different to anywhere else in the grounds.

I have taken a sample of it, and I bribed the man who cleans the boots to scrape the mud off all the size 9's and put each sample in separate envelopes. Later, I shall send them all to an analyst to find the thief. I have already decided that he weighs 190 lb., and has black hair which he parts on the left. He has six buttons to his vest, and he is fond of lager.'

'I believe you're making fun of me,' she said doubtfully.

'I wouldn't dare,' he declared. 'Now, if you really would like to do me a favour, Lady Malchester, I want to measure how far it is from this ladder to that flower bed. Thank you so much.'

He tied a knot in the string at a point which indicated the distance and, coiling it, placed it in his pocket. 'I have to go in to the village now,' he added. 'I shall no doubt have the privilege of seeing you at lunch—if I can manage to get back in time.'

She murmured an assent, and he strode away. Lady Malchester remained for a little while watching his retreating figure, and her grey eyes were more hard and less childlike.

'He's not altogether a fool,' she murmured. Then with a philosophic shake of the head: 'A fool would be less easy to manipulate than a fairly clever man—and less fun.'

There is a newspaper motto, much more closely observed in detective circles than in journalistic life—always verify your facts. Truth is a necessity for the detective, a handicap for the journalist. The foundations of a successful inquiry need more than a brilliant flash of inspiration or deduction. Though Weir Menzies believed he had got a glimmering of the truth, he was too old a hand to expect it to immediately unravel itself. It was probable that a good deal of heavy inquiry work would have to be done before he became clear about the case.

Certain crimes, as all criminologists know, fall into grooves. It is comparatively easy to eliminate those who, either through lack of motive or lack of opportunity, could not have committed them. One can usually ignore a millionaire when investigating a case of pocket picking. An East End loafer would not be capable of a skilled forgery. Most classes of crime show in themselves a particular group among whom to look for the perpetrator.

Here, however, Weir Menzies, on the facts as he knew them, had no very definite arena of search. Holdron's theory, that the robber had only accidentally taken the cipher documents, might be perfectly sound. In that case most members of the house-party were probably above suspicion. On the other hand—and Menzies felt that it was strongly possible—the bank notes might have been taken merely as a blind. There are varying standards of honesty, and if the papers dealt with some big projected financial coup, the thief might just as likely be a peer of impeccable reputation as a professional burglar.

At a tiny village post-office, Menzies wrote a comprehensive wire to his partner in London. There was plenty of material in it to test the singularly complete organisation of their office, for it included a list of every one of Holdron's guests, with a request that as much detailed information as possible might be gathered about each one. It might have seemed superfluous that the detective laid some stress upon the name of his own employer.

As he emerged from the post-office a bronzed little man with a tooth-brush moustache and square shoulders met him in the doorway. He came to an abrupt halt.

'What the blazes are you doing in a hole like this, Mr Menzies?'

Menzies grinned as he shook hands. 'I'm a freelance now, Captain Lackett. Able to pick and choose my jobs a little. If it comes to that, you are about the last man I should have expected to find here.'

'Meaning I'm to mind my own business,' grinned Lackett. 'I'm doing a bit of fishing—got a bit run down, you know, so I thought I'd take a holiday.'

'Queer time to take a holiday, isn't it? War and all that, you know.'

It was Lackett's turn to grin. 'Oh, I don't know. Look me up if you're staying in the neighbourhood. I'm at the Dolphin.'

'I certainly will if I get a chance. So long for now.'

The detective strode out in the roadway with new food for thought. The presence of one of the keenest brains in the Intelligence Service in an obscure Hampshire village, while the greatest war in history was being waged, might be accounted for by a passion for fishing, but on the whole Menzies thought not. He wondered if it had anything to do with Holdron's case, whether the deal this client had mentioned had anything to do with the war. It was a possibility not to be lost sight of.

He reached the house half an hour before lunch and the butler found in him a congenial spirit. Menzies had a faculty for friendliness when he cared to exert it, and he pressed into service an utterly fictitious relative who was bailiff to an earl. Many pumps work on the reciprocal principle. You must pour water down them first. Menzies made no attempt to conceal his identity, and poured a number of reminiscences confidentially into appreciative ears. In return he received a tolerable amount of gossip and scandal concerning Holdron and his friends—for an upper servant knows many things gathered from valets, maids, and keepers. The butler had no conception that he was being made a victim of Menzies's painless method of extracting information.

'There's the first lunch bell, Mr Menzies.' The butler felt himself justified in the subtle avoidance of 'sir'. Hadn't the detective practically admitted that they were on the same social level! 'I suppose you'll be lunching upstairs?'

'I suppose so,' agreed Menzies. 'Just one moment, though, Mr Wringley. I don't want to worry Mr Holdron about this. I want to know exactly where every one slept last night. Can you draw a rough plan for me, marking each room with the name of the occupant?'

Wringley agreed, and five minutes later Menzies, with the plan in his waistcoat pocket, was walking sedately upstairs. He met Holdron on the landing.

'Any luck?' demanded his client.

He shook his head. 'I can't tell yet. I may be closer up tonight. By the way, I may be a little late for lunch or I may not come down at all. I hope you won't mind?'

'Not at all,' snapped Holdron, and with a curt nod resumed his descent.

Lady Malchester gave a gasp that resolved itself into a stifled cry, and her hand went to her heart. Menzies gave her credit for being genuinely startled—almost as startled as he was. He had just taken a pipe from one of the drawers of her dressing-table—a common, straight-stemmed, silver-mounted briar pipe, and so quiet had been her entry that her cry was the first indication he had received of her presence.

He looked up quietly. So far from being disconcerted was he, that one might have imagined him engaged in a most commonplace act instead of being caught red-handed ransacking a lady's room.

'You—you blackguard!' she said tensely.

'Quite so,' he agreed mildly. 'I should come in and close the door if I were you. One cannot tell who may pass.'

She pulled the door savagely open and stood defiantly with fists clenched, a dainty figure of wrath. 'I hope they will,' she flamed. 'You will perhaps be able to explain what you are doing here.'

Impulsively she crossed the room, sweeping disdainfully by him, and laid one hand on the bell. He wheeled to continue to face her, and smiled benevolently.

'You will find that bell act ever so much better if you press the push instead of the moulding,' he commented dryly.

For an instant he thought she was going to strike him. Then she dropped her hand, and her face lost its passion. Her whole attitude changed.

Re-crossing the room she slowly closed the door and answered his smile. 'Really, Mr Menzies, it is difficult to lose one's temper with you. I ought really to call the servants and have you thrown out, and I can't tell why I don't, except that

I'm curious. I may do it yet. Meanwhile, you might gratify my curiosity a little. I suppose I am what you would call a suspected person?'

He liked this attitude of hers somewhat less than that of lofty indignation. He prepared himself for more subtle tactics on her part than a crude bluff of anger. He toyed mechanically with the pipe.

'Undoubtedly,' he said bluntly.

There was an open bureau to which he had already directed his attention. She stood with her back to it, placed both hands upon its surface, and swung lightly to a seat, her satin-shod feet dangling. Laughing lightly she picked a scented cigarette from a box at her side, applied a light, and tried unsuccessfully to blow a smoke ring.

'So I'm a burglar, Mr Menzies—a sort of Lady Raffles.' Her gay eyes met his austere ruddy face in mocking challenge. 'Do you know I'm frightfully interested. What is the right thing to do? You must have had such a lot of experience in these cases. Do I go on my knees and beg you to spare me, or do you snap the handcuffs swiftly upon my wrists and hale me forthwith to the deepest dungeon of the village police station? Or does the village police station keep a dungeon? Perhaps the constable there uses a woodshed. I hope it isn't damp.'

Her badinage embarrassed him more palpably than her unexpected entrance had done. She was something beyond his experience, and she was giving proof of a consummate nerve whether she was innocent or guilty. He had few doubts in his own mind upon the question. She must have suspected a possible search of her room or she would not have returned so unexpectedly ten minutes after lunch had commenced. Nor would she have so calmly acquiesced in his presence there had she no sense of guilt.

'I shall put the facts before Mr Holdron,' he said stiffly. 'It will be for him to decide what steps to take.'

She laughed again. 'It will be a horrible scandal in high life, won't it? Only, of course'—she perched her head on one side like a bird—'you are quite certain about me. Do you know, in every detective novel I have ever read the hero—that's you—explains the steps by which he exposed the villain—that's me. I'd love to hear how you penetrated my subtle machinations.'

He frowned at her. After all, she was not a professional criminal. As a churchwarden and one of the pillars of a suburban constitutional club, Weir Menzies was a staunch believer that the upper classes were the salt of the nation. It pained him, it revolted his sense of womanliness, that she should meet the situation with flippancy. That was almost worse than being a thief. The scent of her cigarette irritated him.

'If you want to know,' he said grudgingly, 'it can't do any harm, as the rest of the facts are bound to come out. I know that you laid that trail of footsteps—you probably wore men's boots over your own.'

She gurgled delightedly. 'How clever of you. How on earth did you get to know that?'

'It was plain enough for a child to see. The size of the tracks did not correspond to the length of the paces. That is where you make a mistake, Lady Malchester. You should have taken longer strides. It was quite clear that the trail had been faked for the purpose of a false scent. Then, again, you were altogether too interested when I was examining them. I had an idea then, and I got you to walk alongside the trail. The length of your stride corresponded exactly to that of the burglar.'

'Wonderful!' she ejaculated. 'I didn't expect to be run to earth so quickly and cleverly. But after all, Mr Menzies, though I don't mind admitting to you that you're right—because I shall deny this conversation later on, and you've got no corroboration—it will be difficult to bring anything against me merely because my stride happens to be the same length as that of a supposed burglar.' She shook a white forefinger at him. 'If you say a word against me there's such a thing as an action for slander, you know.'

'That is silly,' he observed. 'You must give me credit for a little common sense. For instance, this pipe.' He held it up and tapped the stem lightly.

He thought he had scored a point. For a moment the mocking light deserted the grey eyes.

'I—I picked it up on the stairs this morning and pushed it in the drawer, intending to give it to one of the servants to find the owner.'

'I can save you that trouble. It bears the initials W. C. The owner is Mr Walden Concord, a young gentleman whose official salary as a government clerk by no means covers his expenditure. He is a guest of Mr Holdron's, I believe, and a friend of yours. He arrived about ten o'clock last night and was supposed to have retired shortly afterwards. As a matter of fact, he never went to bed at all.'

The woman's self-confidence was rapidly vanishing. 'How do you know that?' she demanded.

He stuck his thumbs into the armholes of his waistcoat and beamed complacently. 'There's no Sherlock Holmes about that, Lady Malchester. I have been talking to the servants. One of them, the butler, tells me he happened to see a figure prowling about the grounds, and investigated. He got near enough to recognise Mr Concord, and, concluding that if any of his master's guests chose to walk about late on a damp night it was no business of his, he was withdrawing when he saw a woman steal out of the house. He recognised her.'

Her cheeks were scarlet. 'Well?' she said.

'Well!' he drawled. 'This morning Mr Concord sent his man out for his pipe, which he had, he said, left overnight in the summer-house where he had gone for a *solitary* breath of air.'

There were great gaps in the structure Menzies had so elaborately reared on the facts he had gained, and no one was better aware of its weakness than himself. But he judged that Lady Malchester's logical strength was breaking down, and he was determined to press his advantages.

She slid down from the bureau and passed a hand in a weary gesture across her brow. Very pretty and very helpless she looked, and if Menzies had not held very rigid ideas of duty he might have felt compunctious.

'That proves nothing,' she declared faintly.

'Mr Holdron will form his own opinion,' he retorted. 'It will probably be the same as mine by the time I have searched your room.'

A flash of spirit seemed to return to her. 'You wouldn't dare,' she exclaimed.

'I'm going to,' he returned doggedly, 'with your permission or without it.'

Something glinted in her hand, and with a swiftness of which his bulk gave no promise he sprang forward and wrenched away a small pistol. He stepped back and dropped it in his pocket. 'This is mere foolishness,' he said severely.

Her slender form was shaking and her hands were in front of her face. 'You—you—forced me to do it,' she exclaimed brokenly. 'I can't stand exposure.' Suddenly she was on the floor at his feet. 'You can't understand what it means. If I give back everything—everything—that's all you want—all Mr Holdron wants. You needn't tell him—'

He raised her gently to her feet and pulled a chair under her. Her emotion seemed genuine enough, and although he was inclined to believe in it he was too wary to be deceived by a new feint.

'I'm afraid I can make no promises. I am acting for Mr Holdron, and he is entitled to know everything I learn. I have no discretion in that way.'

'But if I give up everything—'

He shook his head. 'You must do that in any event.'

But he had pushed his advantage too far. The scarlet lips became doggedly pursed, and her bent figure straightened. 'You can either ruin me by exposure to Mr Holdron or you can recover the papers. You will never find them unless I choose to tell you.'

'We will see,' he said grimly.

He resumed his methodical search of the room as calmly as though she were not present. Yet he felt that it was hopeless. Even under the best conditions no man, however skilled, can hope to thoroughly search the smallest room when time is limited. It is largely a matter of luck if he finds an article, even if it has not been hidden. And Lady Malchester seemed very confident. Once, while he was rummaging the papers in the bureau, out of the tail of his eye he caught a glimpse of her in the mirror. He could have sworn she was smiling. Yet when he wheeled swiftly she was still sitting meekly, hands folded in her lap, with downcast eyes and despondent face. He closed the bureau with a snap that showed he was a little irritated, and thrust his hands into his trousers pockets.

'Mr Menzies,' she said tremulously.

'Yes.'

'If I return the money and the papers, will you give me one day's grace before you tell Mr Holdron?' Her voice was very low. 'That can't hurt you much. I could not stand—the—the disgrace if I were here. Give me a day to get away and I shall not mind so much. Surely a single day can't be very important?'

There were tears in her voice and in her big, childlike, grey eyes. He gnawed his moustache while he considered her appeal. It was not so unreasonable. He had scarcely hoped to clear up the affair so completely even in two days. If he refused he might get the documents before the next day or he might not get them at all. The compromise seemed the wisest policy.

'That is outside my instructions,' he said, 'but I will do it.'

The criss-cross of lines that marred her white forehead disappeared. 'Thank you,' she murmured. 'Will you turn your head for a moment?'

He obeyed. There was a rustle of garments and then a crackle of papers. It was obvious that the things had been concealed in her stocking. The hiding-place had all the merit of simplicity and accessibility. She held out the papers.

'I am very much obliged, Lady Malchester,' he said formally.

Holdron paced impatiently to and fro across the library, and Menzies noticed that his fingers were twitching. He was quite clearly in a high state of nervous tension. His eyes dwelt malevolently on the detective as though he meditated wresting the secret from him by force.

'When you're satisfied with this melodramatic nonsense perhaps you will condescend to tell me what you mean,' he snarled. 'If this is a trick to enhance your fee it doesn't go down with me.'

'It is unusual,' admitted Menzies. 'But you're a reasonable man, Mr Holdron, and you'll see the difficulty of my position. I have got the papers and have solved the mystery, but I could have done neither if I had not passed my word that you should not receive my report till tomorrow.'

The other came to an abrupt halt. 'The papers, man! You have the papers? Give them to me.' His hand fell on a bronzed elephant used as a paper weight.

'Tomorrow,' said Menzies with determination. 'I will post them on from town tonight.'

So unexpected was Holdron's next movement that the detective was almost taken unawares. He saw the hand with the bronze elephant flicker upwards, and divined the other's intention as the missile left his hand. He sprawled sideways, chair and all, and so saved his face. But a numbing shock in the right shoulder told him that his assailant had not entirely missed. The next moment Holdron was upon him, fighting with a dynamic energy that more than made up for the difference in weight and muscle.

In any ordinary encounter the city man would not have lasted a second against the burly detective, but Menzies was on the ground and still entangled with his chair. Moreover, his right arm was for the moment useless.

It was all over in five seconds. Strong, lean hands twined about his throat. He jerked his elbow up into the other man's stomach and heard a groan. Then his head was thrown violently backwards against one of the legs of the chair and a red mist swam before his eyes. Thereafter he lost consciousness.

He awoke with a sharp tang of spirit in his throat, and at once all his senses were keenly alert. A bronzed face with a toothbrush moustache was near his own and Captain Lackett's arm was supporting his head. He sat up abruptly and met the composed, smiling face of Lady Malchester. She was comfortably tucked up in a big arm-chair, her knees crossed and one foot rhythmically swaying.

'You come to life like a Jack-in-the-box,' observed Lackett, straightening himself. 'How d'you feel? Here, let me give you a hand up.'

'I'll be all right in half a minute,' said Menzies. His eyes lighted with inquiry on Lady Malchester. She was smiling whimsically at him as she had done when she had first come across him examining the footprints. He tried to resolve the problem, but his brain was clear enough to show him the impossibility. 'Where is Holdron?' he asked.

'Sitting in a cell by now wondering whether he is going to be tried by court-martial or by the civil power,' said Lackett.

Menzies rubbed his eyebrows and took a long breath. A swift and appalling foreboding that he—sometime chief inspector of the C.I.D.—had been used as a tool by the unscrupulous intelligence officer flashed across his mind. The details were hazy, but he had no doubts of the main facts. There was evidence in the vibrant grey eyes of Lady Malchester, in the lurking smile under Lackett's tooth-brush moustache.

'That so?' he remarked blandly. 'Well, you had better luck than I did.'

Lady Malchester giggled. 'Stung!' said Lackett.

'The old war-horse smells the battle and won't admit that he's lame in the off foreleg. Now, Menzies, be a sport. Admit that you've been done down for once and we'll admit you into the secret. You earned that, anyhow.'

'I seem to have broken in on you somehow,' said the detective. 'I'll own that I'm guessing. The secret service is on top this time. Now then. And I apologise to you, Lady Malchester. You stung me neatly. You're a credit to the service, if you don't mind me saying so. Still, if I'd been given a hint—'

'Lady Malchester is not in the service,' said Lackett. 'She assisted me for—'

'Love,' interjected Menzies, and had his reward. A crimson tinge crept under the tan of Lackett's countenance. Lady Malchester was unmoved.

'If I had known what Captain Lackett has since told me,' she said, 'I might have taken you into my confidence. But I didn't know you, and it was simpler to take no risks—the more especially as I took good care to see you did all you were wanted to.'

'I seem to remember you on your knees begging me not to expose you.'

'That was the transpontine touch,' she smiled. 'Do you know, I wouldn't have had you go away without those papers for anything. I wanted you to think you forced them from me.'

Menzies pushed his hands widely, palms outward. 'Am I drunk or is the room only standing on its head? Things seem to be spinning round. All I know is that Holdron is a spy, and that you are the lady who was so naïvely interested in detective work. I never associated you with Captain Lackett.'

'These are the facts,' said Lackett. 'Holdron, of course, was a spy, or as good as a spy. His financial interests have been largely bound up in Germany, and it's only lately that I ran on to his tracks. During the last few years he's been making many friends in official circles—not the very biggest men, but people with access to confidential information—this man Concord, for instance.

'There had been leakages which could only have come from someone inside, and once I was on the case it was easy to suspect Concord, who was spending a deal more than his small private income and smaller salary. I wanted to get at the man behind, so I waited before jumping on Concord. I had had him closely watched, and naturally there wasn't a letter he mailed or received that didn't come under my eye. The only correspondent he had who was at all doubtful was Holdron—but there was nothing to take hold of, you understand. Holdron was too clever for that. That was where Lady Malchester came in. She found mutual friends and got an introduction. She even managed—she has her own methods—to secure an invitation to this dinner-party, which, though we didn't know it then, had been arranged for a definite purpose.

'Mark the cunning of the man. Yesterday Concord was to take copies of certain cipher documents which showed a strategic plan to be put in execution next week. It was essential that they should be passed over to Holdron as quickly as possible, yet suspicion might have been aroused should it be observed that a Government clerk had been in definite communication with him, and they, of course, daren't trust them to the post. But a house-party to which Concord had been invited long before—you get me?

'Anyway, there we were—Lady Malchester watchng our friend Holdron, I keeping an eye on Concord. When Concord caught a train down here last night, I was behind him. You see, I didn't want any accident to happen to him while he had those papers.'

'You knew he had them, and yet—'

Lackett leaned forward and emphasised his point with a forefinger. 'Yes, it wasn't quite so simple as merely getting them back. You see, it had been arranged that information—of a kind—should reach the enemy—I had duplicate documents which I wished to transfer for the genuine ones unbeknown to our young friend.'

Menzies smacked his thigh. 'That's the point that's been worrying me. Of course you want the scheme to be carried out so that you would know its workings. By gum, why didn't I think of it!' He was seriously annoyed with himself.

'Because it was no more likely to occur to you than a million other hypotheses, I suppose. Anyway, I failed. Mr Man had a motor waiting for him at the station, and I hoofed it in to the village. I knew that Lady Malchester would pick up the end without any help from me, and I didn't want to risk being seen fussing about the house.'

Lady Malchester took up the story.

'That was where I took the stage. My maid—you're not the only one who knows the value of servants as agents for collecting information—had become rather friendly with the chauffeur here, and consequently I knew the exact time of Concord's arrival, but in case of accidents I had the combination of the safe—Holdron keeps it on a slip of paper at the back of his watch, and I arranged that he should sleep soundly the night before last.'

'You drugged him and entered his bedroom? Well, you've sure got a nerve.'

There was a gleam of mischief in the childish face. 'Something had to be done,' she said, as though that settled the matter. 'It was only just the tiniest little drop in his wine. So you see I was all ready for emergencies. I and my maid between us kept a close eye on Concord after he arrived, and when he went out into the grounds I followed. You rather jumped to conclusions about that, Mr Menzies.'

'You didn't disillusion me.'

'That would scarcely have been policy,' she smiled. 'Anyway, I shadowed him—that's the technical term, isn't it?—to the summer-house, where Holdron was already waiting. I suppose the rendezvous had been arranged beforehand. I heard all I wanted to, and the papers passed over. Concord left his pipe and I was silly enough to pick it up. I got back to the house, unseen as far as I know, and found Holdron with his guests. Then I made an excuse, slipped into the library and opened the safe, collared all the papers I could see, and walked out quite openly. At the worst the papers wouldn't reach the enemy.'

'She had no duplicates to replace them,' explained Lackett. 'I had not seen her then.'

'No,' said Lady Malchester. 'Well, it was sometime after midnight that the car started out, and I heard from my maid there had been a robbery, and that Holdron had sent a car to London to fetch a well-known private detective. I didn't learn your name till next day. It seemed a pity that you shouldn't have a clue to work on, so at four this morning I borrowed a pair of boots—there were plenty outside the bedroom doors—and laid a trail. I must say you used it rather cleverly.

'Naturally I surmised that Captain Lackett would not be far away from Concord. They had been accustomed to my taking a solitary walk before breakfast during the few days I have been here, and today was no exception. He, as a matter of fact, was looking for me, and we had a chat.'

'I was rather chagrined,' said Lackett. 'Luck seemed to have been against us for, though it was important to recover the documents, we seemed to have lost all chance of following up the means that were to be used to get them away. Then it was that Lady Malchester thought of you—of allowing you to recover the false papers.'

'I do think,' grumbled Menzies, 'that it would have been more simple to have taken me into your confidence.'

'Now don't be peevish, Mr Menzies,' said Lady Malchester, with a little grimace. 'You were a stranger to me. It was so much more convincing for you to run the criminal to earth yourself. If you had been at fault I was prepared to make the clues plainer—but you seemed to have picked up the right scent at once. It would have been harder to stage-manage with a duller man. You will remember that I never pledged you not to return the papers to Holdron at once, but only not to disclose the identity of the thief. I didn't want him to have any suspicion that I was helping the secret service till he'd passed the bogus information on. He'd have known at once, of course, that I was in no need of money.'

'That's where you jumped the rails,' observed Menzies. 'I misunderstand my pledge and refused to give him the papers. That's how he came to lay me out.'

'All to the good,' grinned Lackett. 'He couldn't have had any suspicion of the papers when you were so anxious to delay his re-possession of them. Well, the result has been this. He'd got a regular pigeon-loft in a derelict lodge among some shooting covers he rents at Stoner, ten miles away. We followed him there. He made six copies of the cipher on tracing papers and turned loose half a dozen pigeons before we collared him. Concord, by the way, was captured on his way back to town.'

'And the result?' said Menzies.

Lackett rubbed a finger along his stubby moustache.

'Germany,' he observed, 'will mass troops to meet our reinforcements some ninety miles from where the real attack will take place. By the way, I hope you got your fee from Holdron?'

'Oh, blast the fee,' said Menzies. 'I really beg your pardon, Lady Malchester.'

VIII

THE SEVEN OF HEARTS

ALLINFORD rubbed the end of a penholder against the bald patch at the back of his head and played a heel-and-toe tattoo with his boot on the floor. For a second time he compared the paragraph in 'Printed Informations' with the written document in his hand.

'It's a nightmare,' he declared aloud. 'I shall wake up presently. You can't tell me that on the same day two people are going to lose two distinct diamond necklaces, each with the same number of stones set in the same way, of exactly the same description, and with the same value. It's ridiculous; it's beyond reason.' And he reached for the telephone.

For ten minutes he held an animated conversation with the chief of the Criminal Investigation Department. At last he replaced the receiver, thoughtfully folded the documents, and put them in the breast-pocket of his morning coat. Two minutes he spent with a velvet pad polishing his silk hat, which he finally adjusted on his head at the fashionable angle, picked up a pair of lavender-coloured gloves, and with a glance at himself in the glass, went out into the sunlit morning.

As a divisional detective-inspector, in charge of an important district of the West End, he always made it a point to dress well. In the department he was known as 'Beau Allinford.' His carefully kept grey moustache, his square shoulders and well-tailored clothes on his tall figure, gave him the appearance of a retired military officer.

His way led him to the Durbar Hotel, and the manager of that caravanserai greeted him with a handshake of relief. 'Come into my private office,' he invited. 'Have you been able to make anything of it yet? I needn't tell you that the hotel will be grateful if it can be cleared up without any unnecessary publicity—though, of course, we're not strictly responsible, as Mr Verndale kept the diamonds in his own rooms.'

He was a rotund little man. His bright little inquiring eyes were fixed with some anxiety on the detective. A robbery at an hotel is apt to have serious results on its patronage.

'You don't expect me to touch a button and produce the thief and the gems, do you?' inquired Allinford irritably. 'It's not an hour ago since I was here and first heard of the robbery.'

'No, no; of course not,' said the manager soothingly. 'I'm quite sure you'll do your best.'

The ruffled Allinford sat down. 'Let me tell you my trouble, Mr Lanton,' he said. 'Perhaps you can help. Here's Mr Rex Verndale, a customer of your hotel—'

'Shall we say a client?' interrupted the little manager, with dignity.

'Very well, a client, if you prefer that. Between six o'clock last evening and nine o'clock this morning Mr Verndale lost from his room a diamond necklace valued at five thousand pounds sterling. Now,'—he took 'Informations' from his pocket and tapped it with a white forefinger,—'this morning it was reported to headquarters that a burglary was committed at Sir Rupert Helton's town house in Mount Street, and that the thieves got away with Lady Helton's jewel-case, which contained, among other things, a diamond necklace worth five thousand pounds sterling.'

'You don't say so!' exclaimed the manager, with astonishment. 'What an extraordinary coincidence!'

'I believe you,' said Allinford grimly. 'What's more extraordinary is that the descriptions of the two necklaces tally, even to the weight of each individual diamond. Now I'm going up to see Mr Verndale again, but I wanted to ask you what you know about him beforehand.'

The manager thought he saw a subtle suggestion in the

question. He made a gesture deprecatory of suspicion. 'He's undoubtedly a gentleman,' he said, laying a slight stress on the second word. 'He's stayed with us for three months or more in every year for more than five years now. He's travelled a great deal, I believe. He is very well known among some good people, and has a private income of his own. He's extremely well-off, I should judge. You don't believe'—with a recollection of a scheme of which he had heard—'that he's trying to work an insurance fraud?'

'That's one of the points,' said Allinford. 'The jewels were not insured. First time I've heard of anyone with a valuable heirloom—which he says it was—which was not insured. You don't know where he gets his income? No? Well, it doesn't matter. I think I'll go up and see him now. I'll look in later on you.'

Mr Rex Verndale occupied a suite of rooms on the first floor of the by-no-means-inexpensive Durbar Hotel, in itself a proof of ample means, if, as the manager said, he had occupied them for long terms over a period of years.

His manner, as he received Allinford, was loftily austere and patronising. He was a young man of thirty or thereabouts, tow-headed, with a clean-shaven face, alert eyes, and an over-powering odour of scent. The detective detested a man who used scent.

He raised his eyebrows languidly as the official explained the coincidence that had arisen. 'That's very extraordinary—very extraordinary indeed!' he drawled. 'How do you account for it?'

'I can't!' said Allinford bluntly. 'Do you know Sir Rupert Helton or Lady Helton?'

'My good man'—Verndale stretched out a well-fitting boot and rocked to and fro as he admired it—'I'm not sure whether I do or not. I may have met them—I can't say. One sees so many people.'

'There's one other point—you'll forgive me for mentioning

it. You told me those diamonds had been your mother's. Do you know where she got them?'

Verndale sighed wearily, as one patiently tolerating a bore. 'They were given her by my father, on their wedding-day,' he said. 'My father was the second son of the eighth Earl of Mulchester. I don't believe he stole them.'

Allinford stolidly ignored the sarcasm. 'It isn't clear to me, either, why you had them here. Surely they'd have been safer in the bank.'

'Perhaps they would,' agreed Verndale, still as if talking to a persistent child. 'That idea had occurred to me, Mr—er—Allinford—thank you. In point of fact, they were in Chancery Lane Safe Deposit up to yesterday morning, when I took them out. I am suffering from—ah—a temporary financial stress at the moment, and it was my intention—you understand?'

'Thank you. I think I do. Now, Mr Verndale, you said you had a few friends in to bridge last evening. I should be obliged if you would let me have a list of their names.'

Verndale sat up. 'But they are people quite above suspicion,' he said stiffly. 'I can't have them annoyed. I would rather drop the whole thing. Really, Mr—ah—er—yes, Allinford.' He shook his head reprovingly.

'I assure you they shall not be annoyed. It is necessary or I would not ask you.'

Verndale moved to an inlaid writing-desk. 'Oh, well, in that case—' He scribbled a few minutes and handed the list to Allinford. 'And now perhaps you will excuse me,' he said.

As Allinford went out, he noticed something on the floor, half hidden under the curtain. He stooped to pick it up; it was a playing card—the seven of hearts.

There is always a certain sameness in the steps taken to investigate a crime. Indeed, a great part of the work of the investigator is usually done before the actual commission of crime—done by an organisation which compiles every ascertainable fact about a probable criminal, from, his finger-prints to the state of his finances, his methods of working to his latest address.

For the time being, Allinford was too busy to devote much thought to the coincidence of the second robbery. It was his duty to find how Verndale's jewels had disappeared, and to that end it was an obvious step to find out which of the known jewel thieves could have committed the theft and then to eliminate them, one by one, until the right person—if it really was a professional thief—was known.

He had twenty men under his immediate command, and the case afforded, work for all. To each man he indicated a line of inquiry, and then he caught a bus for Scotland Yard. He was wishful to find out exactly what had happened on the parallel inquiry of Lady Helton's necklace.

It was on the narrow stone flight of stairs, leading upwards from the back door of the Metropolitan Police Office—which is the official name for Scotland Yard—that he met the burly familiar figure of Weir Menzies, one of the chief inspectors of the department.

Menzies grabbed him by the elbow. 'That you, Allinford? I've been expecting you this last hour. You're handling the Durbar Hotel jewel case, aren't you? I've got the Lady Helton end. What's the latest?'

'The latest, sir,' said Allinford, slowly and deliberately, 'is nothing. We've not got fairly started yet. I was hoping you'd be able to help.'

'Come inside,' said Menzies. He pushed his colleague into the chief inspector's room and dragged forward a chair. 'I may help or I may mix things up. I've finished my job. That part of it was simple.'

'Finished?' repeated Allinford.

'Yes, finished. Tell me—is your man—Verndale—a friend of the Heltons?'

'I asked him. He isn't even sure that he knows 'em.'

Menzies looked meaningly across at the other. 'Sure to say

that. What I mean is, he didn't know the lady before her marriage—old flame, and that sort of thing?'

'I don't know.' Allinford glanced at his watch. 'I may be able to tell in three or four hours' time. I've got two men collecting all they can about him. How about the Helton case?'

'It didn't take long to burst that up. I got down to Mount Street early and saw the lady—a fine woman she is, too! You may have seen her picture in the society papers. She was in tears, and Sir Rupert was raving up and down, cursing burglars and police and servants indiscriminately. It seems he had asked her to wear the necklace at the ball he is giving tonight. She got it out of the bank yesterday, according to her story. One of the lower windows had been left open, and it was through that that the burglar entered. Her bedroom is on the first floor and adjoined by a dressing-room. She had left her jewel-case on the dressing-table. She woke up early this morning, heard a noise in the dressing-room, and raised an alarm. The thief got clear away—with the jewel-case. The household theory was that he'd gone through the open window.

'Sir Rupert fixed the time of the robbery. He had looked at his watch; it was ten-past five. I of course, went and had a talk with the constable on the beat. Now here was a curious thing. He had placed a private mark on that window when he went on duty. He had gone by the house at five o'clock and it was undisturbed. About thirty yards along he met his section sergeant, and they were there talking when the alarm was raised.'

'Fake?' asked Allinford.

'Fake, all right! I didn't beat about the bush. I put it to Sir Rupert and Lady Helton. She denied it, of course; he took her side, and you can take my word for it he didn't gloss over any defects he could find in my character. I was ordered out of the house—he told me to go before I was kicked out—and he's going to get me hounded out of the service.' Menzies grinned as though the prospect did not greatly daunt him.

'Then it comes to this,' said Allinford thoughtfully, 'the necklace that has been stolen from Verndale was originally Lady Helton's, and it must have passed out of her hands to him, directly or indirectly.'

'That's how I make it!'

'She faked the robbery because she didn't want to tell her husband what she had done with the jewels. You're thinking of blackmail, Mr Menzies, of course?'

Menzies nodded. 'That's the drift. How do we know he hasn't been bleeding her? I'd look into it from that point of view, if I were you—though, after all, it doesn't much matter how he came by the necklace if you can't prove anything. If it's blackmail, Lady Helton, who's the only possible witness, won't speak. No, take it all around, Allingford, I'd stick to safe lines. All that ought to worry you is—who stole the jewels from Verndale?'

'H'm—yes! About your own affair, sir,—the necklace was insured?'

'Yes, I was talking to Lloyd's assessors just before you came in. No claim has been put in yet. If it is'—his jaw became grim—'there'll be trouble for Lady Helton. But it's not likely. She won't be such a fool.' Wherein Menzies, for once, showed himself no prophet, for by four o'clock that afternoon a representative of Lloyd's had informed him that a formal claim of the loss of the necklace had been put in.

Menzies had insisted that the coincidence of the two necklaces was a side issue, with which Allinford need not concern himself. If the robbery from Mount Street had been faked—and of this the detective had no doubt—the claim on the insurance companies was an attempt to obtain money by fraud. It might be possible to prove this on the facts known to Menzies. But to clinch the matter beyond doubt, it became necessary to show that Verndale's stolen necklace was actually identical with that that had belonged to Lady Helton.

Allinford heard of the claim by telephone. He sat back, took out the seven of hearts which he had picked up in Verndale's rooms, and examined it minutely. He could not rid his mind of the thought that the card held the key to the mystery. It was pure intuition—and intuition is often more likely to mislead than to guide in most investigations. Presently he shrugged his shoulders and pressed the bell. A broad-shouldered young man, whose face and bearing were those of a City clerk of athletic possibilities, answered.

'Ah, Swain!' said the inspector, 'I've got a little job for you. You had Verndale under observation till four o'clock, hadn't you? Ah, good! Tell me where he was when you were relieved.'

'He was at 704 Granville Street, Piccadilly. Been there since twelve o'clock. Must have lunched there.'

Allinford smashed his open hand down on his thigh, and his eyes narrowed. 'That's it!' he exclaimed. 'I'll be dashed if that isn't it.' But he volunteered no explanation. 'Look here, Swain,' he went on, 'I want you to go to the Durbar Hotel and see if you can get hold of a pack of cards out of Mr Verndale's room. I'm relying on you not to do anything foolish. You needn't go to the manager—understand? I want this done quietly. Bring 'em to me as soon as you can.'

The young man gave a business-like assent and disappeared. In half an hour he was back. He laid a pack of cards on the desk, and the inspector picked them up with a word of thanks. He asked no questions.

For half an hour Allinford went through the cards with a steady scrutiny; then he carried them nearer to the window and examined them in pairs and threes, by what photographers call 'transmitted light.' A little chuckle broke from his lips.

'What a Dutchman I was not to think of it before. This begins to explain things.'

The door pushed open and Menzies entered. The usually smooth forehead of the chief was corrugated into a frown. 'What's the game?' he asked. 'Are you taking up conjuring tricks?'

'Something of that sort,' smiled Allinford. He replaced the

cards in their case and put the case in his pocket. 'If all goes well, as I think it will, we'll know where we are by tonight.'

'That's all right! You got my telephone message?'

'About Lady Helton—yes. The woman must be mad!'

'It's not the woman so much; I imagine she would be pleased enough to let the whole thing drop. It's Sir Rupert. You see, technically, the necklace is his, it's insured in his name and he's put in a claim. He's one of that honest, mutton-headed, obstinate, fiery kind of men, and he's not going to be dictated to by any blessed common policeman—that's me—from Scotland Yard. I thought I'd call in, as this was on my way back, and let you know how things are.'

'What are you going to do?'

Menzies spread his hands out hopelessly. 'What can I do? Sir Rupert's honest enough. He believes in his wife. Of course I might charge them both with an attempt to defraud, but it could never be brought home against him—and as it would have to be brought against both of them together, the charge against her would naturally fail, too. If it had been her own necklace and she had put in the claim in her own name, it would have been different. The insurance company will have to fight, I expect; it's none of our funeral.'

He yawned and stood up. 'Well, I thought you'd like to know how things are. I'm going on to the Yard and then home. Goodnight!'

Allinford sighed as he reflected that his own connection with the case gave no promise of immediate leisure. He had formulated an idea, but if that fell through it might be days or weeks before he would be able to settle things. He called Swain again, and gave that intelligent young man long and earnest instructions. Then he went out to a frugal meal of weak tea and dry toast. He was troubled with his digestion at times. He ate abstractedly. At last, with the air of an idle man who was not quite sure what to do with himself, he sauntered out and strolled towards Shaftesbury Avenue.

There is a famous theatrical outfitter in one of the side streets of that thoroughfare. And the urbane, frock-coated proprietor came forward, rubbing his hands.

'Good-evening, Mr Allinford. Been a beautiful day, hasn't it? You're looking very fit.'

'Yes, it's grand weather,' admitted the detective, and with that concession to conversation he got to business. 'Say, can you turn me out as a doctor in half an hour? That's all the time I can give you. I want something weather-proof and fool-proof—something that isn't obvious. I won't have a false beard. You know the kind of thing I mean.'

The costumier measured him with a professional glance. 'I know,' he said. 'I can make you so that your own mother won't know you.'

The art of disguise—especially facial disguise—is one that is very rarely used by officers attached to the Criminal Investigation Department. There is indeed a make-up room at Scotland Yard where men may transform themselves into anything from coal-heavers to guardsmen, but it is used only when the ordinary attire and manner of the detective would be so entirely out of keeping with his surroundings as to attract attention. A dirty muffler, unshaven face, and corduroys work a transformation more difficult of detection than the most cunning use of grease-paint and wigs.

It is only when an officer is to be brought into personal contact with some who knows him, and by whom it is essential he should not be recognised, that he goes to the extreme and very risky length of altering his face.

Allinford was critical and exacting while expert hands transformed him. When the disguise was complete, he examined himself with the mirror and gave a grunt of approval. His grey, drooping moustache had become well waxed and auburn, with pointed ends. His scanty hair also had a tinge of the same colour, and had been brushed so that it appeared twice as luxuriant as it was in reality. A razor and dye had worked wonders with his eyebrows. He wore his own clothes and was as neat as ever, but it would have needed keen eyes to detect any likeness to the man who had entered the establishment.

'Yes; I think that ought to do,' he commented.

Unless a person were keenly observant or suspicious, he would be very unlikely to guess that the front door of 704 Granville Street, Piccadilly, had not been out of sight of officers of police for six or seven days.

It was a quiet house, solid-looking and respectable—a residence which would not have shamed a Cabinet Minister. A luxurious motor-brougham had just driven away when Allinford walked briskly up the broad stone steps and pressed the bell. The door swung smoothly back, and a ponderous footman, in olive-green livery, confronted him.

The detective fingered a card. 'Will you take this to Mr Glenston, please. Mr Roberts, a friend of mine, suggested I might call.'

Now Roberts is a fairly common name. That is why Allinford had used it. He knew that the house had many visitors, and it was possible that a Roberts might be among them, or, alternately, that the occupant might not feel certain that he had not a client named Roberts. On the card the footman read:

AUDREY LATIMER, M.D.
GREAT SOUTHERN HOSPITAL

His eyes wandered from the card to its owner, in a measured scrutiny that might have seemed offensive had not Allinford been prepared for it. He met the look with bland arrogance.

'Very good, sir,' said the man. 'Will you come this way?'

He ushered the detective into a reception-room furnished in keeping with the solid character of the house, and left him. For ten minutes Allinford waited, drumming his fingers on his knee. He knew very well what was happening, but he had taken precautions. When he had assumed the name and title of a hospital doctor, he had arranged that the hospital authorities should not betray him. If the muscular footman with the inquisitive eyes was ringing up the Great Southern Hospital to verify the visitor's identity, he would soon be satisfied.

He returned in a little. 'It is all right, sir. Will you walk upstairs—the first door on the right. It's rather early now. Most people drop in after dinner or during the afternoon.'

'I expect I shall find something to amuse me,' said Allinford, and while the man held open the door, he passed out and up the thickly-carpeted stairway.

There were a dozen or more people in the room which the servant had indicated. It was a big apartment, and its furniture and fittings were rather those of a club than of a private house. Prominent at one end was a kind of bar partly shielded by curtains, and with two or three small tables in front of it. Some of them were occupied. One woman—she was scarcely more than a girl—with delicate tinted complexion was drinking tea with an older companion of her own sex, a soft-faced woman with a heavy jaw.

A little group of men were clustered around another table, laughing and chatting, but their drink was not tea. In the body of the room was a large roulette table at which the croupier sat idle in his high-backed chair. Nearer the window half a dozen men and women were seated round a *chemin-de-fer* table, watching the dealer.

Decidedly it was a slack time of day. There was none of that hectic excitement which the picturesque writer about West End gambling dens loves to depict. It was all very decorous. As Allinford moved up to the baccarat, one man signalled to the waiter and scribbled a cheque. The detective noted the amount with an inward gasp. It was for five hundred pounds.

He observed Verndale among the group at the bar and moved towards them. Refreshments—even to the most costly of wines—were free. But he contented himself with a modest cup of tea. He wanted to keep his head clear.

'Yes,' Verndale was saying, in his arrogant, dogmatic way, 'baccarat's all very well to a point, but I'd nearly as soon play pitch-and-toss. It's a children's game. Give me poker—or auction bridge, for that matter—something with more life in it.'

One of the group—a tall young man with a weak chin and a scrubby tooth-brush moustache—grinned feebly. 'There's life in your poker, Verndale.'

'You ought to know,' chuckled a second man. 'For my part, I'd sooner buck against him at poker than auction. There's a little woman who's paid for her bridge lessons—eh, Verndale?'

Verndale frowned. The last hint seemed to have touched a sore point. 'That's enough, Devine!' he said curtly. Then, more amiably: 'You can't afford to be chivalrous in a card-game, you know; there's a difference between sportsmanship and quixotry. Most women are fools. If they had the sense to stick to a pure gamble—something where no skill is required—they would sometimes win. Talking about poker, I'm willing to sit in. But we can't play here. Suppose you people come up to my rooms. How many of us are there—four? Five would make a better game.'

His gaze rested on Allinford only for a moment. The detective was quick to see the invitation. 'I should be happy to sit in, if you will allow me,' he said. 'My name is Latimer.' He proffered a card.

Verndale bowed. 'Pleased to know you, Dr Latimer. My name is Verndale. Let me introduce Lord Tiverley, Sir Richard Hopville, Mr Granger. Well, we might as well have some taxies.'

'He thinks he's roped a new mug,' meditated Allinford.

Verndale indeed seemed to have taken a fancy to the stranger. He insisted on the doctor's sharing his cab, while the other three took a second vehicle. By the time they reached the Durbar Hotel, the two might have been, judging from their manner, the friends of a lifetime.

The game began slowly enough, but Allinford had fears that the ten pounds with which he had provided himself would not go far. He played cautiously. Hopville, the weak-chinned young man, was the plunger of the party. His futile attempts at bluff, at times, awoke the derision of the others. Verndale seemed to be feeling his feet. The detective judged him to be measuring the game of the others. He was winning a trifle.

He was a lavish host too, for a servant was continually filling up glasses at a side-table; but it was noticeable that he himself drank little.

Allinford had lost five pounds, and he was still no further advanced than when they had begun. He bit his lip. All his plans depended upon his proving Verndale to be a cheat, and yet, to all appearances, the man was playing honestly enough. The worst of it was that he might go on playing honestly. The skilled cheat most often only falls upon unfair methods in a game like poker when luck runs against him. While it holds he is content with his expert knowledge of the straight game.

As the game warmed up, Hopville's luck turned. He took risks; he broke every law of the safe game. Yet he won. He seemed able to do nothing wrong. The stack of chips in front of him mounted higher and higher, and he grinned inanely over his cards. Verndale too was losing. Allinford's small capital ebbed away until only a sovereign was left. He sat tense and watchful.

'Now, Doctor,' said Verndale, smiling as he picked up the cards, 'I am going to give you a real royal flush. Just keep your eye on me.' He dealt slowly.

As the last card fell from his fingers, Allinford suddenly rose, reached across the table, and wrenched away the pack. 'One moment, gentlemen!' he cried. 'Hold your hands!'

Verndale's chair overturned with a crash, as he leaped to his feet. 'What the devil do you mean?' he demanded. His white hands were opening and shutting, and his face was flushed. 'Are you making any suggestion against anyone present?'

'I am!' said the detective sharply. 'Sit down!'

'You're a liar!' stormed Verndale. 'Get out of my house or I'll have you thrown out.'

'I think not,' said Allinford quietly. 'I should advise you to sit still till I have finished. Gentlemen, the cards are marked! You, Mr Granger, hold a pair of aces, a pair of fours, and the king of diamonds. You, Lord Tiverley, have the four of clubs, one knave, four, three, and the deuce of spades. Sir Richard Hopville has three queens. Mr Verndale, I observe, has dropped his hand on the floor, and as I am not quite expert enough to have read them, except slowly, I can't tell you what they were. My own are a pair of knaves, the three of diamonds, six of spades, and the seven of hearts.'

'We've got a blessed conjurer!' laughed Sir Richard Hopville.

No one paid him any attention. Granger and Tiverley turned their cards face upwards and looked gravely from Allinford to Verndale. The latter was breathing heavily. He tried to laugh.

'You know me, Granger,' he said; 'so do you, Tiverley, and you, Hopville. I don't quite know what this man's idea is, but it looks like blackmail. If the cards are marked, he has managed to introduce them himself. Why,'—he brought his fist down on the table to emphasise his remark,—'I've lost money myself.'

'That's true!' said Hopville. 'A pot!'

'Before we go any further,' said Allinford, 'I may explain that I am a police officer. That will dispose of any question of blackmail. Perhaps you will hold a card to the light, Lord Tiverley. Thank you. You will notice a small spot near the top left-hand corner. Now put the card down. That spot has gone. It looks like an optical illusion, doesn't it? You could be told the cards were marked and search for a week if you didn't know what to look for. You will find that spot in a different position on each card, according to the suit and value. The person who marked them had a full acquaintance with the virtues of aniline dye. An expert could read them as they were dealt as easily as though they were face upwards. He could do more than that, with a little experience. He could deal any hand he wished to any person at the table.'

Tiverley towered over Verndale.

'I think I've heard enough,' he said. 'I ought to have been less simple. I am obliged to you, Mr—er—er—?'

'Allinford,' said the detective.

'Thank you, Mr Allinford. I assume—ah'—he paused, embarrassed—'I assume you are not acting in your professional capacity—that is, I shall not be required to give evidence.'

'I hope not, my lord. Indeed, I may say I think it unlikely.'

Verndale pushed out a detaining hand. 'You don't really believe this preposterous thing? It's so utterly ridiculous.'

Lord Tiverley brushed by him, with head erect, and Granger followed. Hopville sprawled, with his arms over the card-table. ''Pon my soul,' he ejaculated, 'it's like a scene out of a melodrama. A stage detective and all!'

'Including the wicked baronet,' retorted Allinford quickly. 'You may drop your pose, if you please, Sir Richard. This is serious, and you will be wise to recognise it. Do you think your change of luck was not noticeable directly a new pack of cards was introduced?'

Hopville sat upright. 'So he's in it too, is he?' sneered Verndale. 'Look here, Mr Detective, we've had quite enough. I don't suppose you're a rich man but it will take every penny you've got when I commence an action for slander. You've wormed your way in here in disguise, and you've accused me of card-sharping. Now go—if you've finished!'

Allinford moved to the door, turned the key, and thrust it in his pocket. 'I haven't quite,' he said coolly. 'Now listen to me.' He pulled out his watch. 'It's now ten minutes to nine. At nine o'clock a police raid will be made on 704 Granville Street, and certain people will be charged with assisting to run a gambling-house. Now there's nothing on earth that can prevent you two being charged as proprietors. Don't trouble to deny it. There will be plenty of evidence. The place has been watched for days. I don't suppose a fine of a few hundreds—which is what it will probably amount to—will affect you much but if you're wise you'll come off your pedestals and listen to plain sense. There's another charge it may be in my power to prefer—receiving stolen goods.'

'Go on!' laughed Verndale. 'Accuse us of murder while you're at it.'

'Oh, very well,' said Allinford nonchalantly, 'only you may as well know that the jewels you had from Lady Helton were not her property. They were stolen from her husband, and a bogus robbery arranged to account for their absence.'

To casual observers, Verndale's appearance remained unchanged, but a slight distension of the nostrils showed Allinford that his shot had told. 'I do not admit that I had the necklace from Lady Helton,' he said.

'Come,' said Allinford bluntly, 'you're not such a fool as you'd wish me to think. Would you expect a jury to believe that? Lady Helton has been at Granville Street day after day for weeks on end. She had an ample allowance for all ordinary purposes. She made over the jewels to you either as a payment or as security for a gambling debt. If she didn't, it's worse for you, for you had stolen goods in your possession for which you can't account. You must remember you signed an exact description of the jewels.'

Hopville whistled a tune. Verndale laid his head on his hands and stared thoughtfully into space. 'You've got me in a corner,' he admitted. 'What is it you want me to do?'

'I want you to return the necklace,' said Allinford. 'No,'—as Verndale would have spoken,—'don't trouble to put up another bluff. It's easy enough to see what's happened. Lady Helton wanted the jewels returned so that she might wear them tonight. You refused, and, fearful that she would become a nuisance in the future, arranged that they should be apparently stolen. Unluckily for you, she had the same idea of a bogus robbery. Now—'

'If I give it up, will you promise me nothing further shall be done?'

'I can't promise. The gambling-house prosecution will go forward in any case. If the necklace is returned, however, I doubt if Sir Rupert Helton will prosecute.'

Verndale rose, crossed the room, and, unlocking the secretary, took out a red morocco case which he placed in the hands of the detective.

'Yes, sir,'—Allinford was speaking to Menzies,—'luck and bluff carried it through. When I heard that the Helton robbery was bogus, I began to get a glimmering, because I had picked up a marked card in Verndale's rooms. Then, when I heard he had gone to Granville Street, I began to be sure, more especially as Lady Helton had been seen there. The games in the gambling-house were straight enough—it wouldn't have paid to run anything crooked—but Hopville and Verndale used to pick up likely young fools there and carry them off to Verndale's rooms.

'I'll own Hopville had me guessing, at first. He looked a regular pigeon—instead of which he was a rook. Of course, it wouldn't have done for Verndale to have won heavily at his own place. But no one was likely to suppose him in with Hopville. As soon as I was sure, I shook them up with my composure. After that I bluffed for all I was worth, and they fell into it.'

'I see by the papers,' said Menzies inconsequently, 'that Sir Rupert and Lady Helton are going abroad for a protracted period.'

'Exactly!' smiled Allinford.

IX

THE GOAT

BIG RUFE DEVLIN and Goat O'Brien moved on different planes of the criminal hierarchy. There was all the difference of status between them that there is between an ambitious curate and an archbishop. For while Rufe was merely a sneak thief of parts, the Goat was one of the potentates of crime with a fat bank balance and little fear of the police. Yet Rufe it was . . .

You might have passed the Goat a hundred times in the street without giving him a second glance. He was a slim-built, slouched-shouldered little man of seventy, with a trim grey beard and a deprecating manner, who wore well-made clothes untidily. His record ran back through fifty years of subtle and audacious rascality in three continents. Now, in his old age, he had promoted himself from the executive to the less risky but more profitable administrative side of crime. He was, in fact, a receiver, and it was the misfortune of the Criminal Investigation Department that he should have settled down to exercise his talents in London.

It is only in books that a man of the Goat's reputation can avoid the suspicions of the police. And O'Brien, who knew every trick on the board, had no illusions on the subject. He knew that time and again the keenest men of the C.I.D. had taken the warpath against him only to retire at last baffled and chagrined, with the futile headache which comes from battering brains against a stone wall. He knew that the department had sworn to have his scalp, and at times he would smile grimly into his little grey beard. They might know he was at the back of half a dozen burglaries, not only in London but in Paris and Amsterdam, that his money had provided the resources, that his brains had planned the coup, that his fingers dipped deeply into the proceeds; but juries require concrete proofs, and proofs were just what were lacking.

More than once a surprise descent of officers, armed with a search warrant, had been made on his cosy flat on the north side of Regent's Park. He would receive them mildly, with a resigned shrug of the shoulders, as one who is the subject of unjust annoyance, against which no protests would avail. On the last occasion it was Almack, newly promoted divisional detective-inspector of the 12th Division, who was confident that the Goat knew a great deal more than he ought of a weekend robbery of specie from a West End manufacturing goldsmith. He dropped swiftly down upon the flat with a couple of his staff. Three thousand ounces of gold cannot be disposed of in a hurry, and he hoped by rapidity of action to catch O'Brien before he had time to get rid of it.

It took a full five hours to convince him that wherever else the gold was it was not in the flat. The Goat, with a subtle irony that was not lost on the inspector, produced champagne.

'You've got your duty to do, gentlemen, and I don't complain. I've been a crook, and I've got enough to live on. I've no need to get in the game again. I just hate to see you wasting your time.'

Almack wiped his damp brow. The shifting of furniture is heavy work for amateurs.

'We'll get you, Goat,' he said definitely. 'You're clever, I own, and you've done us down this time, but we'll get you. Don't you make any error.'

The Goat shook his grey head reprovingly. 'I believe you would—if you got a chance,' he admitted. 'But, as I said, I've enough to live on, and I'm side-stepping all work on the cross. It would save your people a lot of trouble if you'd believe me. Well, here's promotion.' He lifted a thin-stemmed wineglass and sipped lovingly. 'Did I ever tell you how I lifted a parcel of diamonds from the Rietfontein post office?' He sighed. 'That was in the old days. And mind you, the diamond field police were smart men.'

He saw them urbanely off the premises, even offering to send for his car to take them back to headquarters. But Almack was in no mood to accept further civilities. 'A bus will do for us, thanks,' he retorted. 'See you again some other time. So long.'

'Drop in whenever you're passing,' said O'Brien. 'Always pleased to see you or any of your friends, Mr Almack.'

Not until they were out of hearing did Almack say the things that were burning within him. To fail was bad enough. To be taunted by the old man in the presence of his subordinates was worse. But worst of all was the knowledge that the department would know that he, the last created 'D.D.-I.,' had wrecked a lance against the Goat and been ignominiously unhorsed. He swore fervently.

The 'under-world,' as the pictures call it, is no freemasonry society of brothers. It is only by chance that its inhabitants get to know one another, for there are no obvious signs by which a crook betrays himself as other than a law-abiding citizen. Consequently, when a mild-looking, little old man moved slowly out through the swing-doors of the Great Southern and Northern Bank in Holborn and signalled a bus, Big Rufe had no conception that he was beholding in the flesh a fellow-crook as far above him as the stars. All that he saw was, in his own vocabulary, a possible 'mark.'

Times were bad with Rufe, and though his trousers were carefully creased and his sleek black hair was parted in the centre as definitely as though by a sword cut, he had only five small silver coins in his pocket. For seven days he had sat before the same marble-topped table at a restaurant that commanded a view of the portals of the bank and spent most of his time chewing a toothpick and watching. Three times had he seen the feeble little man with the vague face enter and emerge, and from the mass of the bank's customers he had decided that this was the one Providence indicated as the instrument which was to provide him with the means of life for a period.

His hand dropped to a pocket. Rufe's limitations might have been gathered from the fact that he carried a heavy seven-shot automatic. No big professional criminal, in England at least, carries arms as a usual thing. It makes a big difference in the sentence to be found with a weapon. There are other ways of offence and defence.

One minute later he had swung himself on to the bus that contained O'Brien, and the listless eyes of the old man rested on him indifferently as he took his seat. Rufe met them with equal indifference, and presently stooping, picked up a coin from the floor. 'Did you drop this, sir?' he said politely.

The Goat stretched out a thin hand. 'Thank you very much. Must have slipped down while I was paying the conductor.'

Rufe saw one-fifth of his worldly wealth vanish into the pocket of his destined victim. Though he mentally condemned him as a 'tight wad,' he smiled philosophically.

After all, it was an investment. He flashed a hand forward—a hand that boasted a big imitation diamond set in a gold ring.

'Rotten weather, ain't it?' He imagined he had the society accent to perfection. 'Looks as if we hadn't finished with the rain yet. Say, is it always wet like this in London?'

Not a change in O'Brien's face showed that he recognised the awkward gambit of the unskilled confidence man. Rufe had conveyed that he was a stranger in the metropolis. The big diamond on his finger showed that he was a man of wealth. His accent was meant to show that he was a man of culture.

The Goat folded up the paper which he was reading. 'Sonny,' he said gently, 'if you get off this bus you will soon find a constable. Tell him you've lost yourself, and get him to hand you over to your nurse. She'll take you home and tuck you up in your little bed. London's a big place for an innocent youth to get lost in. There's a lot of wicked characters about, and you never know when you might get taken in.'

Rufe's jaw dropped. For a second the devil peeped out of his green eyes and his fists clenched. His chagrin and disappointment were plain for anyone to witness. He spat out a malevolent oath. The Goat's eyes half closed as though he had lost all interest in the incident.

'You—' Words failed Rufe, and he choked.

'Count twenty slowly,' advised the Goat solemnly.

Rufe could have broken the frail body of the older man between his two hands. He pushed his head forward until he was within a couple of inches of the other's face.

'Say you,' he demanded, with all the intensity of malice he could inflect into his voice. 'You gimme back my shilling or I'll eat you up.'

O'Brien folded his thin hands in his lap. 'I think not,' he said placidly. 'I think not.'

Had he shown anything like aggressive defiance, Rufe was in a state of mind to carry out his threat. But the cool confidence of the Goat somehow deterred him while it did not lessen his anger. A sort of vanity which is one of the distinguishing characteristics of men of his type was hurt at his designs being frustrated. He glared inarticulate.

When the Goat descended from the bus he was aware that six feet of wrath was dogging him. He walked homeward serenely contemptuous. It did not even amuse him that he had been selected for the crude experiment of Big Rufe. He knew that the other was raw at the game, otherwise he would not have lost his temper. He knew, too, that Rufe was keeping him in sight in hope of finding an opportunity to give physical effects to his passion. That, too, worried him little. In streets as well policed and as frequented as those through which he had to pass, no assault could be committed with impunity. He had other affairs to think of than this trivial encounter with a minor crook.

That contempt was where the luck which for half a century

had been his handmaid deserted him. Had Rufe been the rawest detective patrol, the most stupid of plain-clothes constables, the Goat would have been warily on his guard. If he thought of the matter at all, it was merely that his follower's passion would evaporate when he found that there was no chance of violence. He slurred into his block of flats without even turning his head.

Now five minutes or more before, Rufe, who was not altogether a fool, had resigned himself to seeing his victim escape for the time being. He recognised that he had made a mistake, and though he was still sore, his first anger had passed. He was capable of more or less sound reasoning. He had no very clear idea, but he was certain that somehow, if he could hit on it, there was a way of digging money out of the little old man who had not only bilked him out of his money but administered such a nasty jolt to his self-esteem.

He walked boldly up to the lounging janitor at the doorway.

'What's the name of that bloke that's just gone in?' he demanded bluntly. 'Skinny little chap with a grey beard.'

'What y' wanto know for?'

Rufe was more in his element at this kind of thing. He lowered his voice mysteriously, and glanced round with melodramatic emphasis.

'Sh. I'm a split—a "tec," y' know. I can't tell y' all about it, but he looks like a man we want. I'm not sure. I'm only going by what I remember of a photograph.'

'I reckon you've made a bad miss this time,' said the attendant. 'He's no gaol-bird. His name's O'Brien, and he's got pots of splosh. Runs a motor and Lord knows what all. I've been here six months and always found 'im a perfect gentleman. You'd never guess he was an American.'

The name O'Brien is a fairly common one. It never occurred to Rufe to associate it with the Goat, otherwise he might have hesitated. He pulled at his top lip.

'Looks like a bloomer, don't it?' he said frankly. 'We all make mistakes. Still, you can't be too sure. Since I've wasted me time comin' here I shall have to make a report. Tell me what you know about him.' Another of his precious shillings passed.

This time, however, he was satisfied with his investment. He had pumped the janitor dry before he walked thoughtfully away. His idea was beginning to take shape. He was no pendent specialist. When he wanted money, methods didn't matter. Results were all that concerned him. And he wanted money badly.

Exactly at half-past two in the morning Big Rufe drove his fist on to the point of the jaw of the drowsy night porter whose sleep for a couple of hours thereafter was sounder if no more refreshing. But ten minutes later the Goat awoke.

It was a proof of the soundness of his nerves that he merely opened his eyes and made no motion, although he was perfectly certain that there was someone in the room. He continued to breathe with audible regularity, but eyes and ears were tensely on the alert. For several minutes the ticking of the little bedside clock was the chief sound in the room. But the Goat knew what was happening. The intruder had clumsily made some sound and was now waiting, motionless, until he could be sure that the sleeper had not roused.

Presently there was a faint click and the darkness of the room became less intense. The Goat instantly shut his eyes, and the next second felt a beam of light searching his face. Then it was gone, and he felt rather than heard a stealthy footfall.

Slowly, with deliberate caution lest the rustling of the bedclothes should attract attention, he began to turn over so that he should face the burglar. He was not at all alarmed, but he was curious. There were several friends of his—business friends—who were quite capable of deeming him worth a professional visit. It had not been unknown for a thief to recover in the night the stolen goods he had sold in the morning.

He could see dimly a black formless figure moving stealthily about the apartment and the pencil of light from the electric torch darting searchingly over the various articles in the room.

The Goat raised himself on one elbow. His visitor's back was towards him, and in the farther corner of the room were half a dozen walking sticks. Many a time in his younger days had the Goat's liberty depended upon his soft-footedness, and his old cunning had not yet deserted him. He lowered his feet gently until they touched the carpet, and noiselessly and swiftly crossed the room.

He had reached the corner and his hand encircled a malacca cane when the beam of light suddenly wheeled round. Instinct seemed to have warned Big Rufe of his danger. The Goat blinked his eyes as the circle of light blinded him, and then found himself looking down the barrel of a heavy automatic.

'Keep your yap shut or you'll get it,' said the steady voice of Rufe.

It was then that O'Brien recognised him. He did not venture to move, but he gave a thin, harsh cackle of laughter.

'Hello! You come to collect that shilling? Say, son, I'd sooner have you as a con man than a burglar out of the funny papers. Take my advice and give up being a crook. It will pay you better to open cab doors for a living.'

'Shut it,' ordered Rufe peremptorily. 'You know what I want. Where d'you keep the stuff? Come on. Cough it up or it'll be the worse for you.'

'You're surely some tough,' taunted the Goat. His grip on the stick shifted and tightened. 'Gosh, but you've nearly got me frightened. Who trusted you with a great big gun like that? Do you know what would happen to you if it went off while you're pointing it at me? You would be hanged by the neck until you were dead, and your mummy would have to buy nice new black clothes for you.'

'That's enough,' growled Rufe. 'I don't want to be hard with an old man like you.' The pistol muzzle dropped. There were men who could have told Rufe that the only time the Goat could be considered safe was while one had him at the end of a gun. But this knowledge he had yet to acquire.

A man more astute might realise that the Goat's gibes were intended to distract attention. In fact he was only waiting for that pistol muzzle to drop.

Rufe understood too late. The Goat lunged with the stick as a fencer with a sword, and the other doubled up like a clasp-knife as the ferrule caught him on what the doctors call the solar plexus and boxers the bread-basket. Even while he was gasping the cane swished again through the air twice in rapid succession. He dropped clumsily forward and lay still.

O'Brien switched on the light and, replacing the stick, opened the door and listened. Presently he went a little way along the corridor, tapped at another door, and pushed it open.

'George!' he called softly. 'George, come here!'

A sleepy grunt answered him, and a moment later a middle-aged man with immature side-whiskers had leapt out of bed. He was chauffeur valet to O'Brien as far as the outside world was concerned. He was also general assistant in a variety of affairs of which the public knew nothing.

He followed O'Brien back to his own room, and his employer jerked his head to the prostrate figure.

'Woke up to find that tough here. Had to lay him out,' he said succinctly.

George expressed no surprise. He went to the unconscious man and rolled him over. 'Hit him precious hard, didn't you?' he commented, noting the bruise on the temple.

'He had a gun on me. Not croaked, is he?'

George turned a serious face upwards. He was holding Rufe's pulse. 'He seems mighty bad. What do you reckon we'd better do? Shall I phone for the doctor?'

'Don't be a blamed fool,' said the Goat with asperity. 'That'd mean giving the bulls a chance to come in and out here all the time they were hanging up a case against him. Go and get some clothes on. We'll dump him out in the street and trust to luck.'

'There's the night porter,' remonstrated George.

'I know all about that. You go and get dressed.'

The Goat himself hurriedly flung on some clothes and reconnoitred down the stairs. He found the night porter breathing stertorously in a corner of the little partitioned-off office, and nodded sagely. He knew now all the steps that Rufe had taken, and he understood how he had got possession of the master-key which afforded him entrance to the flat. He returned upstairs.

With jerky reluctance the tape machine rattled out a message, and Divisional Detective-Inspector Almack, who had lingered on his way upstairs to his own office to chaff the sub-divisional, idly tore off the message and glanced at it.

'In consequence of an outbreak of swine-fever at Cheam the Board of Agriculture have prohibited . . . Hello, what's this?' His eye had fallen to a later message.

There is a constant interchange of police news day and night between the ten-score police stations of London—by telephone, by motor, by official newspapers, and by the tape machine. It may not seem essential that a constable at Ewell should know that a burglary has been committed at Bayswater—but the burglar may live at Ewell. News—swift news—is the life-blood of the greatest police organisation in the world, even as it was in the old days of hue and cry.

Almack twisted his reddish moustache absently and, passing the strip of tape abruptly to the sub-divisional inspector, strode off to his own department. One of his sergeants, a broad, ruddy-faced man, was sprawling against the mantelpiece, and a clerk was writing beneath the barred window.

'Mornin', Horand,' said Almack. 'I've just got a hunch that we may get a line on the Goat after all.'

'Huh,' commented Horand, and spat in the fire. He was a veteran of the old days who had never troubled to attempt the further examinations preliminary to higher promotion, and was a pessimist in certain ways. He had known many campaigns against the Goat, and he had small faith that the young 'D.D.-I.' could achieve anything. Still, discipline is discipline, and he said nothing.

'We'll get right over to Regent's Park again,' went on Almack. 'There's a report just come through on the tape that's put me thinking. Ever run across Big Rufe Devlin?'

'I have so,' admitted Horand, struggling with his overcoat.

'They've picked him up outside High Cliff Mansions—that's the Goat's place—badly knocked about. He's in the infirmary now, and he won't say who put it across him.'

Horand stared at his chief with something of contempt. 'There don't seem much to that to drag us right across London. I know Rufe and I know the Goat. They'd no more have anything to do with each other than—than a banker with a confectioner's assistant.'

Almack had a respect for his senior assistant, but he sometimes wished that his common sense was not so arrogant. It blunted enthusiasm. 'All the same, it's deuced funny that he should be picked up practically on the Goat's doorstep. It needs looking into, anyway. A bit of fresh air will do you good.'

Horand ventured no further comment. By the time they had reached the infirmary and stood by Rufe's bed he had become bluffly genial. He had his private opinion that they were on a wild-goose chase, but that would not prevent him from loyally carrying out any steps that Almack might initiate.

'How do, Rufe? You remember me? My name's Horand. Heard you'd been banging yourself about and thought I'd give you a look in. Friend of mine—Mr Almack.' He seated himself with the familiarity of an old friend on the bed.

The crook glared at him resentfully. 'You ain't troubling about my health,' he said suspiciously. 'I'm about sick of you blokes pushing your noses into my private affairs.' He ostentatiously turned his back, and tried an ineffective snore.

'Slip along to High Cliff Mansions and see whether you can

pick up anything there,' whispered Almack. 'Now Devlin,'—his voice was tinged with incisive authority—'listen to me.'

'Oh, blazes,' said Rufe wearily, and turned over again. 'You rozzers don't give anyone a chanst.' Ever since a couple of constables had picked him up and brought him on an ambulance to the infirmary he had been parrying questions and wondering why his assailant of the flat had not handed him over straight away to the police.

'How did you manage to get that?' Almack jerked his head to the bandage that encircled the crook's head.

'Blind to the world,' ejaculated Rufe crisply. 'Must have tumbled over something and smashed myself on the pavement. You know how it is, guv'nor, when—' He broke off as he encountered Almack's disbelieving smile.

'So you said when you were picked up. Do you know what the doctor here says? He says you couldn't have done that by a fall. Somebody hit you—eh?'

Rufe expressed the opinion that the doctor was a condemned fool.

'Now see here, Mr Devlin'—Almack's tones were honeyed—'I want to know what really did happen. Perhaps I can help you to get one back on the man that sacked you.'

'I reckon not,' said Rufe doggedly. 'There ain't no man.'

Since by some miracle his exploit in the small hours had not been brought to the notice of the police, he considered that he would be a fool to disclose it himself. And Almack began to feel that there was something solid behind his 'hunch.' The crook would not be so clumsily secretive if his injuries had not come about while he was engaged in some illegal business. He idly watched Rufe's face as he sprung his next question.

'Then it wasn't Goat O'Brien?'

Rufe sat sharply up in bed, his green eyes glittering with interest. He knew of the Goat, naturally, and an explanation of the recent events in which he had been concerned hit him like a blow with the detective's casual question. It restored something of his self-esteem to realise that he had been worsted by a master of the profession although he remained none the less bitter against the other. But the police were dangerous men to confide in, and he slipped back into a recumbent position and shook his head. 'I've never seen the Goat.'

But Almack was satisfied so far. An unqualified assent could not have carried greater conviction. He leaned sideways towards Rufe and, though he was smiling, his voice had an indefinable menace.

'Listen here, Rufe,'—he judged the time was right to drop the Mister Devlin,—'you've got a rotten record, haven't you? Our people pick you up at three this morning in a street of residential flats. That looks bad, you know.' He shook his head solemnly.

He was within the letter but outside the spirit of the law. It is absolutely illegal to intimidate a man into incriminating himself. But for his eagerness to run the Goat down he would never have hinted—as he had done—at the possibility of arresting Rufe as a suspected person. The shot told.

'You wouldn't do that, guv'nor!' exclaimed Rufe in alarm, shifting himself to allow for a better view of the stern, clean-cut face. 'You wouldn't do that?'

'I'm not saying what I shall do,' said Almack with careful vagueness.

Rufe hesitated a second. Either of the two alternatives by which he was confronted seemed to lead directly to the dock—but if he spoke the police would probably deal with him gently. He took the plunge. Aided by a shrewd question now and again the whole story came out. He held his clenched fist out of bed as he finished, and shook it vindictively . . . 'And if it was Goat O'Brien, as you say, guv'nor, strike me . . .'

'Just so,' said Almack. 'You say it was a malacca cane he used. You're sure of that?'

'Dead sure,' said Rufe. 'Didn't I hold him up for Lord knows how long. It was a light yellow malacca cane.'

*

For a staid divisional detective-inspector Almack felt uncommonly youthful as he passed out of the grimy courtyard of the infirmary. He felt like doing a step-dance on the pavement.

'Luck—incredible luck,' he murmured joyfully. 'I can't be wrong—I simply can't be wrong.'

And then the burly figure of Horand came in sight. The sergeant accosted his chief with an 'I knew it' air.

'Nothing doing yonder,' he reported. 'No one knows anything about this business. The Goat leaves for Paris by the two-twenty.'

'Horand,' said Almack expansively, 'I'm going to buy you a drink. By the Lord High Muck-a-Muck I'd make you drunk if I didn't want you on duty. Then you go and keep your eye on O'Brien until I send a relief. See?'

Horand paused in the act of lighting his pipe and shot a quick inquiring glance at his chief.

'I see,' he muttered slowly. 'Do you mean to say you've actually got a tip from that yob?'

'Do you think,' said Almack, 'that a little snipe like the Goat could lay a man like Big Rufe out with a malacca cane?'

The lighted match burnt the sergeant's fingers. He dropped it hastily and wrinkled perplexed brows. 'What's the point?' he asked.

'Oh, nothing. I'd just got an idea, that's all. Come and have that drink. I don't want to leave the Goat alone too long.'

After he left Horand, Almack swung cheerfully back to his division. He was young enough to feel tempted to ring up Scotland Yard and expound his idea, but he resisted the temptation. He had very little that was tangible to go on, and there was always the possibility that he was wrong. He decided to wait.

He pulled down a much-thumbed copy of *Whitaker's Almanack* from a shelf, propped it open at a certain page, and with the aid of a pad of paper became absorbed in a series of calculations.

Presently he lay back in the chair and surveyed the result of his labours discontentedly. 'That would take months,' he grumbled, 'months and months and months. I'm dashed if I can see where I'm wrong.' He stood up and strode up and down the narrow office, hands thrust deep in his trousers pockets. 'I'll see it through,' he said resolutely. And then a new train of thought occurred to him. He literally jumped to the telephone, and his fingers played an impatient tattoo while he waited for a reply.

He was satisfied, when at quarter-to-two that afternoon he arrived at Charing Cross Station, that every precaution had been taken. He felt a premonition of success, and he chuckled grimly to himself as he loitered near the bookstall in a position which commanded an unostentatious view of the barrier for the Continental train. Somewhere among the throng which congregated the station were three men he knew he could rely on. It only remained for the Goat to walk into the trap.

O'Brien was punctual. As a business man he knew the virtue of always being in time. He and George descended from a cab outside the station just five seconds before another cab that carried Horand and a colleague.

'We're barking up the wrong tree,' proclaimed the sergeant to his companion. 'We'll not get the Goat this trip. The gov'nor's got some wild idea in his head, but I bet you it don't come off. They haven't got the goods on 'em, anyway. All their luggage is those two kit-bags—come on.'

He strolled off in the wake of the other pair as they moved towards the barrier. Then he saw Almack step out smilingly and greet the old man.

'Why, Goat, you're never leaving London. Who'd have expected to see you here?'

'Hello, Mr Almack. This is good of you. You've come to see me off, haven't you? There's a couple of your men been tracking us here in a taxi. We've been quite a procession.'

Almack laughed. 'You're not losing your eye-sight, Goat. Let's go along and have a stirrup-cup. You too, George,'—they were becoming the centre of a little group of uninterested men,—'we'll just take a peep inside those bags of yours, if you don't mind.'

The Goat smiled his humble smile. 'Why, sure.' he ejaculated. 'You're an active young man, Mr Almack. You ought to get on. Fancy springing this on us.'

'I've had a waiting-room kept empty,' said Almack, hooking his arm into O'Brien's, while someone performed a like kindly office for George. 'We won't be long.'

'I hope not,' said the Goat easily. 'I don't want to miss that boat train.' He took the holdup quite as a matter of course.

In the waiting-room he surrendered his keys docilely, and waited while Almack rummaged the bags perfunctorily. The inspector relocked them and made a half-bow as he handed the keys back.

'Just one minute,' he exclaimed, and made a snatch at the thick malacca stick the Goat was carrying. Even the alert O'Brien was taken unawares and for the moment his nonchalance deserted him. He made a wild spring at the inspector, but big Horand caught him in mid-air and swung him back.

'No wonder poor Rufe was knocked out,' said Almack, balancing the stick in his hand. 'It's as heavy as a bar of lead.' He swung the stick by the ferrule twice against the solid fender. At the second blow the silver knob gave way and a quantity of yellowish pellets trickled like hail on the floor. 'I think, Goat, we'll have to trouble you to put off that trip for quite a while.'

'It was Big Rufe gave me the idea,' said Almack, making a verbal report to the superintendent of the Criminal Investigation Department. 'He was so certain that he'd been knocked out by a malacca cane—and there was only one supposition—that the cane must have been loaded. As a fact, when we'd made a search the previous day we'd noticed a collection of sticks, and I'd picked up one or two about which there was nothing apparently abnormal. We find that most of the sticks were honest enough, and even if we'd hit on one of the prepared ones there was nothing to give it away before it was filled up. These sticks just had a hollow steel lining, and those we took away from the Goat and George held just over three pounds of gold apiece—worth in all getting on for £300.

'As you know, sir, the Goat hasn't often received any bulky stuff, and that confirmed my impression about the walking-sticks. But I'll admit it puzzled me as to how he could have stowed away three thousand ounces of gold. That would have needed a whole armoury of sticks. Then it occured to me to make sure if he often went to Paris. I rang up, and had the word passed to Horand to make inquiries. He found that either the Goat or George—mostly George—was away from the flat every weekend. I guessed that meant Continental trips, and that they probably intended to get the stuff over piecemeal.

'That was all there was to it, except when we went over the flat again today we knew for sure that the stuff was somewhere and it wasn't where we had looked before. Of course we had tapped for secret panels and all that sort of thing, but it occurred to me that the one place that neither we nor anyone else had ever looked at was the windows. As a matter of fact, most of the woodwork of the windows was just a thin veneer over steel boxes and tubes—all made to open and all full of gold. They had remelted it to the most handy shape for their purposes. That's all there is to the business, sir.'

'I really think'—the superintendent beamed at the divisional officer—'that we may get a conviction this time.'

'There seems to be a probability, sir,' agreed Almack dryly.

X

PINK-EDGED NOTEPAPER

ROCKWARD'S hand was shaking, and his strong, heavy face was quivering as he finished. Yet he was held by common repute a man completely beyond human emotion—a man whose soul was wrapped in the collection of millions.

'If it is blackmail, why haven't they demanded money in the letter? I'd have paid anything—anything rather than the girl should run the risk. Here's three days gone since she vanished.' He was working himself into a petulant anger, unusual for a man of his temperament. 'If your people had taken it in hand at the first you might have done something. As it is, I've employed two confounded agencies, and we're not an inch nearer finding her.'

'I'm sorry, Mr Rockward,' said Barraclough. 'If we had known when you first reported it that your daughter had been abducted we might have handled it. You see,' he went on soothingly, 'more than ten thousand people are reported missing to the police every year. Very few of them have committed any criminal offence, and in the majority of cases there is some perfectly natural explanation of why they went away. There'd be no end of trouble if the department went chasing after each one. All that can be done is to circulate a description and have men keep their eyes open. But you can rely that now we have something to go upon in Miss Rockward's case she will turn up safe and well in the end.'

The millionaire proffered his cigar-case.

'Forgive me, Mr Barraclough, I'm a little over-strained. I know you will do your utmost, and if you want money, call upon me—never mind for how much.'

Detective-Inspector Barraclough did not often smoke half-crown Havanas, and he took one now with gratitude. He could understand the millionaire's feeling in the circumstances and make allowances. But in spite of his professional optimism—a detective, like a doctor, is bound to have a surface optimism in dealing with outsiders—it was with a perplexed mind that he made his way back to headquarters to lay the matter before his chief.

'It's a bit out of the ordinary run, sir,' he said in the privacy of the superintendent's room. 'Rockward's half off his head, and I don't wonder. Miss Elsie Rockward's a young girl—she'll be nineteen next June—and the old man would have spoilt her if he could. That's nothing to the point, though. As a matter of fact, she went out, according to the servants, at eleven o'clock on Monday morning—three days ago. She was believed to have been going to Regent Street. Anyhow, she's not been seen since. This morning Mr Rockward had a letter. This is what it says.' He produced it from his pocket, and read:

'"Sir,—This is to inform you that your daughter is safe and well. She will be permitted to return to you unharmed in probably less than a week from today, provided you comply with a certain request which may be made to you, and which will cost you nothing. This is not blackmail. You will be wise to remain quiet and not approach the police."

'The letter is unsigned and in palpably disguised handwriting. It was posted at Winchmore Hill, and is postmarked midnight yesterday. That, of course, only means that the one place we're certain the writer will not be found is Winchmore Hill.'

'There's more than one kind of blackmail,' commented the chief. 'In some City deals, for instance, if Rockward could be induced to throw his weight one way or the other it would tip the balance.'

'Yes.' Barraclough sucked in his lower lip. 'Of course, I've not lost sight of that. I suppose I have a free hand?'

'Entirely. Go ahead and good luck to you.'

Barraclough went away to begin pulling the obvious wires necessary to an investigation. There was the already circulated description of Miss Rockward to be gone over, to see that nothing was omitted, from the colour of her eyes to the texture of her stockings. Two photographs of the lady he sent down to have sufficient copies made to supply every divisional section of the Criminal Investigation Department, to say nothing of the more important provincial police forces.

In their little studio on the second story the staff photographers were busy with the letter that had been sent to Rockward. One of the shirt-sleeved assistants came to tell Barraclough that all was ready. He followed the man up to a windowless room, at one end of which stood a square white screen. The photographer touched a switch and the screen alone remained illuminated. Then he inserted a slide in the magic-lantern, and the letter, magnified enormously, leaped into being.

Very carefully Barraclough examined the enlargement, word by word and letter by letter. He had had the thing thrown on the screen, not because he had any definite idea as to what he was to look for, but on the general principle that it should be submitted to the minutest possible examination. At last he came to the final word and drew back.

'Thanks,' he said. 'It doesn't help much, but that isn't your fault. By the way, have you got the focus right? The edges of the letter seem to be in the shade.'

The photographer switched on the light.

'That's not the focus, sir. That's on the letter itself. There's a kind of pinkish shade on the margin.'

'Oh, yes! I was forgetting,' said Barraclough.

The tint around the margin of the letter had not escaped his notice, but it had not impressed him particularly. He went back to his own room and considered the original closely. There was a decided, uneven pink border, shading off irregularly into the cream colour of the paper itself. Moreover, the envelope showed the same peculiarity.

He called Cranley, the first-class detective sergeant who was his invariable assistant in his investigations, and handed the sheet to him.

'Notepaper good—vellum, very best quality, I should say,' commented Cranley. 'It's an educated writing, though it's disguised. No fingerprints, sir? That's a pity. I imagine whoever wrote this is not an ordinary crook. Maybe one of Rockward's friends in the City.'

'Oh, shut up!' said Barraclough irritably. 'It may be the butler of one of Rockward's friends, or it may be the Lord Chancellor, but we don't know. You're a good chap, Cranley, but carrying deductions too far will bring you into trouble one day. An anchor tattooed on a man's hand doesn't prove that he is, or has been, a sailor, but it's a mark of identification.'

All of which Cranley knew as well as Barraclough. Being a wise man, however, he recognised that he had laid himself open to rebuke, and apologised with a certain degree of humility.

'What we want,' went on the inspector, 'is something that'll save us guessing. I don't object to guessing when you can't do anything else, but if it's possible to *know,* I prefer that. Who's a good paper manufacturing firm?'

'I'll go and find out,' said Cranley.

He went away, and in a little returned with a ponderous directory. He planked it on the table, and with a stubby forefinger turned over the leaves till he came to the trade section.

'There's Rogerfelt's in Upper Thames Street,' he said. 'They're about the biggest people in the trade.

'Right you are. I'll go along to see them. You'd better stay on tap here till I come back. I may want you.'

*

When Inspector Barraclough emerged from behind the yellow-stained partition which shielded off the sanctum of one of the departmental managers of Rogerfelt's from the common herd, his face betrayed a supreme content. The most hardened campaigner does not seek discomfort. If he can sleep on a bed instead of the bare ground he does so. Equally so a detective does not enjoy being baffled. He prefers to see his way as clearly as possible. He does not climb a fence if he can open a gate.

Barraclough knew that his quest was still far from simple. Nevertheless, he had at last something to go upon, something definite to unravel. He made his way to a public telephone call office and called up Cranley.

'Yes, it's me, Barraclough. I want you to get through to the division. Find out if they know of any wrong 'un who's been ill lately, or who's had illness in the place where he's staying—it doesn't matter what for. I can't tell you over the wire. Get on to it as soon as you can, sonny. Get someone to help you if you can. Me? Oh, yes, oh, yes, I'll be about. I'll either drop in or ring up. I've got a lot of business to do.'

He hung up the receiver and wended his way eastwards. It was a warm day, and by the time he had reached the Convent and Garter off the Commercial Road he was glad to turn into the gilded and plated saloon. He ordered a lime-juice and soda, and leant against the bar with the air of a man to whom nothing mattered. All the while his eyes were quietly searching the groups of customers.

Presently he beckoned to a group of three, and they greeted him with deference. One would never have guessed from their joyous manner and their anxiety to pay for his drinks—which he would not permit—that they were each mentally checking off any secret exploit of theirs that might have excited the attention of a staff man from Scotland Yard.

Something of the same scene was enacted at Blackfriars, at Islington, Brixton, and half a dozen other districts of

London. Barraclough was always genial, willing to buy drinks and talk over affairs. There was nothing of the stern, iron-handed, clumsy officer of police, beloved of the novelist, about him. Had he not strictly confined himself to non-intoxicating drinks it would have been a drunken man who reeled back to headquarters. As it was, disappointment and physical weariness were plain on his face when he dropped into his chair.

'If you offer me a drink, Cranley, I'll hit you,' he said. 'I'm full up to the lid with lime-juice and ginger-ale, and ten thousand other poisons. Who says we don't earn our pay?'

'Any luck, sir?' queried Cranley.

Barraclough shook his head.

'Not a ha'p'orth. How about you?'

His subordinate handed him a sheet of paper, which the inspector perused with wrinkled brows. Ultimately he crushed it up and, with a gesture of disgust, threw it into the wastepaper-basket.

'Not a bit of good,' he declared. Then, as Cranley's puzzled gaze met his: 'I meant some infectious disease—I ought to have made that clear. Ah, well!' He yawned wearily and drew out his watch. 'Feel inclined to make a night of it, Cranley? It's eight o'clock. Let's have a bit of dinner and drop into the Alhambra and forget all about things for an hour.'

Doggedness is one of the most valued attributes a member of the Criminal Investigation Department can possess, and Barraclough had a reputation for that quality. He had a bull-dog tenacity in following up the case until he had shaken it to pieces that had on occasion served better than a thousand brilliant inspirations.

At ten o'clock he and Cranley had commenced a fresh tour—this time of the supper-rooms and restaurants of the West End. Cranley was puzzled—more puzzled than he would have cared to admit. He could have grasped it if they had been seeking some particular crook who could have given definite information. But apparently Barraclough was merely questing around in search of a scent. With the reticence which he sometimes displayed even to his most intimate colleagues, he would vouchsafe nothing beyond that he wanted to find a criminal who had recently been in some house where there was an infectious disease. For the life of him Cranley could not see how an infectious disease could be connected with the threatening letter that had been written to the millionaire.

But everything has an end. A string band was making an undercurrent of melody to the laughter and conversation of hundreds of men and women clustered in twos and threes about little tables under shaded lights, as they descended into the basement of one of the great supper-rooms—where no one ever dreamt of taking supper. A frock-coated under-manager caught a glimpse of them out of the tail of his eye, and promptly threaded his way towards them. Barraclough laughed.

'Just having a look round, that's all,' he explained. 'Nothing to get alarmed about. We know you're always pleased to see us.'

The official smiled and rubbed his hands. The proprietors liked to be on good terms with the police.

'We're very careful. You know that, Mr Barraclough.'

'Of course,' agreed the detective cheerfully. 'You've got your licence to consider. I suppose you'll give a certificate of character to every one here—men and women?'

'We see that every one behaves themselves,' said the under-manager. 'Where would you like to sit?'

Cranley was looking over Barraclough's shoulder into one of the big mirrors.

'There's Big Billy sitting at the eighth table on your right,' he said.

'We'll go and have a talk with Billy,' said Barraclough.

He picked his way along the tier of tables and dropped a hand heavily on the shoulder of the fat man who was seated with his back towards them.

Big Billy sprang to his feet with a start, and a liqueur-glass tinkled in fragments on the carpet.

'Snakes!' he ejaculated. 'Is it you, Mr Barraclough? You shouldn't do that. You gave me the jumps.'

'Sorry, Billy,' said the detective penitently. 'I'll be more careful another time.' He sat down and indicated another chair for Cranley. 'How's things? I haven't had a talk with you on business for a long time.'

The twinkling little ferret eyes set in the heavy, broad face became a trifle apprehensive. Big Billy did not like the officer's tone. His nerves had been a little shaken by the sudden manner in which Barraclough had announced his arrival.

'Business!' he said, with a laugh that ill concealed his nervousness. 'I didn't know that you wanted to talk business with me or I'd have called on you before this.'

Barraclough crossed his legs.

'Oh, it isn't exactly business, Billy. We spotted you just now, and we thought we'd like a talk over old times. I'm sure your lady friends will excuse us for ten minutes.'

'Right you are. Run away for a little while, kids,' said Billy.

The two girls who had been enjoying Billy's hospitality seemed inclined to resent this abrupt dismissal. Cranley, however, had half turned his head, and the under-manager was rapidly approaching. They rose, and swept away, haughtily contemptuous.

'And now what'll you have?' said Barraclough.

'Absinthe will do me,' said Billy. And as the detective gave the order: 'Now, gov'nor, what's the lay?'

There are few more hoary untruths than that which insists that there is honour among thieves. If the axiom held, the work of the professional detective forces of the world would be tenfold more anxious and arduous than it is. In isolated cases now and again criminals will keep faith one with another. But such occasions are very rare. Weakness, jealousy, revenge, the mere desire to curry favour with the police are motives upon which it is possible for the tactful detective to play. The devious channels of information that run to Scotland Yard from the underworld are a great asset in the preservation of law and order.

'Oh, nothing much, Billy.' Barraclough lay idly back and began to toy with an empty glass. 'Seen anything of Dongley Green lately?'

The fat man wrinkled his brows. He was all alert to fathom the detective's intentions, and whether any harm to himself was coming. He sipped his absinthe.

'Dongley!' he repeated. 'Why, Dongley went down at Nottingham for six years three months ago. Didn't you know that?'

'Come to think of it, so he did,' said Barraclough. 'It had slipped my mind. He always was unlucky, was Dongley. Do you remember that jewel business in Bond Street? You were on top then?'

The reminiscence was apparently not pleasing to Big Billy. He shot a malevolent glance at the detective. He remembered how Dongley and he had concocted a neat little scheme to attack a certain five-hundred-guinea ring; how Dongley, in the neatest of morning dress and with a small piece of chewing gum in his mouth, had walked into the shop inspecting trays and trays of gems; and how he had at last failed to properly fix the ring he had abstracted to the ledge of the counter with the chewing gum, whence Billy was later on to take it when he strolled in as an independent customer after the trouble had died down. Dongley had worked all right up to a point, but while he was being searched the ring and the chewing gum had dropped from their hiding-place. It had been a narrow shave for Billy, against whom nothing could be proved.

'He was a clumsy dog,' he growled.

'Wasn't he in with Gwennie Lynn for a time?' queried Barraclough, with the air of one trying to keep up a languishing conversation.

Big Billy settled himself heavily.

'That old hag always seems to slide along, but anyone who works with her seems to catch it,' he growled. 'There was Dongley. Now, poor old Brixton George is in for it. Yid Foster has been staying at her place down at Tooting, and he pretty well died of typhoid or measles or something. I'd like to wring her neck.'

Cranley shot a glance significant at his superior, who seemed to be suppressing a yawn. Here was the information that Barraclough had been seeking, and yet it seemed to make little impression on him.

'Ah, yes!' he said. 'Brixton George! He was committed for trial a week or two back with one of the bank clerks. The Great Southern Bank forgery, wasn't it?'

'That was a neat job,' broke in Billy. 'Someone's split up a hundred and twenty odd thousand, and all you get is George and the stool-pigeon. That is, unless you've got someone in line.' He looked cunningly across the table.

Barraclough smilingly shook his head.

'I'm not handling that case. Well, we won't keep you any longer from your friends. So long!'

He thrust his arm through Cranley's as they got outside, and hurried him with long, quick steps to Trafalgar Square, where they picked up a taxi. 'The best piece of luck I've had today,' insisted the inspector, more than once.

At Great Derby Street the cab halted, and Barraclough hurried into headquarters. When he returned ten minutes later he brought with him a third man, a sloping-shouldered individual with shrewd eyes and a light moustache.

'Three of us ought to be enough even for Gwennie,' he said. 'I've sent someone to drag Watford out of bed—he's looking after the Great Southern Bank case. But I doubt if we shall want him.'

Cranley tugged at his moustache.

'I'm not quite clear what the point is yet, sir,' he said.

Barraclough's eyes twinkled and he regarded the other whimsically.

'I'm too old a bird to show my hand until I'm dead sure,' he smiled. 'I'll tell you all about it sometime—when it's needful for you to know.'

The car whizzed on and conversation languished. In half an hour it drew up panting at the corner of one of the neat, respectable streets of villas that fringe Tooting Common. Barraclough laughed as he got out, and cast a glance down the row of tiny front gardens arranged in geometrical designs of calceolarias and geraniums.

'Civil service clerks, small business men, and maiden ladies,' he commented. 'Wonder what some of the neighbours will say when they learn who Gwennie is? Come on, boys. You'd better wait, driver.'

Not a soul did they meet as they sauntered down the dimly-lighted street, scrutinising the numbers on each side. At last Cranley lifted his hand in signal and his companions joined him outside the gate at which he was standing.

'No. 107, sir,' he said.

They advanced up the path and Barraclough plied knocker and bell. In a little a light was switched on at an upper window. They heard footsteps. Then a light sprang up in the hall and the door opened.

A skeleton of a man with deep-sunken eyes and a dressing-gown hanging lankly about him stood peering out at them. 'Well,' he demanded curtly, 'what is it?'

Cranley leant nonchalantly against the doorpost so that it was impossible to shut the door. Barraclough, dazzled somewhat by the sudden glare of electric light, wrinkled his brows at the interlocutor.

'That you, Velson?' he said, as he picked out the features of the man. 'How's Gwennie?'

'I don't know you,' retorted the other. 'And my name's not Velson.'

Barraclough stepped inside.

'No, very likely not,' he admitted coolly. 'Shall we cut all that out?'

A sudden blaze of wrath flamed in the dull, sunken eyes of the little man. He withdrew his right hand from beneath the folds of his dressing-gown, and the blue barrel of a revolver showed in the electric light.

'No funny business!' he warned them. 'You guys can't play it on me.'

Cranley leapt swiftly. The revolver crackled noisily as he overbore the little man, and they fell a wriggling heap on the tiles. But Velson stood no chance. In rather less than sixty seconds he was disarmed, pulled to his feet, and handcuffed.

Barraclough picked up the revolver.

'I knew you were a gun man, Velson,' he observed quietly, 'but I didn't think you were a fool. You wouldn't have pulled out the weapon unless you were mighty frightened that something was going to happen.'

'You go to blazes!' said the prisoner sulkily.

'All right.' The inspector added the formal warning. 'No need to tell you we're police officers. Anything you say may be used as evidence, you know. You look after him, Conder. Take him into the dining-room. Cranley, you'd better stay at the door.'

There were movements upstairs, the shuffling of footsteps, the sound of voices. Then the authoritative tone of a woman could be heard apparently ordering the frightened servants to bed.

As Barraclough reached the foot of the stairs the woman descended, dignified and self-possessed. She was somewhere about fifty years of age, not uncomely—indeed, at one time she must have been possessed of striking beauty. Her complexion was as delicate as a child's, and only the grim mouth and an indefinable quality about the velvety-blue eyes gave any plausibility to the supposition that she was a crook.

There had been plenty of time for her alert wits to gather

what had happened. Her face showed no sign of perturbation. She smiled sweetly at Barraclough.

'Good-morning, Gwennie!' he said urbanely. 'It's a pity to wake you up. Suppose you know what we've come about?'

The smile persisted.

'Good-morning, Mr Barraclough! I see it's gone one, so it is good-morning!'

If Barraclough had hoped to surprise any admission out of her, he was disappointed.

'Is there anyone else in the house?' he asked.

She shook her head.

'Only the two servant maids. But you won't take my word for it, I know. You'll search anyway.'

'That's so. You're a sensible woman. Come on.'

He half led, half pulled her into the dining-room, where Conder and the other prisoner were seated. She took a chair with composure.

'You've overdone it this time, Mr Barraclough,' she said. 'What are you pulling us for?'

Barraclough shrugged his shoulders.

'You'll learn that a little later on,' he said. In point of fact, he was still uncertain himself as to what the charge might be. 'Meanwhile, if you will tell us where Miss Rockward is it may save trouble.'

She elevated her eyebrows.

'Miss Rockward! Who is she?'

The detective turned abruptly away.

'I'm going to search the house,' he said. He went through all the twelve rooms that composed the villa to make certain that Gwennie was speaking the truth when she said that there was no one else in the place but the maid-servants.

From the two servants, all in a flutter by the unexpected raid, he extracted little. Mrs Frankton—which was the name by which they knew Gwennie—had employed them for about six weeks—that was since she had taken the house. They understood that she was going to conduct it as a boarding-house. There had been only two boarders so far—Mr Green (Barraclough understood that Velson was meant) and a Mr Shilworth. Mr Shilworth was a commercial traveller. He was now away on business—had been away for four days.

Here was food for thought. Miss Rockward had been missing for three days. Barraclough shot a question at the more intelligent and least flustered of the two girls. Yes, Mr Shilworth had been away before—sometimes for one day, never more than two. He was a middle-aged man with a scar on the right temple, had a pointed beard, slightly auburn, and light hair, tow-coloured.

Barraclough got them to point out the rooms which had been occupied by Gwennie herself, by 'Green,' and by 'Shilworth.' It was in the drawer of a writing-table in the apartment of the commercial traveller that he came across what he wanted. He descended to the dining-room and addressed the two prisoners.

'See here, you two people. You know as well as I do that I've no right to question you, but I may as well tell you that I'm not on the bluff. I've got evidence that you were concerned in the abduction of Miss Rockward, and I know *why*. You can't do any good by holding her up any longer. We're bound to find her—and Yid Foster. Now, where is she?'

'You're a wise guy,' sneered Velson.

'Shut up,' ordered Gwennie imperatively, and the little man relapsed into scowling silence. She fixed an appraising gaze on Barraclough. 'You're a gentleman, Mr Barraclough,' she said. 'Will you let up on us if we put you on the line?'

'I can't make bargains, I'm afraid,' said Barraclough.

Gwennie placidly crossed her arms.

'Then you'll have to work out your own business,' she observed.

Detective-Inspector Watford faced Detective-Inspector Barraclough as they sat in two of Gwennie's softly-cushioned arm-chairs. Gwennie and Velson were safely on their way by taxi-cab to King Street police station, and a more minute search of the house than Barraclough had been able to make was being systematically conducted by the three men Watford had brought with him.

The latter tapped the bowl of an empty pipe thoughtfully upon the heel of his boot.

'I wish I was sure you hadn't dragged me out of bed on a wild-goose chase,' he observed. 'It seems to me like a dead end. We can't prove that they had anything to do with the Great Southern Bank business, and that's my funeral. You may feel sure about the abduction, but you haven't got the lady. I'm not quite comfortable. I own it freely.'

Barraclough stood up.

'Of all the infernal gratitude! Why, man, it's as clear as crystal! Here's this forgery committed. You suspect one of the bank clerks and keep young Elsleigh under observation. You find him colloquing with Brixton George, and, like a sensible man, you send 'em both down. They're both as tight as oysters, and there's a hundred thousand of the best stowed away somewhere that you can't lay your finger on.'

'Well?' said Watford dryly.

'Well, it stands to reason that there's something behind it. They've briefed Luton, K.C., to defend them at the trial. Somebody's finding the money, and that somebody has got the hundred thousand stowed away in an old stocking. Now, you told me the other day that the defence intend to apply for an adjournment to the next sessions when the case comes up at the Old Bailey.'

'Well?' repeated Watford.

'There'll be an application for bail,' went on Barraclough. 'The rest of the gang know Brixton George. They've got to get him out if they want him to save their own skins. He would talk too much if they deserted him. That's what Luton is for—to get bail—and then George could slip the country. Now the judge is bound to want a person of reputation as well as financial standing for bail—a man like Rockward, for instance.'

His colleague moved till he was upright in his chair.

'I see your theory. Miss Rockward has been abducted to force Rockward to go bail for Brixton George.'

'That's it. It's certain that Brixton George has been in close touch with Gwennie and Yid Foster. Add it all together, and you couldn't get a likelier gang than Gwennie, the Yid, Velson, and George for a job of this kind. And why did Velson draw a gun?'

A tap at the door and the entry of one of his men prevented Watford from answering. He took from him a couple of letters and three bank pass-books, and looked them through. The creases smoothed out of his bronzed face.

'By the great horn spoon, you're right!' he cried. 'Here's letters from the Yid. Why on earth Gwennie kept them I don't know. Where did you find then?'

'Stuffed between the mattress and the springs of her bed,' replied the other.

'Listen to this,' said Watford. He read: '"You're a real wonder, Gwennie. After you had given the girl the dope in the tea-room in Bond Street I got her away to Charing Cross as simply as A.B.C. She kept up her daze right across the water, though I got a bit of a shock at Boulogne when I thought she was coming round. However, it was a false alarm. We got here safe enough to your friend at Rue Vaillant 24."

'Then there's the other letter: "I went round to see the kid this morning. She's a little tartar, but I guess T. will learn her to be good. I am staying at the Bristol, and am feeling a heap better. Have you fixed up about Chelsea yet?"'

'The Bristol!' remarked Barraclough. 'That's going some. I suspect the Yid will have worse lodgings before long. Will you go out and burn up the wires, or shall I?'

'I'll go,' said Watford.

*

The unravelling of a skein, once the right end of a mystery is found, proceeds rapidly. It was ten o'clock in the morning when Barraclough and his assistants finished ransacking the house at Tooting. A bath and a shave effaced the traces of a sleepless night, and Barraclough made his way to Scotland Yard. He found Watford in his room with a packed bag in one corner.

'Paris?' he asked.

'Yes,' replied his friend. 'I'm off to fetch the Yid. The business is well weighed up now. Those bank-books show that all the money has been paid into the account of Gwennie and her pals, and we shall have no difficulty in proving the case. The Brigade de Sûreté have nobbled Foster and found the girl. She was in a little house cooped up with an old hag named Templeton, who was with Gwennie in a swindling ladies' bank in the States some years ago. Rockward is going over with me. He asked to be remembered to you, and said that if the commissioner approved he would like to hand you over a cheque.'

'That so?' said Barraclough wearily. 'Good!'

Watford tapped him on the shoulder.

'See here, old man, I'm puzzling how you got on to this in the first place. You might tell.'

Barraclough sighed, and dragged the note that had been sent to Rockward out of his pocket.

'See how that's edged with pink?' he said. 'That's what got me on to it. Of course, that edging was bound to attract anyone's attention. I didn't know whether it was important or not, so I took it to the people most likely to know—a firm of paper merchants. They told me that the paper—technically a cream-tinted vellum—was made of esparto grass, and that aniline sulphate solution would turn it pink. That didn't seem to help much. I asked if anything else would have done it. Then I got my tip. It seemed that sulphur fumes might have done the trick—they had heard of a case where it had happened when a room had been fumigated.

'I hit right on to that. A room would probably be fumigated after some infectious disease, and that was what I had to look for. I had gone right over London before I hit Big Billy and got the straight tip. That's all there was to it.'

'Quite simple, my dear Barraclough,' grinned Watford. 'There's the guv'nor in his room waiting to pat you on the back.' He looked at his watch. 'Crikey! I'll have to run to catch that train. Good-bye.'

'Good-bye,' said Barraclough.

XI

THE STRING OF PEARLS

HELDON FOYLE dropped his cigar on the pavement, crushed it under his heel, and went thoughtfully on his way as the woman stepped into a taxi-cab. In the distance some public clock faintly hammered out the stroke of twelve.

A touch of imagination if it be harnessed to common sense does no harm to a detective. It was just that quality of imagination which had caused Foyle of New Scotland Yard to pause for a second at the point where Clarges Street runs into Piccadilly. It was his common sense that took him on.

From one of the houses in that street of austere respectability a woman had emerged, closing the door behind her with infinite caution and listening before she descended the steps. It was her caution that attracted Foyle's closer attention. He noticed that the house was in utter darkness. The woman was in evening dress of some dark fabric, and the wrap over her head had been drawn close to shield her face. Once, as she crossed the road, she had thrown a furtive glance over her shoulder as though she feared she might be followed. She had halted a passing taxi-cab with an air of furtive haste.

Now there was no man more acquainted with queer happenings in all grades of society than Heldon Foyle. Years of experience at Scotland Yard had made him slow to jump to conclusions. But it is not usual for well-dressed women to steal surreptitiously at midnight from houses in a fashionable quarter. The thing touched his imagination. He was stirred to speculation.

One of the great street electric lights shone down on him as he lit a fresh cigar. There was nothing of the police officer about him—he would have considered himself unfitted for his business if there had been. He might have been between thirty and forty. Tall, with broad shoulders and indomitable chin, a carefully-kept brown moustache and steady, shrewd, humorous blue eyes; he was dressed scrupulously but unobtrusively.

Coincidence is by no means a negligible asset to Scotland Yard. To Heldon Foyle the next day there was announced Count von Haussen, whose card bore in one corner the number of a house in Clarges Street. The chief detective gave a little whimsical whistle as he deposited the reports which he had been busy perusing in a drawer, and prepared to receive his visitor.

The Count von Haussen was a slim-built man with a lean, sallow face, which was now twitching with some strong emotion, so that he seemed to be perpetually readjusting the eyeglass that he wore. His morning coat accentuated the thinness of his figure, and he wore spats over his sharp-pointed, highly-polished boots.

'Mr Heldon Foyle?' he asked in quick staccato tones, as he shook hands. 'You are the chief detective here?' In spite of his German name and title his English was perfect.

'The superintendent of the Criminal Investigation Department,' answered Foyle. 'Will you sit down? What can I do for you?'

Count von Haussen placed his silk hat and gloves on the corner of the table.

'It is a case of robbery,' he declared, plunging at once into his subject. 'I have had a string of pearls stolen, taken from my safe somehow—it seems like magic. They were there two or three days ago; this morning they were gone.'

Foyle nodded and lifted the telephone receiver from its place.

'Get through to Grape Street,' he said quietly, 'and ask Inspector Milford to come up here as soon as he can.' He put back the receiver. 'Milford is in charge of our West End fold,' he explained; 'we may want him. Go on, Count. What are these pearls worth?'

'I don't know. They have always been in my family. They are insured for £3000, but their value is more than that. The queer thing is that the safe was not broken open. It is quite a small one, but the makers assured me it was absolutely burglar-proof. I last went to it, I believe, three days ago. The jewels were all right then. This morning, an hour ago, I had to go to it again. They were gone.'

The detective stroked his chin, a habit he had when considering a problem. 'You mean to say that someone opened it with a duplicate key?' he asked.

'That is impossible. There is only one key, and that never leaves my possession.'

'You are sure you didn't leave the safe unlocked?'

'Quite certain.'

A head showed round the corner of the door. The chief of the department beckoned with his forefinger.

'Come in, Mr Milford,' he said. 'This is Count von Haussen, of Clarges Street, Piccadilly. He has had some valuable pearls stolen. I wish you would go into the matter. Take a description and the Count's statement. Let me know when you are ready, and we'll go down to Clarges Street together.'

Milford bowed ceremoniously at the introduction, and disappeared with the Count.

In the next twenty minutes Heldon Foyle did many things which made several of the six hundred men under his charge exceedingly busy. He knew that the sooner the great machinery which he controlled was set to work the greater the chance of solving the problem that had been set him. A swift pursuit often saved long labour.

A list of those expert professional thieves who were known to have been in London on the day the jewels were last seen was instantly to hand, and a little army of men set to trace and check their movements. Reports were called for from the departmental men continually on duty at the London termini; from the watchers at the ports—Harwich, Dover, Folkestone, Southampton, and other places, including the Continental ports.

These were all first steps in routine, to be amplified or modified by instructions as developments might occur. A known jewel thief leaving London would scarcely have escaped the notice of the triple line of observers, and once his trail was picked up he would be watched until his guilt or innocence was reasonably settled.

A cable to Amsterdam, to which place it was likely that stolen jewels might be sent for disposal, advised the police in that city of the robbery.

There may be more sport in fishing with a rod and line, which is what the single-handed detectives in books do, but there is more certainty about a net. Foyle always regarded the capture of criminals as a business matter, and, as far as possible, adopted business methods. All his precautions might go for nought—the thief might not be a professional at all—but they left him free to deal with any matters that might arise in the course of the investigation.

The chief detective had five minutes to think over events when his last order had been despatched over the private telegraph wire. For the first time he allowed his thoughts to ponder over the mysterious woman he had seen leaving Clarges Street the night before.

Milford stalked in at last, a big sheet of foolscap paper in his hand. Heldon Foyle began to put on his hat and coat.

'Well?' he asked. 'What do you make of it?'

The divisional inspector shook his head.

'Nothing at present, sir. It's odd, if what the Count says is right.'

'Do you know anything about him?'

'Only what he tells me. His father was a German, but he's lived in England all his life. The pearls—there were eighteen of them—were a kind of heirloom. He is rather vague about them, but I phoned through to Halford and Jones, the assessors to Lloyd's, who tell me that the man who examined them for insurance was struck by their individual purity and the way they were matched. They're worth a lot more than the money they're insured for. I've got a full technical description.'

'Is this gentleman married?'

'No.' Milford referred to the paper in his hand. 'The only people living in the house besides himself are a Miss Ethel von Haussen—a girl who comes of Devonshire stock, whom he adopted as his daughter nine years ago—and four servants—a housekeeper, two maids, and a page-boy.'

The chief detective rubbed his chin.

'Right you are, Milford. You'd better let that description go out at once. Hurry up. We'll take a taxi.'

He joined von Haussen, who was waiting in the corridor. There were few men who could turn a stranger into a friend or who knew more of the art of indirect cross-examination than Heldon Foyle. The dapper little Anglicised German was as empty of all information as a wrung sponge by the time the cab drew up at Clarges Street. Foyle had learnt much of the character and history of each person in the house—not excepting Miss Ethel and von Haussen himself.

A little hitch of the shoulder was all the sign he gave as he recognised the house from which the mysterious woman had emerged. His keen eyes noted the Yale lock on the outer door, and the couple of heavy bolts which secured it at top and bottom. Von Haussen led them through to a room at the back. It was furnished as a sitting-room. He drew aside a small curtain in a recess.

'This is the safe, you see,' he said.

The two detectives stooped to examine it closely. Foyle inserted the key and, turning the handle, swung back the heavy door. As the Count had said, there was no indication that it had been tampered with, Even their expert scrutiny could find nothing likely to prove of use to the investigation. Foyle shrugged his shoulders and Milford made a few notes in his official pocket-book.

'You would like to question the servants?' demanded von Haussen.

'Mr Milford will see to that,' said Foyle. 'Perhaps you will introduce me to Miss von Haussen first if she happens to be in.'

'Oh, certainly,' said the little man. 'She is probably in her room. Will you come with me? Excuse me for one moment, Mr Milford.'

Heldon Foyle found himself ushered into a dainty boudoir and bowing to a slim, girlish figure who rose from the depths of a big arm-chair as they entered. Miss von Haussen was a girl whose wholesome beauty would have attracted attention anywhere. Her exquisitely moulded cheeks were stained with a touch of scarlet as she bowed in response to the introduction. She stood uncertainly gripping the back of a chair, but her brown eyes met those of the detective steadily. Von Haussen had returned to Milford.

'I do hope you'll be able to recover the pearls, Mr Foyle,' she said. 'It's terrible to have lost them like this. As you know, perhaps, they were to have been mine in six months' time.'

'We shall do our best, Miss von Haussen,' he said smoothly. He was scrutinising her with subtle care, making up his mind how to deal with her. There was nothing in what von Haussen had told him that would have afforded any explanation of the midnight excursion, yet he felt sure that she was the woman he had seen.

He was becoming aware of a penetrating scent that filled the apartment. He glanced at the window. It was wide open.

'Can you tell me if you suspect anyone?' he asked. 'I won't conceal from you that my present idea is to believe that the robbery must have been carried out by someone in the house—someone who could have gained access to Count von Haussen's keys.'

She spread out her hands—they were firm white hands—in an expressive gesture of hopelessness.

'There is no one,' she said. 'With the exception of Robbins, the page-boy, they have all been with us for years. It is ridiculous to suppose that any of them had a hand in it.'

Again that whiff of scent. It was the pungent odour of smelling-salts. Foyle's eyes dropped for a second to the empty fire-grate. He raised his expressionless face to the girl's.

'What time does the household retire?' he asked.

'Usually about eleven.'

'You—pardon me—are not engaged?'

She shook her head laughingly.

'Oh, dear, no. But I don't quite see what that has to do with it?'

The detective laughed frankly and held out his hand.

'It wasn't mere vulgar curiosity, Miss von Haussen. I wanted to know if there might be any privileged visitor by any chance. Good-bye, and thank you so much.'

He bowed himself out with an idea beginning to germinate in his mind. But he did not permit whatever theory he might have formed to possess him entirely. Neither he nor Milford left the neighbourhood of Clarges Street until a telephone call had brought a couple of unobtrusive young men from the Grape Street police station. Foyle met them a little out of view of the house, and gave them curt, definite instructions. For the rest of the day one or the other of them was never out of sight of the Count von Haussen's house.

Milford was cynical over the whole business.

'It looks to me like a put-up job,' he confessed frankly. 'The servants haven't had a hand in it, that I'll swear. But we know that whoever got at that safe did it with a key. I'm inclined to think that the Count could say where those pearls are if he wanted to. But he'll draw the insurance money before they'll turn up.'

The chief detective chuckled.

'Don't you think that if this was a bogus business the safe

would have been ripped to pieces?' he asked. 'Just take my tip, Milford, and let everyone who comes out of that house be kept under observation for a while. We'll get those pearls back or call me a Dutchman. Hello, here's Bond Street! I'll leave you here. I want to go and get some smelling-salts.'

He strode away. Milford pulled at his moustache.

'Smelling-salts?' he repeated to himself. 'Well, I'm hanged.'

On the mantelpiece in Heldon Foyle's room at the Yard stood three green bottles of smelling-salts. Since his first visit to Clarges Street he had been content to leave the investigation of the missing pearls case to Inspector Milford. He knew that an inquiry on parallel lines had been opened by the corps of detectives employed by Lloyd's assessors. He rarely interfered personally in a case unless it was of extreme importance, or unless it came beyond the ability of the man in whose charge it was.

But the Clarges Street developments he watched with considerable interest, so far as the formal daily reports of those engaged allowed. And at last, after three days, came Milford, his face wrinkled and worried.

He sank into a chair that his superior indicated with a long breath that was almost a sigh.

'Well?' demanded Foyle.

The other brushed back his hair from his forehead.

'It's that von Haussen affair, sir. That girl's at the bottom of it somehow, though it beats me how. The night before last was when we first began to get on to her. She came out of the house about half-past eleven or so, and took a taxi-cab. Perring, who was on duty, followed her. She went to a place in Bloomsbury Street and let herself in with a latch-key. She was there ten minutes or a quarter of an hour, then she returned home. Of course, we made inquiries about the people staying at the place, and they all seem decent folk enough. I had it out with Miss von Haussen the next day. She declared that I was drunk or mad—and that she knew no one in Bloomsbury Street, and that at the time she was supposed to be there she was in bed. Of course I had to go cautiously, for Perring did not see her face, although he's certain that it was she. What does she want gadding about at that time, and with the latch-key of a strange house too?'

Foyle was turning over the pages of a report that the inspector had given to him. Attached to it was a list of the occupants of the boarding-house, with pithy remarks giving detail of their avocations. He ran a finger over the list meditatively.

'There's nothing to indicate which of these people she went to see, I suppose?' he asked.

Milford's heel tapped the floor.

'There are nine boarders there—seven men and two women. We have questioned them all, and they all deny knowledge of the girl. There's no reason to suppose it should be one person more than another.'

'I've a mind to look at this place,' said Foyle. 'Let the matter rest till you hear from me, Milford.'

It was an hour after this conversation that a military looking man who used a walking-stick to assist a slight lameness, whose gold-rimmed eyeglass encircled a blue eye, and whose moustache had been carefully waxed, limped along Bloomsbury Street. It was very exceptional for Heldon Foyle, or any of his men for that matter, to use disguises that might get out of order. It is wonderful what a change can be wrought in a man by a change of clothes, a different method of arranging the hair or moustache.

The card sent into the house he at last selected bore the inscription:

MAJOR JACOB DAVIS
WRINGTON

It brought him into the presence of a stern-faced, broad-built lady, whose black silk dress rustled as she rose with all the stateliness of a Bloomsbury landlady to receive him. His story had been well prepared. He had just been invalided from the Indian army, and wanted to secure permanent rooms. He had heard of her from a friend of his whose name he could not recollect.

Thus it was that Major Jacob Davis, otherwise Heldon Foyle of the C.I.D., became a lodger in the boarding-house of Mrs Albion.

He was a popular guest. Every morning he would limp away—to his club, he said, returning at half-past six in the evening. He would play chess, take a hand at bridge, discuss politics, or tell stories of Indian frontier life with an engagingly modest air. He became the recipient of many confidences, but he seemed drawn most of all to Mr Horace Levith, an artist, whose bedroom adjoined his own, and who used one of the top attics of the house as a studio.

Gradually the two became in the habit of smoking a farewell pipe together after the others had retired, and once or twice they shared a bottle of wine together in the privacy of Foyle's bedroom. Levith was not averse to a bottle of Beaune at anyone's expense, and Major Davis was an enjoyable companion.

But never was the soldier invited into Levith's private room; and he knew, by demonstration, that the doors of both the studio and the bedroom were invariably kept locked. To a man of Foyle's calibre, however, that mattered little. He merely bided his time.

There are always ways and means open to a man of determination who is willing to take risks. In France and other countries a detective is covered by law in whatever he may do. In England an officer has sometimes to commit a technical illegality to achieve his ends.

Heldon Foyle had no shadow of legal right to use a false key to gain access to Levith's room. Strictly, he was stealing when he took a photograph from the dressing-table, smiled at the inscription on the back, and put it in his pocket.

Only one other thing he did before he left. A green-tinted smelling-salt bottle stood on a small dressing-table. He lifted the stopper, smelt it, and squinted within. Then he compared it with those three green bottles which had for a time adorned the mantelpiece of his office at Scotland Yard.

'It's not exactly the same, but it will have to do,' he muttered.

Then he left, locking the door carefully behind him.

It was with Milford that Heldon Foyle called upon Count von Haussen. He was quite sure what might happen, and a reliable witness could do no harm. The dapper little German received them at once.

'No news, I suppose?' he asked gloomily.

Foyle smiled at him.

'Did you ever hear of a Mr Horace Levith?' he retorted.

'I don't recall the name,' said the Count, frowning, a little puzzled. 'Wait a moment—no, I can't remember it,'

'Well, he is an artist living at a Bloomsbury boarding-house. I have taken the liberty of ordering him to be brought on here as soon as he returns. Ah, there is a ring! That should be he now. Perhaps you'll answer the door, Milford?'

The inspector slipped out. When he came back he was accompanied by two men—one a detective-sergeant, the other Levith. The artist was pale, and stared at Foyle with unfeigned astonishment as he came into the room.

'What is the meaning of this—this outrage?' he demanded angrily.

But Count von Haussen had leapt to his feet.

'It is Ethel's drawing-master!' he exclaimed. 'Levith—yes, that is the name. I could not remember. Why have you brought him here, Mr Foyle? Did he steal the pearls? Is—'

Foyle quieted him with a wave of the hand.

'Keep still a minute, Count,' he said. 'He did not steal them; but he received them.'

'It's a lie!' burst from the artist. 'I know nothing. You can search me—search my rooms. You can't prove it.'

Ignoring him, Heldon Foyle brought from his pocket a green smelling-salts bottle. He removed the stopper and shook the contents out on the table. Glowing iridescent against a green tablecloth was a string of pearls. Levith clutched at a chair to support himself.

'You see that I have already searched your rooms,' Foyle said coldly. Then turning to von Haussen, he continued: 'There were reasons why you should have an explanation before we charge this man. It was luck that gave me a hint before I knew that the jewels were gone. As soon as I knew all the particulars it was obvious that the robbery must have been executed at least with the connivance, if not actually by, someone in the house. I had seen a woman, whom I afterwards learnt to be Miss von Haussen, surreptitiously leave one evening—sit still, Count, I have not finished yet! That gave me an excuse for regarding her with suspicion when I knew a crime had been committed. The servants might have been guilty, but their opportunities were limited compared to hers.

'I was not satisfied with her manner when I questioned her, and it was then I came to the conclusion that my suspicions were well founded. I noticed that a bottle of smelling-salts had been recently emptied in her fire-grate. It had not been broken, for it and the salts would have been removed at the same time as the broken glass. Evidently she had emptied a smelling-bottle for some purpose. If it were needed as a hiding-place for the jewels, I could understand it. A smelling-bottle would not arouse suspicion.

'I let the matter rest, and had her watched. Once again she left the house surreptitiously, and was traced to a boarding-house in Bloomsbury. There we were at a loss for a time because there were many people in the house, and we could not definitely determine which she had gone to. I took apartments there myself and for a week made myself acquainted with all the inmates. One of the reasons that made me fix on Levith as the culprit was that he always kept his rooms locked. I got him out of the way on a pretext, and, as I expected, I found the jewels hidden in a smelling-salts bottle. I left a similar bottle so as not to arouse his suspicions should he return before I was ready.

'I had got from him some particulars of his life. He had been a drawing-master. He was a Devonshire man. He was, I knew, hard up. It was not difficult to suppose that Miss von Haussen had been his pupil at some time, and that they had become lovers. You would have objected to your adopted daughter becoming engaged to a drawing-master, I suppose?'

'Most decidedly,' said von Haussen, his lips tightening.

'I thought so. It was, as I say, evident that the man was hard up. Whether he persuaded her or she did it on her own initiative, I don't know, but the fact remains that she got the jewels and they were taken to him. I suppose they were only waiting for a suitable opportunity to dispose of them. Here is a photograph I found on his dressing-table.'

It was a portrait of Ethel von Haussen, and scribbled on the face of it were the words: 'To my husband.'

Von Haussen wheeled round on the artist.

'That is so?' he demanded. 'You are married?

Levith bowed his head.

'Yes,' he replied. 'It is all my fault. We were married two years ago. I should have dissuaded her when she wanted to take the jewels. She argued that it was only anticipating matters, they would be hers anyway in a little while.'

The Count bit his lip, and stared straight in front of him. Presently he rose and abruptly left the room. He returned in a few minutes.

'It was not what I had hoped for my daughter,' he said dully. 'But what is to be will be. At any rate, I have to thank you, Mr Foyle.'

The chief detective was standing.

'Not at all,' he returned. 'I take it you will refuse to prosecute this man?'

'Of course. Good-day, Mr Foyle. Good-day, Mr Milford.'

'Good-day, Count von Haussen.'

Out in the street Foyle jerked his head back at the house.

'At any rate, we've saved those people the airing of a scandal,' he said.

XII

THE 'CON' MAN

IT is not every man who can stare unexpectedly into the business end of an automatic without changing countenance. I say unexpectedly, for Bond Street at midday is the last place in which a hold-up is liable to occur. Yet Detective-Inspector Ansoll smiled as he lounged opposite the broad-shouldered man who held a pistol peeping from under a well-cut morning coat.

No one of the hundreds passing to and fro paid more than a casual glance to the two men outside the tobacconist's window engaged in apparently idle conversation. For Coyne's pistol was invisible to anyone but the man whose attention it was meant to engage, and he seemed unconcerned.

'That you, Wolf?' he said serenely. 'I shouldn't play about with that sort of thing. It's liable to go off, and think what a horrid mess it would make. I didn't know you were a gun man.'

'I reckon it is liable to go off,' agreed the other grimly. 'Especially if you try to put any of the funny dope over on me. See.'

Wolf Coyne did not look like a desperate character. There were a thousand men abroad in the West End that morning who might have stepped out of the same mould as he. He had kindly hazel eyes, thick iron-grey hair, a well-kept iron-grey moustache, and there was no man living who could dress better or assume better manners at will. Just at present he had dropped his manners and something of his carefulness of speech.

'Look here, Ansoll,' he went on. 'I've been after you a long time, and this has got to stop right now. I'm not putting any bluff across. You're gunning for me, but I don't stand for it—see.

I'm trying to cut loose from the old game, and sooner than be driven back by any grafting son of a policeman who tries to fasten his teeth into me I'd shoot hell into you.' He thrust his face forward viciously. 'Get that. I wonder I don't get you now while I've got a chance.'

Ansoll made a deprecating gesture. 'I shouldn't, Wolf,' he said mildly.

No one would have guessed that he took the other's threat seriously. Coyne had only one defect from the crook's point of view. He sometimes lost his temper. Indeed, some thousands of miles away, in the United States, there were at least a couple of men who would bear the marks of his anger to their dying day.

'They say it's an unpleasant death,' went on the detective cheerfully. 'They've got a contrivance to strap you up, and they read part of the burial service over you while you're still alive, and then you stand on the drop and they put a white cap over your face—Why, hello, Jimmie! Shake hands with Mr Coyne. Wolf, this is Mr Cotterill, one of my sergeants.'

The menacing muzzle of the pistol had disappeared as though by magic into Coyne's trousers-pocket. His face lighted with a delightful smile that had charmed many hundreds of pounds from unwary pockets. He thrust out a delicately-manicured hand.

'How do you do, Mr Cotterill?' he said pleasantly. 'Pleased to know you. I've got to run away now. We'll run across each other sometime, I suppose, Ansoll. So long.'

He strolled away, tapping gently with his gold-headed cane at the side of his boot. Ansoll grinned as he looked after him, and saw him warmly shake hands with a middle-aged, eye-glassed man on the other side of the road.

'See that, Jimmie! I wonder what Lord Dalgaren would say if he knew that his pal had a gun on me a few seconds ago, and was half a mind to batter my brains all over Bond Street. It looks to me as if he's getting worried, Jimmie.'

*

Mr James Arthur inhabited a suite of rooms overlooking the river on the first floor of the Palatial Hotel; and since the Palatial Hotel charges its guests sixpence a breath, it will be evident that Mr Arthur was a man of means. If one had been sufficiently curious one might also have learned that he was a man of standing, for his intimates stretched right away into the topmost pinnacles of society. Still further one might have learned that Mr James Arthur had unimpeachable introductions from generals, from bishops, from the High Commissioner of a remote settlement, and from the President of a South American Republic.

Knowing all this, one would have been surprised to learn that Scotland Yard took an interest in Mr James Arthur—so great an interest that, since he stepped ashore at Liverpool, he had been watched over with as much paternal care as if he had been of Royal blood. The attentions of the detectives had not been obtrusive, but Mr James Arthur *alias* Wolf Coyne, had felt worried by an observation which he divined rather than saw. It is so harassing to one's plans to be treated like a gold-brick man.

The essence of Mr Arthur's grievance was, that he *was* a gold-brick man. So he was classed in the archives of Mulberry Street along with sawdust men, green-goods men, and other crude practitioners who could as easily have sprouted wings as have attained to the eminence of the Palatial Hotel. Yet since a knowledge of human nature is the greatest asset of 'con' men, whatever their degree, Mr James Arthur was rightly classified. He had a genius for divining a man's (or a woman's) weak point, and a facility for using the knowledge to his own advantage.

It had been Detective-Inspector Ansoll who had met Coyne at Euston and warned him that London was an unhealthy place for prolonged residence. Coyne, who had never been convicted in his life though he had had some narrow escapes, smiled blandly, declared that the officer had made a gross mistake, and passed on.

He had some reason for his confidence, since those introductions were genuine. It is astonishing how far personality and nerve can carry one in the remote corners of the earth. Moreover, acquaintance with many detective bureaux, and the knowledge that the victim of a confidence-man—whether he has merely bought a ‘stolen’ razor from a man in the street or a ‘gold’ mine with a questionable title from an urbane City man—rarely has the courage to talk about his folly afterwards, had brought him to despise threats. England is a free country, and it is a delicate business to interfere with a person merely because he has a reputation.

Yet Coyne had not been long in London before he felt the influence of the machine. There was no overt act to which he could take exception. If he had not known the quality of his own nerves he might have supposed that his imagination was betraying him. Somehow he was beset by an atmosphere of all-pervading watchfulness until all his plans threatened to go awry.

Now, in fact, there was nothing miraculous in Scotland Yard’s arrangements for ‘covering’ him—merely large resources and common sense. There were half a dozen men who did little else than glean details of his daily life—in the hotel smoking-room, among the servants, among his acquaintances. Coyne was too big a fish for Ansoll to take any risks, and the men he had put on to deal with the ‘con’ man had been picked with care. It was not easy work this method of trying to follow the mobile fluctuations of a subtle man’s brains. Yet in the end some hint of his intentions must inevitably materialise. Not till they had proof that he had committed some illegal act could they do anything else.

All this simmered through the ‘con’ man’s brain as he sat moodily in his big sitting-room with an iced-drink and a big cigar after his fruitless attempt to terrorise Ansoll. The kindly eyes were hard and his jaw was set. He was not, he told himself, going to be put out of the game—not if they turned a thousand bone-headed bulls to try and stack the deck against him. Once he had carried his plans through, he could laugh at them and his victims. The chief obstacle in his path was the man who was organising the opposition campaign—Ansoll. In which Wolf Coyne made an error of supposition, for Scotland Yard is never dependent on any one man.

He touched the bell.

'I'll get him,' he muttered viciously, 'I'll get him.' On the soft-footed valet who answered his summons he turned abruptly.

'Get me a telegraph form,' he ordered.

Within an hour afterwards he had a visitor—an old young man who moved with stealthy alertness, and whose eyes were incessantly roving to and fro. He gripped a clean-shaven chin and nodded guardedly to the 'con' man as he was ushered in, but not a word did he speak till the door had again closed behind the servant.

'Say bo,' he declared at last. 'Is it really you? You certainly are making good, Wolf, since I saw you last. This is some luxury.' His eyes wandered appreciatively about the chamber.

'How are you, Freddie?' said the other genially. 'Sit down. You got my wire all right?' He rose, crossed the room, and turned the key in the door.

'I got your wire,' agreed Freddie, picking up the cigar-case which lay on a table and helping himself. 'I guess there's something moving.' He crossed his legs and struck a match. 'Well, you know I've always admired your talents, Wolf, though if you'll forgive me saying so, you're a little too inclined to play a lone hand. You need a partner to balance you like—to help with the heavy work. I'm somewhere around it, eh?'

'Don't pull any of that dope on me,' said Coyne sharply. 'What I want you for is no partnership gag. You'll get paid for what you do, and it won't take you a couple of hours. It's worth just a hundred to me and not a penny more. That'll perhaps save argument.'

'You always was harsh, Wolf,' said Freddie in hurt remonstrance. 'What are you going to pull out of it? What's the stunt anyway?'

'I'm going to pull out of it just what I can make,' snapped Coyne. 'You'll get a hundred—and easy money at that—or you'll get nix. Now listen. Been on the boards lately?'

'The stage,' lamented Freddie, 'is infested with knights. There's no chanst in the legitimate, and demean myself to vaudeville—'

'Cut it out,' advised Coyne. 'Do you know Ansoll—the boss bull of the 14th Division?'

'Do I know you?' retorted Freddie. 'Why, Ansoll is the friend of my youth, my long-lost uncle. Hasn't he pulled me twice, once because I stood outside a bank wondering what I would do if I had all the money that was in the safe, and once—But say, if he's on to you count me out of the game.'

'You're yellow,' sneered Coyne. 'I thought you had some nerve, Freddie. But if you can afford to throw away a hundred jimmies . . .' He crossed over and laid a hand on the locked door.

'Don't be hasty,' urged Freddie. 'Tell me what it is and I'll consider.'

Coyne resumed his seat. 'It's simple enough. There's not a ha'p'orth of risk in it for you. All I want you to do is this . . .'

Freddie's solemn face expanded in a grin as he listened. He nodded his head in delighted appreciation.

'You're sure a top-liner, Wolf!' he exclaimed. 'It's the nuttiest move I've heard for a long time. You put him in bad and you have your swell witnesses, an'—lor' lumme, I'd like to see his face when you open out on him.'

'That's all right then. You'll be on hand seven-forty-five to the minute. And mind, Freddie, no soaking. Here's a fiver. Get down to it.'

Luck is a great handmaid to the detective—though he invariably has her on a lead. She must not be confused with coincidence, for example. It was no blind luck that had caused the clerk at the desk to scratch his head when a visitor applied for Mr Arthur. That was due to the persuasions of a couple of very ordinary-looking young men who for many days past had spent much time loitering in the palm court of the Palatial Hotel.

Nor was it luck that they happened to be there. That was a very simple precaution of Ansoll's. The only piece of luck in the whole business was that Wolf Coyne should have overlooked their possible presence. Thereafter everything became more or less inevitable.

For while Coyne and his satellite were planning the downfall of the inspector, a man in one of the telephone boxes below was talking over the wire to Ansoll. And when Flash Freddie, actor by profession, and what the United States calls 'sneak' by vocation, stepped out of the elevator and moved jauntily on to the rubber-paved courtyard, he had no supicion that the young fellow who looked like a bank clerk and brushed by him was at all interested in his mission.

He whistled cheerfully as he turned into the Strand and bent his steps westward. The young bank clerk dropped farther and farther behind, but an acute observer might have noticed that his relative position to Freddie was maintained by a heavy-jawed man who, if suddenly addressed, might have answered to the name Jimmie. And ten yards behind Jimmie Cotterill, smiling and bland, a red rose in his button-hole, strode Detective-Inspector Ansoll.

The procession maintained its order till Freddie turned down a street off Charing Cross Road. Then Ansoll closed up on Cotterill and the two moved up on Freddie. His foot was in a doorway when the inspector's hand dropped lightly on his shoulder. One glance he took, and then recoiled with every evidence of dismay and terror.

'Well, Freddie!' said Ansoll. In the quiet, gentle voice the other man read a menace that did not exist.

'Gawd, Mr Ansoll!' he cried. 'You scared me.'

'Sorry,' apologised Ansoll. 'You don't mind a joke, old son?' He linked his arm lovingly with that of his quarry, and Cotterill ranged up on the other side.

Freddie made a half-hearted attempt to disengage his arm. This encounter was altogether too pat upon his interview with Wolf Coyne to be to his taste. He was almost superstitious about it. But the ruling gambit of the crook came automatically to his lips.

'There's nothing you've got up against me. You lemme go. You ain't no business to interfere with me.'

'Freddie!' remonstrated the inspector. 'You seem frightened of something. What's the matter with you? We only want to buy you a drink. You never used to be as shy as this.' His grip tightened.

'I'm not frightened,' declared the other, raising his voice so that there should be no mistake. 'What I got to be frightened about? Only I've got an appointment. You've got no right to hold me up like this. I'll report you.'

'Report away,' agreed Ansoll. 'We like it. But come and have a drink all the same.'

Somehow Freddie found himself impelled away from the costumier's. The prospect of the drink did not entice him. He was possessed by too wholesome a fear even for that. His restless eyes sought vainly for enlightenment in the inspector's face. It wore an air of beaming benevolence.

In the cellar-like saloon of a near-by public-house Freddie found himself seated on a high stool with a detective on each side. Ansoll paid for drinks, and his unwilling guest found the taste of a liqueur brandy grateful and comforting. Ansoll talked idly in general. When Cotterill insisted on a second round Freddie was a little less suspicious of their motives. With a brand-new five-pound note burning in his hip-pocket he was not to be outdone in hospitality, and again the barman replenished the glasses. Freddie began to see how he had misjudged his hospitable companions. By the fifth round he was calling Cotterill 'Jimmie', and had dropped the 'Mr' when he addressed Ansoll. It escaped his notice that since the second round they had confined themselves to temperance beverages.

'You're a good sort, Anse'. I sort o'—hic—thought you had it in for me. My mistake. Y' heard o' the sweat-box, eh? No 'fence. Same again?' He put down his empty glass.

'Same again,' said Ansoll. 'No, Freddie, the third degree don't go in London. We're all for pleasant methods. Own up now. We've never put a crooked deal up on you, have we?'

Freddie gravely shook his head. 'No. I don't owe you no grudge. When you've been after me you've always played the straight game. But—hic—say, Anse'—he hooked a couple of thin fingers on to the inspector's middle waistcoat button—'you folk want somethin' outa me now.' He leered cunningly sideways. 'That's so. I ses to meself—hic—when I lamped y' firsta all, "Anse's got something on—something doing, eh?" I was a bit peeved 'cos I'd gotta' 'pointment—matter of hundred jimmies t' me boy. But I'm glad I missed it now, because—hic—because you're a good f'llah. Have another?'

'Sure. That appointment now. Something to do with me, was it?'

Freddie grinned confidingly. 'Y' betcha shirt it was. Say, Anse', some of the boys are savin' it up for you. But I'm not in it now. I'm goin' back to Wolf Coyne and tell him to count me out. You're a good f'llah—better f'llah than Wolf any day. Let him keep his hundred.'

Ansoll raised a lemonade and angostura to his lips and took a slow drink. Over Freddie's head he saw Cotterill deliberately close one eye. That was all the sign that either was vitally interested in Freddie's babble.

'H'm,' commented the inspector. 'Wolf's gunning for me, is he? Well, I wish him luck.'

'He's a mean man. He thinks he's got it all under his own thatch—'stead of calling in those that's forgotten more of the game than he ever knew. Told me I was yellow, he did—*me* yellow.' His half-fuddled wits were working a grievance against the 'con' man. 'But you're a good f'llah. I'll show him whether I'm yellow—him and his swell suckers.' He scowled at the fresh drink which had been placed in front of him.

Ansoll pulled at his reddish moustache. 'Called you yellow, eh? I suppose that hundred pounds was so you might try and croak me. Why on earth Wolf Coyne should be putting it across me, I don't know.'

'Croak y',' Freddie laughed scornfully. 'No, I don't fall for that sort of business. I'm nobody's fool to run my head into a rope. No, it's like this, Anse'. You're crowding Wolf, and he's a man that don't like to be crowded. So he fixed it with me to play a little game with you—something that'd keep you too busy thinking about yourself to interfere with him till he made a get-away. Now, Anse', you're a good f'llah, Wolf was going to give me a hundred of the best—what's it worth to you if I put you wise?'

Ansoll stiffened. He stood up, and his smiling familiarity vanished. 'You're talking through the back of your head, Freddie,' he sneered. 'I thought you had more sense than to pitch me a cock-and-bull story like that. Say, honest now, have you ever met Wolf Coyne in your life? What do you think of him, Jimmie?'

Cotterill humped his shoulders scornfully. 'What you take us for, Freddie? Just a couple of piecans? Want to make a fiver by telling us a tale? Try it on someone else, my lad.'

Freddie gulped angrily. This change from good fellowship to rank incredulity had been well-timed. Too ready an eagerness would have made him anxious to extract terms, or, worse still, might have aroused his slumbering suspicions. But this attitude of the officers was nicely calculated to make a nearly drunken man blurt out all he knew. Freddie eyed them in fierce resentment.

'Telling the tale, am I? Don't know Wolf Coyne, don't I? You bulls think you're mighty smart—I don't think. Would you believe it if I was to tell you . . .'

Twenty minutes later he was being whirled in a taxi-cab towards King Street. To his protests both detectives listened with no trace of emotion.

'It's all right, old son,' said Jimmie Cotterill soothingly. 'We're not going to hurt you. We're just going to hold you safe till you're feeling better. A nice, strong, hot cup of coffee is all you want—then a stiff soda water. Now, you cheer up and you'll be as right as rain.'

They put him in the detention room at King Street—'detained for inquiries' was the official explanation—and adjourned to the dingy little C.I.D. office on the second floor. There they sank into chairs facing each other, and the little wrinkles round the corner of Ansoll's eyes grew more intense. He gave a short cackle of laughter.

'Wolf Coyne is It.' He chuckled. 'The one and only It. He meant having me. But I think the surprise packet he held for me will be nothing to his astonishment when he finds it go off in his hand. Now, Jimmie, we've got to get busy.' He reached for the desk telephone. 'Give me C.I.—Ansoll speaking.'

With the dismissal of Flash Freddie, Coyne felt that the Ansoll problem was in a fair way of being settled. It had been a flash of inspiration—almost of genius—that had shown him the way out. He regretted now the access of temper that had made him seek out the inspector and show a gun. In that he felt he had been foolish. But this—this was different—something worthy of the man who, before the week was out, would, barring accidents, be worth a hundred thousand pounds.

He chuckled to himself as he dressed for dinner. He had that touch of vanity in which most criminals, big, and little, are alike—though, unlike smaller men, he was content with his own admiration of himself.

As his man brushed him down he gave a glance at himself in the glass, and with a satisfied nod moved to the private room he had ordered for dinner. He did credit to his tailor, and his tailor was worthy of him. His wanderings and a certain natural ability had given him an air. He was distinguished even without the three orders that dangled on his lapel—a man of whom you might be sure at first glance as standing in front rank of whatever profession or society he adorned.

He welcomed his guests—there were only three—with that charm of manner that had stood him in good stead in multifarious enterprises. If you had raked London you would not have found three persons less likely to be duped by an adventurer than those whom Coyne was entertaining. There was Lord Dalgaren, millionaire, owner of fifty thousand acres in Yorkshire and two hundred in London, and reputed one of the best business men in the House of Lords; Sir Henry Palton, builder of the big enterprise that shrieked at you from every hoarding 'Palton's Preserves'; and young Rupert Dainton, M.P., who had been left £15,000 a year and a big political future.

It was over the coffee that business was introduced. Up till then Coyne had given no indication that this was any more than a matter of hospitality. He lit a cigar with dainty care.

'Well, Palton,' he said, 'I've had a cable today. You people have had plenty of time to make sure of my credentials. This ought to be fixed up now, or before we know it we'll be pushed aside. These American Republics are slippery folk to deal with. We don't want anyone to get ahead of us.'

Palton adjusted a pair of eyeglasses and looked gravely over their rims at his host. 'It would have been better if you'd got the concession signed before we put up the money, Mr Arthur. Of course I can understand the difficulties of the position, but—'

Coyne drummed on the table absently. It was Dainton who struck in. 'My dear Palton, we've been over that ground a dozen times among ourselves. It isn't as if it was a gamble. It's a perfectly reasonable proposition.'

The 'con' man interrupted. 'I want to be clear with you gentlemen. You perfectly understand that I don't risk a penny of my own money. I would like you to be in on this, but of course if there is any difficulty about raising the money, I can take the proposal elsewhere. If you had my experience of South America you would know you can't do these sort of things on hot air. You can get this concession to build a railway through one of the biggest South American republics if you are prepared to put up a hundred thousand as a guarantee that you really will build. It seems, as Mr Dainton says, perfectly reasonable. If we were the only people on the market—'

'Put that point aside for a moment,' said Dalgaren. 'What I think, I tell you frankly, is that you are asking us too much. We're putting up the money, and the contract you want us to sign agrees that for services rendered you are to receive not less than one-fourth of the ordinary shares when we go to allotment.'

'That's it,' agreed Palton. 'It's too much. You agree with us, don't you, Dainton?'

Coyne leaned back in his chair. He was too old a hand to make the mistake of lowering his terms. 'I think we might perhaps drop the discussion.' he said amiably. 'You know how it stands. One hundred thousand to be paid to me here and the concession to be signed directly I cable that it's done. I take one-fourth of the ordinary shares or nothing.'

'You're a hard man, Arthur,' sighed Palton. 'Have you got the contract?'

'I'm a business man—that's all. I've got four copies all made out, and we'll sign 'em presently. You can pay the money over to my bank in the morning.'

*

A waiter placed a card in front of him. He looked at it frowningly for a moment and then nodded. 'Show him into my sitting-room in five minutes.' He held the card in his hand as the servant left, and turned with a smile to his guests. 'This happens rather opportunely. I don't suppose any of you can tell me the etiquette of the occasion. It's a little matter of blackmail.'

'Someone ferreted out the black pages of your past, Arthur?' said Dalgaren. 'Or is it a woman?'

'Neither,' said Coyne. 'It is a gentleman who apparently holds an official position here.' He read from the card: 'Detective-Inspector J. C. Ansoll, Criminal Investigation Department.'

Dainton whistled. Palton readjusted his eye-glasses. 'Do you really mean that this police officer is trying to blackmail you?'

The 'con' man nodded. 'He's got wind of this concession business somehow—just enough to make him believe there's something fishy. He came to see me this morning, and threatened to tell you all the horrid details, Palton. It was an awkward fix, because, though I didn't mind him going to you, I did not want the scheme talked about till everything was watertight. Publicity might have killed it. So I temporised—told him to come back some other time and we'd talk it over.' He spoke with just the right air of amused irritability.

'I say, this is serious,' said Dainton. 'A detective officer levying blackmail. We'll have to do something you know. The Home Secretary—'

'Do what you like after we've got the concession,' said Coyne. 'We can't do anything till then—though we might give him a scare—what? Look here, if you three conceal yourselves, it would be a good idea to have him in here. When he learns that there have been witnesses to his attempt—'

'We can shut him up till the deal goes through,' said Dalgaren. 'I think that's the right idea. What about those *portières* for you, Dainton? Palton, you might take the window—and the screen will do me.'

'That's splendid,' agreed Coyne. 'I hadn't arranged this little entertainment for you folk, but it ought to amuse you. Now, green lights. Enter the villain—or, rather, I'll go and fetch him.'

No one of the three concealed gentlemen could have supposed that their host was filled with contemptuous amusement as he left the room. He chuckled as he received the waiting inspector.

'Gad, Freddie, you're a wonder. If I didn't know, I'd think you were the real thing. Come along.'

Ansoll obeyed with docility. As they passed into the dining-room he straightened his shoulders.

'You'll guess what I've come about,' he said.

'I've a sort of idea,' said Coyne imperturbably. 'I think you've got the wrong man. However,'—he thrust his hands in his trousers pockets,—'what's your price?'

There was nothing forced about Ansoll's grin. He had caught a movement beneath one of the *portière* curtains. 'I fancy you are making a little mistake,' he said pleasantly. 'You can't buy me off. I am a police-officer, as you know, and it is my duty to tell you that unless you can give a satisfactory explanation of certain facts that have come to my knowledge, I shall take you into custody on a charge for attempted fraud. You understand that you are not obliged to answer any questions.'

Three lines bit vertically into Coyne's forehead. He regretted there had not been a more complete rehearsal of the scene they were now playing. Somehow it was running off the lines.

'Fire ahead,' he said.

'You claim to be able to obtain a concession to build a railway across certain districts of Chile, but that, prior to obtaining the necessary signatures, a deposit of £100,000 must be paid to *you*.'

'That is right.'

'You have practically induced three gentlemen to entrust you with that deposit?'

'Well?' Coyne meditatively surveyed a well-fitting dress shoe.

'I have today received information that it is not and never has been contemplated to grant a concession—that the Chilean authorities know nothing about it.'

'I suppose,' said Coyne, 'that all this beating about the bush is for a purpose. You want me to pay to keep your mouth shut. Would you like me to write a cheque?'

'Not exactly,' laughed Ansoll. 'I would like you to prove to me that this is no fraud. Otherwise—'

'Otherwise?'

Ansoll stepped to the door. 'Jimmie,' he called softly. And then to Coyne: 'I think, Wolf, if you tell these gentlemen who are so interested in our little conversation to come out, we can drop the curtain on this farce. You see, Freddie has let you down.'

Not often in his career had Wolf Coyne been taken at a loss. It took him a full second to realise that it was Ansoll in reality and not Flash Freddie. He stared unbelievingly at the detective.

'Hell!' he muttered. 'Hell!'

Then he was galvanised into action. With a couple of strides he cleared the room, jerked the amazed Palton from his hiding-place, and turned the handle of the inner door. But Jimmie Cotterill and Ansoll moved as quickly. They flung themselves upon him and pulled him back. Both were powerful men, but Coyne was no less so, and he was driven desperate. They surged, a tangled mass of humanity, over the soft carpet, the two officers in grim silence, the 'con' man cursing fearfully.

Dainton flung himself into the fray, and received a kick in the face that sent him half-stunned into the fireplace. Ansoll spat out a tooth and took a fresh grip on the place where the collar of Coyne's dress-coat had been. Cotterill, with his knee momentarily on the 'con' man's chest, succeeded in adjusting one cuff of the handcuffs. A second later the flying other end caught him in the mouth.

'Aw,' he gurgled, and clenched a fist.

'None of that, Jimmie,' ordered Ansoll sharply, and the sergeant, who had lost sight of the tradition of the Metropolitan Police, stayed his blow. Two minutes later he got the prisoner's wrists together and the handcuffs clicked again.

Ansoll stood up, breathing heavily. 'I'm not so young as I was,' he sighed. 'In the old days I'd have enjoyed a scrap like that.' He wiped the blood from his lip. 'Now, gentlemen, if you'll follow us on to King Street police station I shall be grateful. You can reckon that this job has saved you at least £100,000.'

To three disillusionised men Ansoll vouchsafed explanations in his office. 'You gentlemen,' he said, 'don't think yourselves in the same class as a countryman who buys a pawn-ticket for a gold watch outside Waterloo Station. Yet, except that it was a concession instead of a pawn-ticket, it's just the same old game that this crook down below has played on you. They say it's better to be born lucky than rich.

'We had Wolf Coyne tipped off to us when he came across. Now, he's a free-born American citizen, and there's no law that we could use against him, though we were pretty sure he had something up his sleeve. He just laughed at me when I warned him off.

'Of course we kept a pretty strict eye on him. We couldn't do anything till he overstepped the law, but we were just watching for a chance. The awkward thing was that we didn't know in just what direction his talents would break out. We could only wait and watch, and the longer we waited the more evident it was that it was a big thing.

'Now, though we could learn nothing of the stunt—all of you took pretty good care to keep that secret—we worried Wolf. He knew that we were right on his heels, and it got on his nerves. You see he was alarmed lest we should get a hint to put you wise before he got his hooks on the money. He actually stood in Bond Street this, morning and threatened me with a pistol. When he found that didn't work he tried something else.

'He sent for a man named Mullins—Flash Fred—who was an actor before he took to drink and went on the cross. That gave us our first hold. When Freddie left the hotel we followed him, caught him up after awhile, and made him drunk. There was very little Sherlock Holmes work in this, I can tell you.

'Well, first we made him drunk and then we got his goat. It all came out like drawing a cork from a bottle. The scheme had all the marks of Coyne's genius. First of all, he wanted to increase your confidence in him. And secondly, lest I should get a line on him, he was to destroy your faith in me. Freddie was to make up to resemble me and then to put up a blackmail show with you three gentlemen in unimpeachable positions as witnesses. Clever, wasn't it? Supposing I'd found out afterwards, and come to you with a story that Coyne was cheating you, would you have believed me? To make the blackmail convincing he had to entrust Freddie with rough points of the scheme, and that gave us enough to work on.

'We cabled the chief of police at Valparaiso, and got in touch with the Chilean Ministry here—'

'But,' interrupted Dainton, 'he told us that for reasons of secrecy this matter of the concession was being conducted direct from headquarters. There was a matter of a—er—bonus.'

'Bribery, in plain English. The old "con" stuff. When you buy a brass ring you have to keep quiet because it's been stolen from Streeters. Anyway, that stopped you making inconvenient inquiries here. As I was saying, there was never any idea of a concession. A week after you'd made over cheques, you'd have looked in vain for your Mr Arthur. He'd got a pal in Valparaiso who sent the cables that kept you keen, and his other papers are forgeries.

'Well, that's all. We rearranged things a little and I took the principal part instead of Freddie.'

'I wish, Mr Ansoll,' said Palton dryly, 'you had chosen some other method. For men in the public positions of ourselves it will be a little—ah—humilating to have to confess how we were duped.'

'Why,' smiled Ansoll, 'that's exactly why I did it. Wolf has had too long a run to escape again because—forgive me—three suckers hate to tell how close they came to being stung.'

XIII

CROSSED TRAILS

'THE fact is,' said Mr Harold Saxon, cheerfully, brushing a speck of cigar ash from his white waistcoat with two fingers, 'somebody's trying to murder me.'

Both tone and manner were so casual that the assertion was robbed of any appearance of melodrama. Chief Detective Inspector Yerk was too old a hand to be startled. He almost suspected a joke. He checked a smile, and his eyes travelled over Saxon from his spats to the big diamond pin that sparkled in his tie, and thence to the genial white-moustached face with the twinkling blue eyes.

'You don't say so,' he murmured noncommittally. 'Who is it?'

Saxon's brows contracted a trifle. 'Just what I'd like you to find out. I'd hate to be killed without knowing the reason. That's why I sent to Scotland Yard for somebody to sit in in the game.' He pressed a bell on his desk, and a small page boy darted noiselessly to his side. 'Ask Miss Jukes if she'd mind seeing me a moment, sonny.'

It was a slender good-looking woman, somewhere in the neighbourhood of thirty, who moved into the room in response to the summons. She was carrying two or three typewritten documents and halted, irresolutely, as she saw Yerk.

'I want you to know Mr Yerk—from Scotland Yard,' said Saxon. 'Miss Jukes' he explained to the detective, 'has been my secretary for seven years, and she knows more about me and my affairs than I sometimes do myself—all except the present business, which I've rather kept to myself. Say, Miss Jukes, have you ever seen any marked symptoms of insanity in me—anything more than usual in a theatrical producer? I want you to assure Mr Yerk that I'm not suffering from hallucinations.'

She smiled a little uncertainly. 'I think most people would describe you as a very practical man.'

'Thank you. And you've never heard of anyone who wants to murder me?'

The papers fluttered to the floor, and the girl stared in wide-eyed astonishment at her employer. 'I—you're joking, of course?'

'I assure you I'm not. I'm mighty serious. It's no joke for me.'

'Well,' she said emphatically, a slight stress of surprise still in her voice, 'I don't believe you've an enemy in the world.'

'Nor did I think so. I fancied Mr Yerk might like something beyond my word. Thank you, Miss Jukes. You needn't talk of this, you know.'

There were many people who would have endorsed the girl's opinion. Saxon was a popular man and he had not himself believed that there was a person in existence who hated him sufficiently to wish to push him violently off the earth. The wide variety of nicknames which had been affixed to him was, in itself, a confirmation of his popularity. In his clubs he was 'Pa'. Among the chorus, if you were exceedingly annoyed with him, you called him 'guv'nor'; otherwise, he was 'the old duck'. If you ranked a little higher in the theatrical hierarchy, he was 'Uncle Harold'. Only if you were a servant, or a stranger, did you venture the formality of a 'Mr Saxon.' Actors and actresses, of a cynical cast of mind, sometimes wondered how so likeable a man had achieved control of a dozen theatres.

'It beats me, my boy,' he remarked, as Miss Jukes disappeared. 'It really does.'

Yerk was scrutinising him with narrow screwed-up eyes. He was unused to white-haired theatrical magnates who called him 'my boy' on a matter of five minutes' acquaintance.

'Suppose you give me the facts,' he observed. 'I'm a little in the dark just now.'

'That's true.' Saxon seemed distressed. 'Here, have a cigar, Mr Yerk. Care for a drink? Well, perhaps it is a wee bit early. I guess you had suspicions that I am suffering from softening of the brain—senile decay and all that, eh? That's why I called Miss Jukes as evidence.' He chuckled. 'Yes, I'm alive as ever I was—so far. Three times I've been lucky, and I mean to hang on—what? The cinema hero isn't a circumstance to me in coming up smiling. Know the coast of the Bristol Channel at all—round about Weston-super-Mare?'

'Slightly,' admitted the detective.

'Well, that's where the curtain went up. I had motored over from Bristol and walked out alone to Brean Down—that's where all the visitors to Weston picnic in the summer, but at this time of the year it's pretty deserted. It's a promontory jutting out into the channel for a mile or so, and you reach the point over mud-flats and marshes. I was near the old fort on the headland about dusk. There's a bit of a drop from the rocks at one point—only a few yards, but quite precipitous enough to prevent a swimmer landing. That's where my unknown friend got me first. I was standing on the edge looking out to sea when someone pushed me from behind. Had I hit the rocks and been disabled, I should have been drowned. As it was, I fell into deep water.'

Yerk nodded. 'Sure you didn't over-balance yourself?' he asked. 'Did you see or hear anyone near you?'

'I saw or heard nothing. I'm sure it was a push now, though at the time, I felt I was probably mistaken. Luckily, I haven't forgotten how to swim and I managed to get round the point and yell. Someone at the old fort—it's a restaurant now—heard me and fished me in at the end of a rope.

'Now I might have taken no more notice of that, but the day before yesterday I was walking on the darkened stage at the Regal when a trap gave way underneath me, and it was only by luck that I got off without a broken neck. That *might* have been an accident, too. But listen to this morning's limit. The end of the steering rod in my car broke off sharp while rounding a corner off the Strand, and it's a miracle to me now that we weren't smashed to pieces. And, believe me, my boy, that rod had been filed so that any sudden strain would snap it.' He replaced his cigar jerkily in the corner of his mouth. 'I walked here and sent for you.'

The inspector shrugged his shoulders. 'First of all we've got to put a finger on a motive. You say you've got no enemies—that's a bit loose, of course, because everyone's got enemies. But rule revenge out if you like and you come to self-interest. Who would benefit by your death?'

'The hospitals and theatrical charities mainly. I haven't a relative in the world that I know of.'

Yerk's bushy eyebrows came closer together. Unless Saxon was concealing something—and a glance at his ruddy open face made that difficult to believe—the case was going to be less open and shut, as he would have phrased it, than at first he had expected. If some cunning madman was seeking the theatrical magnate's life—and that was the only alternative theory—he would have to seek at large among the immense number of people who, at any time, had any association with Saxon. The detective of actuality bases his work on the fact that, to the ordinary human being, two and two make four. But on a person seeking another's life, from a lunatic caprice, no normal reasoning can bear. He grunted something in his throat.

'I'll take that steering rod away with me if you have it here,' he said. 'I'd like to have an expert's opinion on it. Meanwhile, I guess you want an extra assistant—a male secretary to be in close touch with you. You'd better advertise for one.'

'But'—Saxon's eyebrows went up—'I don't quite see—'

'Among the applications you will get,' went on Yerk, 'will be one from a man named Bronson—F. J. Bronson. You'll engage him on a month's trial.'

'That's all very well,' protested the other a little impatiently. 'See here, Mr Yerk, I don't want to be dry-nursed with a private guard tagging after me all day long.'

'I understand,' said the inspector with suave sympathy. 'Don't you worry. You'll find him a very competent business man. He won't be obtrusive. Now'—his voice became a little harder—'listen to me. If you were consulting a doctor or a lawyer you'd obey them unquestioningly. You've called me in in this business and you'll do what I say or I'll not be answerable.'

Saxon made a gesture of resignation. 'Oh! If you put it that way.'

'I do. One other point. You're carrying an automatic in your jacket pocket. That bulge is pretty obvious. I suppose you got it this morning?'

Saxon clapped his hand to his pocket. 'That's so, I thought it as well.'

'I don't suppose you've handled a firearm in your life before,' observed the detective dryly. 'You might as well—better—carry a pea-shooter. Get rid of it. It's only giving you away as being scared. Now, if you don't mind I'll have a chat with Miss Jukes and perhaps some other of your people.'

It was a very thoughtful chief detective inspector who returned to Scotland Yard some couple of hours later. As he adjusted himself to his desk and placed a little sheaf of notes in front of him, he ran his hand absently through his hair. He did not conceal from himself a feeling that Saxon had rather minimised, than exaggerated, the deadliness of his peril. Thrice, and even four times, he ran through his notes striving to catch some possibility on which he could fasten. The life or death of Harold Saxon would have meant little to him a day before. Now, however, he had a degree of responsibility, and, if the unknown should get the old man— He put the thought from him. Quick work was imperative.

The notes he had made mainly bore on those persons

engaged in the Saxon theatrical enterprises with whom the theatrical man came most in contact. From Button, the general manager, downwards, there was none he could justifiably suspect. But because he was a man who took nothing on trust, within the next ten minutes he had dispatched four subordinates to various parts of London to elaborate his own inquiries. Two more were detailed as shadows for Saxon—a matter of which he had not deemed it worth while to tell the latter, since they were less for the purposes of protection than to follow up any point of investigation that seemed worth while. Then he sought a young alert-eyed man, who ranked as detective-sergeant and answered to the name of Bronson, with whom he held a long and animated discussion. When the convention finished, Yerk lit a meditative pipe. For the moment everything had been done. He could now only wait on results.

Results, however, were slow. As the days went by there gradually grew up in Yerk's desk a mass of material collected by his subordinates, mostly of a negative nature. If Yerk had not known how often seemingly irrelevant evidence switches to a direct bearing he would have destroyed the great bulk of it. The most elaborate inquiries had shown no one person who had had the physical opportunities of making three attempts on Saxon's life. Those who might have tampered with the trap-door in the theatre could not possibly have thrown the theatre owner from Brean Down.

Saxon took the lack of progress equably. 'If they're going to croak me they're going to croak me,' he said philosophically. 'I've put things in your hands, Mr Yerk, and I can't do more. What's the use of worrying? I've got to thank you, incidentally, for that man Bronson of yours. I don't know what he's like as a detective, but he's a darn good personal assistant, and I don't care how long I have him.'

Yerk grinned. 'As things are going it looks as if he's a fixture for life,' he admitted.

The door slid quietly open and the subject of their conversation broke in on them. His face was deathly pale and his left arm dangled limp by his side. He closed the door and locked it.

''Phone to the stage door and the front,' he gasped. 'Tell them not to let anyone out of the house. See there's someone at every exit.' Saxon was busy with the telephone almost before he had finished speaking and Bronson addressed himself to Yerk.

'Glad to find you here, sir, I've had a little trouble—a knife stab, I think. Somebody jumped out on me in the narrow passage leading from the stage door. The light's out there and it's as dark as the pit. I made a grab but I stumbled and whoever it was got away.'

Already Yerk had led the other to a chair and with quick deft fingers was slitting his sleeve with a pocket knife. In a couple of minutes he had made a business-like bandage with three handkerchiefs and Saxon was administering brandy to the injured man.

'Not so bad as it might have been,' he observed. 'You'll have to take a taxi down to Bow Street and see the divisional surgeon.'

'One other thing first,' said Bronson fumbling in his pocket. 'I found this lying on my desk ten minutes ago.' He produced a quarto sheet of paper with a few lines of typewriting upon it.

'We're on to you, you sneaking spy. If you and Yerk try any funny business it will be the worse for you both. Look out.'

The chief inspector whistled between his teeth. 'This can wait,' he exclaimed. 'We've got something else to see to at the moment. Just see him into a cab, Saxon, will you, while I 'phone the Yard.'

It was a matter of minutes before those members of the Flying Squad who happened to be available at headquarters reached the theatre. With every means of egress barred they conducted a rigorous search of the place. As Yerk expected, there were only the stage hands and clerical staff. No one, as far as could be ascertained, had attempted to leave the building, except in the ordinary course of routine. One by one the chief inspector put under a keen, but guarded cross-examination, every person in the place.

He shook his head when he and Saxon were once more alone. 'Nothing very tangible there,' he remarked, 'except—well, I don't quite know. It's plain whoever's mixed up in this is getting more daring—or more desperate. They know we know—and that an apparent accident, as far as you are concerned, won't mislead us. So they're coming into the open—chancing their arm.'

'Well,' drawled Saxon, 'I'm sorry for Bronson, of course, but apart from that, I don't complain. Things were getting a bit monotonous. I've been missing my unknown friends' attempts at assassination.'

The satire was not lost on Yerk. 'You've been reading about detectives who pull a criminal out of their sleeves, as a conjurer does a rabbit,' he replied, with some asperity. 'I'm just a plain police-officer—an ordinary human being, even if I have got a big machine behind me, and I can't do those sort of tricks. Don't forget we're looking for an unknown person with an unknown motive, and you can't make bricks without straw. We're doing our best. I'm too old a hand to ever be certain but it looks as if we've made a start at last.'

Saxon crossed over and patted the detective on the shoulder. 'My dear boy,' he protested, 'I meant no reflection on you. I know your people are doing all that's possible.'

Yerk gave an abrupt nod and dropped the subject. 'I'd like to see every typewriting machine you've got in the place,' he said. 'I'd also like to have, if you'll trust me with 'em, every typewritten letter that you've received for the last month.'

'Just as you say,' agreed the other.

Yerk was no typist, but from every machine that he inspected he contrived to clumsily thump out an incoherent string of words containing most of the letters of the alphabet. With these and a big wad of correspondence he made his way back to Scotland Yard.

With the anonymous note that Bronson had received spread in front of him, he methodically compared every example of typewriting that had been given to him. Only those that were totally distinct did he place aside. When he had finished he had twenty-two letters and three of the scraps that he himself had typed.

Now the print from no two typewriters—even those of the same make and with the same type—is alike. To the trained eye minute differences are as palpable between one and another as the individuality in handwriting. Yerk gave a few instructions and in a couple of hours his specimens were transferred to lantern slides and in the big room which Scotland Yard keeps for such purposes, thrown in vivid enlargement on a screen. Word by word, letter by letter, down even to the punctuation marks, Yerk, and those men he had called in to assist him made comparisons. It was a long tedious job, necessitating often fresh reference to the originals, but at length it was finished. Yerk carefully pinned two papers together and placed them in his pocket.

'That looks promising,' he observed.

Away in Wimpole Street, where those prime ministers of medicine who have overflowed from Harley Street dwell, Chief Detective Inspector Yerk, accompanied by letters of introduction from the medical scientists attached to the Home Office, had a strenuous interview with Sir Ian Pressland, who was a masterful man with pronounced views on the ethics of the profession of medicine. Yerk, a man who liked to get his own way, wiped the perspiration from his brow as the specialist finally spoke.

'Mind you, I've my reputation to consider, Mr Yerk—my standing in my profession. It's a big thing you're asking me but since you say it's in the interests of justice I'll go part of the way with you.' He emphasised the remark with a longer slender forefinger. 'You'll use my name with discretion—the most marked discretion or'—he waved his pince-nez towards the detective—'I'll repudiate the whole affair.'

Always thankful for half a loaf rather than no bread, Yerk withdrew. He was not even sure that he had not attained the whole loaf.

He read with serene detachment the following day a three-line paragraph in the newspapers that, consequent upon Mr Harold Saxon's illness, that gentleman's new London production had been indefinitely postponed. Mr Saxon, it was understood, was suffering from asthma, which had induced serious heart trouble. Curiously enough, the specialist called in was none other than Sir Ian Pressland, who had ordered the patient away to Montreux in France for treatment.

He was whistling happily when the superintendent of the Central Criminal Investigation Department poked his head through the doorway.

'I see there's a little bit of news about Saxon in this morning's paper. Did you get it?'

Yerk grinned cheerfully. 'Was just glancing at it as you spoke.'

The steel blue eyes of the superintendent twinkled. He had not reached his present rank without learning a great deal of tact. 'Wasn't quite sure whether it would affect you or not. I'm asking no questions. You won't be free to handle another case just yet?'

'Hope to be clear in from three days to a week. I don't think Saxon's illness will last long.'

There was an enigmatic quality in the chief inspector's tone that caused the superintendent to jerk his head whimsically sideways as he vanished from the room.

Yerk was right. Saxon's illness did not last long. With dramatic suddenness the news reached his enterprises, four days later, that he had succumbed to a severe heart attack. A wire had early apprised the chief inspector of the fact and he sent Bronson, now once more on duty although his left arm was still in a sling, in a car down to Croydon to catch the next aeroplane for France. For himself he had other work to do.

A taxi-cab bore him to the firm of lawyers who had had charge of the professional and private interests of the dead man. Accompanied by the head of the firm, he first of all paid a visit to the flat of the dead man, and thence proceeded to the offices of the Saxon Syndicate at the Regal Theatre.

Button, the general manager, greeted them with a chastened affability, although Yerk thought he observed an involuntary lift of the eyebrows. Apparently he had not expected the lawyer and the detective to call together.

'Terrible affair, Mr Ladd, isn't it,' he remarked addressing the former. 'So tragically sudden. It's going to make a difference to all of us. Poor old Uncle Harold.'

'The last thing in the world that I expected,' said the lawyer.

Button's eyes were full on Yerk. 'Of course, I know something of what your business had been, Mr Yerk. Mr Saxon had few secrets from me. I feel it,'—his emotion almost overcame him—'as if I had lost an elder brother. I suppose there's no suspicion of foul play?'

'Not so far as I can see,' responded Yerk, fondling his chin. 'As you know, Mr Button, there have been these mysterious attempts on his life, but these heart attacks from which he suffered were, the doctors say, perfectly normal. As I'm on the job, however, I've got to be dead certain. That's why I'm with Mr Ladd, who, as one of the executors, is looking after things.'

'I want to take charge of any private papers he had,' interposed the lawyer. 'Have you the keys of his safe?'

'Miss Jukes, his confidential secretary, has them. I will ask her.'

The girl, her face pale and with large hollows under the eyes as though she had suffered from lack of sleep, surrendered the keys with a word or two of explanations and led the way to the private office. There, with a sort of listless efficiency, she busied herself with assisting the lawyer and the detective as they examined certain of the documents and books in the safe and the drawers of the desk. Button, lounging against the doorway, lit a cigar and looked on.

For half an hour the systematic examination went on. Then from an inner drawer of the safe the lawyer drew a large envelope and gave a low sibilant intake of the breath.

'Ah! This is what I've wanted to find.' He displayed the inscription on the envelope: 'The last will and testament of Harold Saxon.'

Button's hand shook a little as he removed his cigar from his mouth. 'His will. Now I'd be interested to know what he's done with his money.'

Ladd withdrew a parchment paper from the envelope and unfolded it. He rapidly glanced down the legal verbiage and his thin lips compressed to a tight line. With a swift motion he refolded it and placed it in an inside pocket.

'This is scarcely the place or the occasion,' he said dryly. 'I will read it to anyone interested, in my office, at five o'clock this afternoon. If you care to be present'—he turned as if by an afterthought to the secretary—'and Miss Jukes, I shall be delighted. Now'—he lifted his hat and stick—'this practically ends my mission here. I don't know if you, Mr Yerk—'

'No,' said the detective. 'I guess I'll be going too.'

The inscrutability on the lawyer's face gave way to a look of bewilderment as Yerk and he took their seats in a taxi-cab.

'This will interest you,' he said tossing the will into his companion's lap. 'I don't understand it but it is perhaps what you have been looking for.'

Yerk did not immediately trouble to open it. He thrust his head through the window and ordered the driver to change their destination and to take them to Scotland Yard.

Eight or nine people had gathered in the private office of the senior partner of Ladd, Stone, Lincoln & Ladd. The senior partner played a quiet tattoo with his pen on his blotting pad while he waited for them to adjust themselves. Miss Jukes sat immediately facing him. Button, impassive, sat by her side. Yerk was accompanied by Winter, the superintendent of the Central Criminal Investigation Department. The only other woman present besides Miss Jukes was Saxon's housekeeper, a stiff rustling dame, of advanced middle-age. The few men scattered about Button took to be representatives of various charities.

'H'm.' The lawyer cleared his throat. 'I have asked you here, ladies and gentlemen, at the earliest possible moment, to read what purports to be the last will and testament of my late client, Mr Harold Saxon. I should say that, until today, I had no knowledge that this will existed. If this is admitted to probate it destroys all the testamentary dispositions of a will that was deposited with me.'

The lawyer wiped his pince-nez and in a low droning monotone began to recite steadily. There were a few subsidiary legacies and then the will went on:

> '. . . And I furthermore give and bequeath to my dear friend and colleague, to whose loyalty and friendship I owe much, Mr Francis James Button, all the residue of my real and personal estate. . . .'

Yerk had risen and, noiselessly as some jungle creature, had taken two steps forward.

> '. . . And I hereby appoint as my executors under this my last will and testament, Miss Eleanor May Jukes and . . .'

A hand like steel gripped Button's shoulder and a frigid

passionless voice interrupted. 'That will do, sir. Button, you are under arrest for forgery. Anything you . . .'

The manager wrenched himself round and swung his fist. Yerk gave a flick of the head and the blow passed harmlessly by. Somebody sprang forward. Button felt his arms pinioned while deft fingers encircled handcuffs on his wrists.

Yerk imperturbably completed the formal warning, . . . 'may say may be used in evidence against you.'

Button glared round the room in an ecstasy of passion. 'What utter nonsense,' he declared. 'You'll pay for this.'

'I'll take the risk,' answered Yerk quietly. 'Sit still please, Miss Jukes—or shall I say Mrs Button? You also are under arrest. I should hate to use violence to a woman. Most of these gentlemen here are police officers so you will see resistance is futile.'

'Utter ridiculous nonsense,' repeated Button passionately.

'Quietly!' urged Yerk suavely. 'You've been clever over this business, you people, and I'll admit that you nearly had me throwing in my hand. But you made one or two stupid mistakes. The first was when this young lady typed an apparently illiterate anonymous message on her private machine at home trying to scare off the investigation. You may be a little surprised to hear that you can no more hide the characteristics of a typewriter than you can of your own writing. I discovered a note she had written to Mr Saxon among some papers he gave to me and that started some very close inquiries. We know that she was secretly married to you and we found out that you had been plunging heavily for a year. That showed you needed money. You'—he pointed a long forefinger at the male prisoner—'were away from the office when someone made an attempt on Saxon's life at Brean Down. A man answering to your description had lunch at a Weston hotel and was seen walking towards the Down later. I have no doubt we shall be able to get witnesses to prove your identity. You had the opportunity of committing the other attempts. You had the motive and you had the opportunity.'

Button shrugged his shoulders contemptuously. 'There are fifty people who had as much opportunity as I. As for motive I never realised until just now that I was Saxon's residuary legatee. You've manufactured a case that won't hold water.'

'We'll see,' said the detective with silken grimness. 'We'll see if you can explain how this will came to be typed by your wife on her private machine—how it came to be in the safe to which only she, you and Saxon had access.'

The manager had regained control of himself to a large extent although the unevenness of his tones showed he was still shaken.

'You can prove nothing,' he repeated. 'The will is genuine.'

'Listen,' said Yerk. 'When I was convinced you were bent on murdering Saxon I could think of no conceivably adequate motive. I'll admit that the idea of a forged will was not in my mind. I knew, however, that whatever the scheme was it would show its head after Saxon was dead. So with the help of a specialist we arranged a convincing death far enough away from London to prevent any miscarriage. Mr Saxon, as a fact, is as well as you or I. He has spent a short holiday in Paris and is due back in London at any moment.'

The blow went home. All Button's self-assurance collapsed as a pricked balloon. His jaw sagged. 'Saxon alive!' he gasped. 'Saxon alive!'

The door opened and a genial white-moustached gentleman closely followed by Bronson, entered the room.

'Did I hear someone asking for me?' he smiled amiably.

A queer choking noise came from the girl. She pressed both her hands to her temples. 'He—he made me do it,' she choked. 'Mr Yerk is right. I'll—tell—all.'

She collapsed across her chair in a dead faint.

XIV

THE DAGGER

Little Jimson was not beautiful. Weedy, stunted, with a sandy moustache that for long had struggled with adversity, he looked like a grocer's assistant. As one moving more or less in society he had ambitions in the way of dress. Now and again, however, he made those little slips which the best intentions cannot avoid. He had been guilty of a soft hat and brown boots with a morning coat—but they were the best brown boots, and the hat was made by a famous hatter.

You might have known little Jimson for a long while without his provoking more than a smile. If you addressed him unexpectedly he would probably blush like a girl and stutter incoherently.

Yet to many people Jimson represented black tragedy. And Chief Detective Inspector Penny, passing him in the Strand with his arm thrust familiarly through that of Sir Melton Tarson, stopped abruptly before a convenient shop mirror and watched the worried frown on the baronet's forehead.

However, it was no business of his. Detectives of the Criminal Investigation Department, popular imagination notwithstanding, do not dive helter-skelter uninvited into other people's affairs. There are few men with a greater faculty for minding their own business. Penny had his own work to do, and Tarson's troubles were his own.

'That little hawk seems to have got his talons into that chap,' he muttered, and went on his way.

Not till he reached Scotland Yard that evening did he recall the incident to his mind. Loitering nervously in the corridor was the little man he had last seen in the Strand. A clerk pulled him aside.

'This man's waiting to see the superintendent, sir. Mr Foyle's out. Will you see him?'

Penny stopped and dropped a heavy fist on Jimson's shoulder. He spoke without that geniality that had made him one of the best-liked men in his profession.

'Well,' he said hardly, 'what do you want?'

Jimson went red. 'It's a m-m-matter of confidence, s-s-ir,' he said.

'All right. Come along in.' Penny escorted him along to the chief inspector's room and selecting a chair for himself, fixed a harsh gaze on his visitor. He did not trouble to offer him a seat.

'Somebody want to murder you?' he ejaculated.

Jimson fumbled with an inside pocket. 'T-that's it,' he agreed. 'Will you r-r-read these letters?'

'I'm not surprised,' Penny said shortly. 'The only wonder to me is that somebody hasn't knifed you before now. Anyway, let's have a look.'

He took the three letters Jimson handed to him and smoothed them out on the table. There was a glint of ironical amusement in his grey eyes as he read the first. It was typewritten and postmarked from Acton. The signature only was handwritten in blue pencil.

> 'You pernicious little blood-sucker. You have had a long run. It is time someone finished you. You have twenty days to leave the country. The *Themistocles* sails for Australia on the 22nd. If you want to preserve your skin you will book a passage.
>
> 'AVENGER.'

'Sounds like a moving picture plot,' commented Penny dryly. 'Now for the next.'

It was dated a week later and had not passed through the post:

'Have you booked that passage yet?—A.'

'F-found it in my overcoat pocket one n-night,' observed Jimson.

The third was three days later:

'Look out. You are marked. If you remain in England a day after the 22nd you are a dead man.—A.'

'H'm.' Penny was grinning undisguisedly now. 'I said it was a picture palace play. Today is the 23rd. You never did look healthy, my lad, but you don't look a dead man—yet.' He wrinkled his brows. 'You know,' he went on reflectively, 'you're one of those sort of vermin who must have a kind of courage. This isn't the first time you've been threatened if I'm any judge. As I said just now, somebody'll do more than threaten one of these days—and you won't get any wreath from me. What makes you think there's anything in this particular rot?'

The other fizzled for a moment like a newly-drawn champagne cork. 'D-d-didn't at f-first. B-b-but t-they tried to g-get me today.' His stutter vanished as he warmed up. 'Someone nearly pushed me under a motor lorry this morning in Pall Mall. I was all but a goner. Luckily it pulled up in time. I thought it was an accident. Then they tried to poison me at tea. I have a cup of tea at my little flat about four sometimes. My man happened to upset some milk on the floor and the cat got at it before it could be cleared up. It had about two laps and then rolled over as if it had been shot. I took the milk to a chemist who said cyanide of potassium had been put in it. Must have been done when it was left at the tradesman's entrance. So I got alarmed and came along to see you.' He mopped his damp brow with a cream-coloured silk handkerchief.

'Yes.' Penny slowly filled a pipe and rammed the tobacco down with his forefinger. 'Seems as if someone has got it in for you. Of course'—he spoke casually—'you have a pretty good suspicion who it is.'

'W-wish I had,' muttered Jimson disconsolately. 'There's so many people—'

'Give me a line,' persisted Penny, pausing with a lighted match in his hand. 'Tell me one or two likely people.'

But Jimson shook his head. Badly frightened though he was, he had no wish to take a Scotland Yard man too intimately into his confidence.

'I don't know,' he said somewhat sulkily.

Penny had cleared up the work he had in hand and somehow Jimson's case interested him. Otherwise he would have referred it in the ordinary course of events to the divisional staff in the district where Jimson lived. As it was, he had a hankering to see the case through himself—nor did the superintendent of the Central Branch of the Criminal Investigation Department object.

'Might as well look into it,' agreed the superintendent, 'though London would be a healthier place if Jimson were out of it. Maybe there's a woman in it.'

Penny nodded and went away to refresh his memory of little Jimson's career. There are criminals whom Scotland Yard does not dislike. It deals with them when they arouse its attention in an impersonal fashion which has neither malice nor favouritism. On the other hand, there are offenders whom detectives (being, after all, human) despise with all the instinctive abhorrence of clean-minded men for the parasite.

Among these latter Jimson had a place. The Criminal Investigation Department knew him well. Away back for twenty years they had watched his professional career develop and occasionally they had taken a hand in its progress—not often, for Jimson, in spite of his stutter and his blush, was quite capable of taking care of himself.

They had known him when he was yet a mere solicitor's clerk—indeed it was a youthful indiscretion in connection with the petty cash that had first brought him to their attention. Again, six years later, he had been so incautious as to attempt to bluff a well-known financier hardened to threats of exposure. On that occasion a trap had been laid that cost Jimson three painful years but had broadened his experience.

Jimson was, in fact, a blackmailer. Possibly he was the most expert blackmailer in London. Certainly his legal knowledge and his cunning had made him a difficult man to be dealt with by the ordinary police methods. Although fair guesses might be made at highly-placed victims, it would have been mere folly to expect them to help in the cause of abstract justice.

Although, as Penny said, he would have wasted no tears on Jimson's funeral, now that the matter had reached his hands he would have felt it a slur on his competence not to solve the mystery of the anonymous letters. Even a blackmailer's life is entitled to as much protection as can be given.

Two men he detailed to keep a sharp eye on Jimson and his peregrinations. He himself spent the evening in the West End. That a large stock of the information which Jimson found so valuable in his trade came from women was obvious. Penny, the picture of a genial city man on the spree, migrated from restaurant to restaurant and bought innumerable liquers for ladies who were likely to know anything about Jimson's operations.

It was gone ten o'clock at night before he gained the hint that he sought. A fluffy-haired goddess, her fingers armour-clad in meretricious jewellery, sat opposite him, giggling at his jests, muttering inanities and ogling him with sidelong glances under her lashes.

'You know that little chap—Jimson, wasn't his name—that used to knock about here?' he said, as one making conversation. 'What's become of him?'

'Charlie Jimson? I see him sometimes.' She giggled. ''E's a nut, 'e is. Couldn't do enough for me last week. Night before last saw him helping a kid into a motor-car outside the stage door at the Regal. Looked at me as if I was a bit of dirt and didn't even raise his hat. Not that I care—dirty little snipe. Friend of yours?'

He hastened to disclaim the impeachment. 'Just wondered what had become of him, that's all. Queer fellow. Got any idea where he gets his money?'

She glanced at him knowingly over the rim of her glass. 'I can give a guess. Say, I had a boy once—one of the lads—heaps of money. Regular gone on me he was. Believe he'd have married me if he hadn't been married already. He cooled off towards the last and Jimson bought his letters off me for a tenner. What do you think?' There was a knowing grin on her pretty face.

'Little vampire,' thought Penny. Aloud he said, 'I see. Well, I guess I'll be moving. Say, write your address on this envelope, will you? I'd like to drop in and see you one day.'

She complied. She did not know that Penny had a dozen other samples of handwriting in his breast pocket. It was unlikely that the author of the anonymous letters was to be found among her class. Still—one never knows.

Miss Gabrielle Yatdown was struggling into her heavy fur motoring coat when the manager ushered Penny into her dressing-room. She was not a big enough star to resent the unceremonious intrusion and her white teeth flashed in mechanical welcome as the manager introduced them.

'Mr Penny, a friend of mine, Miss Yatdown. Hope you didn't mind my bringing him along to see you.'

She put out a slim white hand. 'Delighted. Won't you sit down, Mr Penny? Are you a newspaper man?'

The manager, a discreet man who had formed his own surmises from the Scotland Yard man's questions, softly effaced himself. Penny hooked his stick on the dressing-table and laid down his gloves.

'No. I'm not a reporter. Fact is I'm a police officer, and I rather wanted to see you about a case in which I'm interested.'

Her blue eyes opened wide in artless astonishment. 'You are a detective.' She trilled with musical laughter. 'And you want to see *me*? What on earth for?'

There was no man who could finesse on occasion more adroitly than Penny. But he was in no mood now for delicacy. There was nothing to be denied in the mildness of his tone but his words were blunt.

'Tell me, Miss Yatdown, how much money have you extorted from Sir Melton Tarson?'

The girl's smile froze on her face and she lost a little of her delicate colour. For an instant she stood speechless and then she blazed into sudden wrath.

'What do you mean? How dare you insult me? I'll—'

Smiling and unmoved, he watched her. 'My dear girl,' he expostulated, as though he had known her as many years as he had seconds, 'what's the use of being silly? You know you've not lost your temper really and these mock heroics don't impress me a little bit. I wish you'd sit down like a sensible child and talk it over.'

She recovered herself. 'I haven't the remotest idea of what you're talking,' she said loftily. 'You are insinuating—'

'Forgive me. I should put it in the form of a statement of fact. I *know*.'

He bore her searching scrutiny with seeming confidence. He had bluffed more astute persons than this dancer. And yet of actual bare facts he knew little. While she was a baby in arms he was being trained in the act of putting two and two together. His self-possession evidently impressed her.

'Have you come from Sir Melton?' she demanded.

'Oh, dear, no.' He seemed surprised at her question. 'I have never spoken to him in my life. I know he treated you rather badly once.'

She laughed again, and he realised that he had underestimated her. 'I suppose that is intended to draw something out of me. I don't quite know what you are hoping to get, but

I have no intention of wasting my time. Good-night, Mr Penny.'

The detective looked after her as she swished with dignity through the doorway. Mechanically he resumed his stick and gloves. Then his face beamed with an expansive smile.

'That's one on me,' he observed aloud. 'Well, that interview doesn't seem to have helped a heap.'

With habitual punctuality Penny was on hand at Scotland Yard next day as nine o'clock was booming from Big Ben. Up in the magic lantern room they had transferred the samples of handwriting he had gained on to slides and now the reproductions were thrown one by one on to a screen while Penny watched closely for any peculiarities that would identify any of them with the signature on the first threatening letter. He was a believer in specialisation as a general rule, but he had small faith in the average handwriting expert. In this matter he preferred to trust to his own judgment.

Long and careful was his comparison, but at last he relinquished it. Not one of the samples—not even excepting that of Miss Yatdown, for he had borrowed an envelope of hers from the manager of the Regal—bore the faintest resemblance to the original signature.

He descended to his own room, his brows wrinkled. There he scanned the reports of subordinates he had put on various avenues of investigation without much hope. Still thoughtful, he at last put on his coat and hat and made his way westwards. He was irritated at his failure to get a grip of the problem.

Jimson inhabited a flat near Jermyn Street, and the detective nodded confidently to himself as he pressed a little electric button on the outer door. Almost at the movement the door flew open and the black menacing muzzle of an automatic was thrust into his face.

For a middle-aged man Penny moved with incredible swiftness. He had no concern just then with the reason for such a reception. He swerved sideways and then inwards. The pistol dropped with a soft thud on the carpet and a moment later its owner was flung crashing against the wall. Penny was angry, and he used all his strength. Only as he released his grip did he realise that the other was Jimson. He stooped and picked up the pistol.

'What in the blazes do you mean by this?' he demanded fiercely.

Jimson sat up, delicately feeling his throat and the back of his head. 'I-I-is t-that you, Mr Penny? Y-You d-d-didn't give me a c-chance to explain.'

'Chance to explain!' Penny's voice was grim. 'I reckon not. I couldn't stop for explanations with a gun under my nose. What do you mean by it anyway? You little rat!'

The other picked himself up and brushed his dressing-gown mechanically. 'I—I didn't know i-it was you. I t-thought it was s-someone else. Will you come in?'

'This job's getting your nerve,' observed Penny.

He followed Jimson through into the sitting-room. The little man's finger was shaking as he pointed to a chair. 'S-Sit down,' he said. Then in a burst: 'They've been at it again, Mr Penny.' He pointed with a dramatic gesture to a desk in a corner of the room. A dagger had been thrust through the writing-pad clean down to the hilt.

The detective turned suspiciously towards Jimson. 'More like a moving picture play than ever,' he commented dryly. 'When did you find it?'

'J-Just before you came in. You see I d-didn't rise very early this morning.'

'Huh! Who else sleeps in the flat? You've got a servant?'

Jimson nodded. 'I—I felt something like that myself after the poisoned milk yesterday. I sent him away last night. It couldn't be him.'

'Did he have a key?'

'I took that from him before he went.'

Penny pulled up a big arm-chair and sank into its luxurious depths. From under his shaggy eyebrows he looked long and steadily at the little blackmailer. 'I don't know if this is something you're putting across on me,' he said sternly. 'I don't believe it is. All the same, I have a kind of idea that no one wants to murder you at all.' He pulled the knife out of the desk and stroked its edge with his thumb. 'Now if they could get in here with this skull and cross-bones business they could just as easily have croaked you as not. What better opportunity could they want? Ever seen this toy before?'

'N-no. I'm not a nervous man, Mr Penny. I d-don't know why I escaped in the night. B-but I feel sure they mean b-business.' He spread out his arms. 'How could anyone get in? I locked the p-place myself.'

'Dunno,' retorted the detective brusquely. 'Seems to me you'd better cough up who you think it is. You can't hurt your reputation with us any, you know. I don't know why you want to hold up information which, you thinking as you do, may help to save your skin.'

Jimson shrugged his shoulders hopelessly, and Penny knew that scared or not he did not intend to put a weapon into the hands of the police that might be used against himself.

Somewhere there was the whirr of a bell. Jimson moved to the door. 'Nuisance my man being away,' he apologised. 'Won't be a second.'

Penny sat still—till his host was out of sight. Then, walking noiselessly, he moved to the portières that shrouded the entrance to the room. In the hall Jimson was holding the door ajar with one hand. The visitor said something that Penny could not catch.

He saw Jimson shake his head. 'I t-tell you I c-can't see you now,' he said curtly. 'T-tomorrow, or this afternoon.'

The detective shifted his position to obtain a view of the visitor. Then he stepped openly forward.

'Good-morning, Sir Melton,' he said quietly. 'May I introduce myself since Jimson here seems to have lost his tongue. I am Chief Detective Inspector Penny of Scotland Yard. Don't let this man'—he indicated Jimson—'put you off on my account. Come right in. I should like a chat with you myself.'

Jimson leaned back against the door-post. Under his scrubby moustache his lips curled in a challenging sneer. Sir Melton stood rigid and erect, and his eyes wavered up and down the detective. He had earned his knighthood by supreme daring in Arctic explorations and had the reputation of a man whose nerves were chilled steel. Yet now he seemed irresolute enough. His lips tightened.

'I believe I will,' he said. 'Mr Jimson will excuse me.'

He stepped in.

Jimson was still smiling when they entered the sitting-room. The nervousness which he had not troubled to conceal from Penny he now had fiercely under control. In his own line of business he was unexcelled, and there emotion had no part. He loved a pose. A casual study of cheap romances had grafted on to his ability as a blackmailer a wish to look the part of the nonchalant society villain. He had little fear that anything the detective might obtain from Tarson would develop to his prejudice, and he felt fairly secure.

Penny was thinking hard. Exactly how the visit of Tarson could help in the investigation in which he was engaged he was not clear. He clung to his main point, which was the matter of the threats. That Jimson had Tarson entangled somehow was a matter quite apart with which at that moment he had nothing to do. He was concentrated on the one thing, and the impulse that had made him reveal himself to Tarson was born of a readiness to catch at anything that might by a chance have some bearing on his work.

All three were men of the world, yet as they entered Jimson's luxurious sitting-room an awkwardness descended on them which Jimson was the first to break through. He produced cigarettes.

'S-Sir Melton and I are old f-friends, Mr Penny,' he explained. His face challenged Tarson to deny it.

Tarson made a visible effort. A look in the detective's face seemed to brace him. 'Not exactly friends,' he protested, a dry, metallic quality in his voice. 'No, I should certainly not go so far as to say that.'

The repudiation took both hearers by surprise. Jimson opened his mouth and his cigarette hung ludicrously from his lower lip. His teeth showed venomously.

'Jimson is not a nice person,' said Penny quietly. 'Confidentially, Sir Melton, I should describe him as the most contemptible rogue in London. Perhaps your association is—shall we say—a matter of business rather than friendship?'

'T-this ain't fair, Mr Penny,' whined Jimson. He had accepted the Scotland Yard man's contemptuous attitude towards him while they were alone together as a matter of course. But by his victims he was accustomed to be treated with either respect or fear after the first hot outburst. Penny's deliberate attempt to humiliate him had got under even his hardened skin. His painfully acquired grammar deserted him. 'This ain't fair,' he repeated.

'You may call it business,' said Sir Melton levelly.

Jimson glowered menacingly in his direction. 'You'd better be careful,' he snarled. 'You know what's likely to happen if you get fresh.'

Penny reached out an arm and gripped the little man's shoulder. He swung him to his feet and shook him fiercely. 'Cut it out,' he ordered sharply. 'You hear me. Drop it.' He pushed him back into his seat. 'Now you sit here for a while. I'm going out with this gentleman. We'll be back in an hour.'

'W-what's the g-game?' demanded Jimson.

'Never you mind. You'll know all about it soon enough. Come along, Sir Melton.'

*

Never a word did Penny say until they were down in the street. A baker's man was outside sitting idly on his hand-cart. With an apology to Tarson, the inspector passed swiftly over to him. Something passed from hand to hand.

'Find out who bought that and when,' said Penny. 'There's a manufacturer's name on it. It ought to help you.'

He returned to his companion. 'Shall we walk this way?' he said idly. 'I shall be glad if I can be of any help, Sir Melton. I've seen enough this last half-hour to convince me that I might be useful.'

Sir Melton twirled his cane. 'Thank you. Had I thought the police could help in any degree, I should have called upon them. It is a matter which must be settled with Jimson in other ways.'

'In plain English, you are afraid of the publicity if you were to prosecute him for blackmail.'

'Exactly.' Sir Melton threw away his half-finished cigarette. 'I don't see why I should deny it.'

'Listen to me,' said Penny persuasively. 'You know perfectly well what is to happen. You pay him once and you'll have to pay him a dozen or a score of times. I don't ask you to commit yourself if you would rather not. I'm not butting into this out of curiosity. If you have ever done anything illegal, keep your mouth shut. I don't want to know it. But if what he's holding over you is something of another kind—well, it might not be altogether necessary to prosecute him.'

A weary, amused smile broke over his companion's face. 'Isn't that a little unusual?' he remarked. 'I thought a high police official would be compelled to let the law take its course. Do you mean that you would be a party to patching up a crime?'

'I mean nothing of the sort. I can't arrest a man for blackmail, unless you agree to prosecute.'

'I see.' Tarson took two or three steps thoughtfully. 'I don't see why I shouldn't trust you,' he said suddenly.

'Not the least reason in the world,' agreed Penny cheerfully.

Sir Melton did not answer for a little. He seemed to be arranging his thoughts. 'You know I have a son in France,' he said at last, 'a boy about twenty-three—as good a lad as they make 'em.'

'Ah!' Penny sucked in his lips thoughtfully. A fresh light was beginning to break on him.

'A year or two ago there was an incident with a music-hall artiste—nothing in itself very serious, but he wrote her a few foolish letters. She kept those letters, and when she ran across him again just before he went to the front, she made the most of them. I was ill at the time and he did a foolish—indeed a criminal—thing. He was short of money and rather than run a risk he paid her by cheque for the return of the letters. That cheque was signed with my name.'

'Forgery?' Penny's tone was serious.

'Precisely. Forgery. Don't misunderstand me. He knew that had I been well he could have had the money without question. He was perfectly innocent of all intention of robbing anyone. In fact, the moment that my health allowed, he came to me with a clean breast and went at once to the bank. The cheque had never been presented. The girl—or those behind her—had guessed.'

'That sounds like Jimson. So I suppose they started to bleed *you* on the supposition that you would go to any risk rather than have the boy charged with forgery.'

'It would kill his mother—if she knew,' said Tarson simply. 'And it—it has hit me pretty hard.'

'Naturally. I'm glad I ran across you this morning, though I should have come to see you anyway. I begin to believe I can straighten it out for you. Will you wait for me a minute or so? I want to telephone.'

The minute or so lengthened to twenty before Penny emerged. He was smiling, and he was even disrespectful enough to clap Sir Melton on the back.

'That's all right,' he said. 'Now pull yourself together. I'm going to prescribe a stiff brandy and soda and then we'll get along and astonish Mr Jimson.'

He was in no particular hurry, however, and to Tarson, who, with tightened brows, was wondering what might be about to happen, he vouchsafed no further explanation. They sauntered back to Jimson's flat. Outside in Jermyn Street, Penny again engaged in private conversation with a man in whom Sir Melton failed to recognise the baker's roundsman of a little while before. Something again passed from hand to hand, and Penny rejoined Tarson, who headed for the steps of the entrance.

'Just a minute before you go in,' said the detective mildly. 'I hate to trouble you, but I would like you to pass over to me a new Colt automatic you are carrying. I am sure you don't intend anything rash, but it will perhaps be safer with me.' He held out his hand expectantly.

'I don't understand,' said Sir Melton icily. He had gone a trifle white.

'Come, it's plain enough,' said Penny impatiently. 'You bought it three days ago in the Strand. I know you have it on you. I am doing what I can for you, but I am not going to run any risks. That's sensible. Thank you. Now we can go in.'

It was not Jimson who admitted them to the flat, but a square-faced man who nodded confidentially to the inspector. 'It's all right,' he said. 'They're all here.'

'Good,' grunted Penny, and passed on.

In the sitting-room there were assembled besides Jimson half a dozen people. Some of them were obviously detectives. Sir Melton started as he met the gaze of Miss Gabrielle Yatdown. She was swathed in furs, and her cheeks were a dead white. A little away was an unshaven, surly-eyed man, whose presence also seemed to disturb Tarson. The only occupants of the room who did not seem restless were Penny and his subordinates.

'You boys can wait outside,' said Penny. 'This is going to be a little confidential conference. I'll call you if I want you.'

He closed and locked the door behind him. 'Now we can talk,' he said suavely. He nodded cheerfully to the sulky man. 'How do you do, Fred? Haven't seen you for donkey's years. Most of you know each other, I believe. The gentleman who looks as if he would like to eat me is Lightning Fred. I forget his other names, but he was well known in pugilistic circles some ten years ago—weren't you, Fred? He had a little misfortune—robbery with violence if I remember rightly. It was just about the time that he came out, that our friend, Mr Jimson, felt the lack of a trustworthy man-servant—a sort of combination of valet and chucker-out who could deal with any obstreperous clients who were beyond moral persuasion. As you see, Fred has more muscle than brain—a fact that perhaps weighed when Jimson selected him. Sit still, Jimson—don't interrupt.

'Now yesterday Jimson came to Scotland Yard. Someone had been threatening to murder him—more, they had in his opinion tried to carry out the threat. I hope, Sir Melton, you won't think it was because we considered his life worth saving. that we agreed to go into the matter. It was our mere duty to prevent murder. We knew that a great deal of misery would be averted if something did happen to him, and it was with a certain amount of sympathy for the opposition that I began the investigation.'

Sir Melton shifted uneasily. Miss Yatdown had pulled off one glove and was absently tearing at it with her fingers. Jimson sat flushed and nervous, and the toe of his patent leather shoe did a quick tattoo on the floor. Penny continued:

'I want to deal with Fred first. Now, yesterday morning he arranged an accident which resulted in Jimson's cat meeting with a quick and merciful death. That shook Jimson up a bit, for he lit on the incident as an attempt at poisoning. You were paid for that little bit of play-acting—eh, Fred?'

Fred scowled at the detective. 'O' course it wasn't meant to murder him, if that's what you mean. I—'

'Never mind. I'm doing the talking for a moment. Those letters must have got on Jimson's mind, for he next fancies someone had tried to push him under a motor. I guess that it was largely imagination. Anyway it riveted in his mind that someone had determined on his doom.

'He was so badly scared that he was taking no chances. He sent Fred away last night, taking his key from him. But for an astute man he made one error. He overlooked that Fred had had plenty of opportunities of having another key made. In fact, that was what happened. Fred could not resist a bribe. Am I right?'

Fred hesitated. 'All right, guv'nor,' he said at last. 'You know what you are talking about. It was . . .'

'Shut up. I guess you'd better wait outside for a while with some of the boys.' He unlocked the door and pushed the ex-pugilist out. Then he relocked it and smiled down at Jimson as he laid a dagger on the small Moorish table.

'The man whom the duplicate key was passed to bought this little toy. Can you guess who it was, Jimson? Or you, Miss Yatdown?'

The blackmailer pointed unsteadily to Tarson. 'Y—you! Y—you'll be sorry for this.' His face was yellow with passion. 'I—I'll see that boy of yours within four walls for this. Yes, and you'll be in it, too. Attempted murder m-means trouble you bet. You're a police officer, Mr Penny. Arrest that man.'

'I don't think so,' retorted Penny calmly. 'Wait a bit.'

The detective menaced Jimson with a stumpy forefinger. 'If you weren't angry you wouldn't be such a fool,' he continued. 'If Sir Melton here goes to gaol, what do you think's going to happen to the pair of you? Bite on that. You know something about law, Jimson. You'd be uncommonly lucky if you got less than seven years.' He thrust his face fiercely towards the blackmailer. 'Why, you little hound, I'm about inclined to let other people take their chance and to send you down anyway. Where's that cheque? Out with it quick before I change my mind.'

'I—I haven't g-got it,' Jimson whined. 'I-it's lost.' Then as Penny advanced on him menacingly, he pulled some keys from his pocket. 'All right, sir. Don't touch me. I'll let you have it.' He moved towards a safe that was shielded by a green curtain and unlocked it. From one of the inner drawers he produced a cheque and passed it to Penny who handed it to Tarson. Sir Melton tore it into fragments and pressed them down upon the fire.

As he was about to close the safe, Penny pulled him away. 'One minute, my lad. I want to look in there.'

'You g-got no right—' gulped Jimson, and found himself flung violently to the end of the room.

'Not the faintest right,' agreed Penny. 'I'm not worrying about rights today. Give me a hand here, Sir Melton.' One by one he went hastily through the packets of papers in the safe and passed them to Tarson who dropped them on the fire. Penny at last swung the heavy door to and attended to the blaze with the poker.

'That ought to do,' he observed with satisfaction. 'You can make a complaint to headquarters if you like, Jimson. Meanwhile, I'll see that you get a society paragraph in the papers—you'll like that, won't you?—saying that by a fire accident Mr Reginald Jimson has suffered the loss of many valuable documents. That'll relieve several people's minds. And Jimson—if I were you I'd clear out of the country. The next time we come after you we'll get you—see? And if I were you, Miss Yatdown, I'd stick to the stage in the future. It's less risky than this kind of get-rich-quick game. Good-morning. Coming, Sir Melton?'

Out in the street Tarson stretched out a hand to Penny. 'I can't say what I think,' he said. 'Believe me, I'm grateful. How you did it is beyond me.'

'I'm no Sherlock Holmes,' smiled Penny complacently, 'but

I'll own I did that rather neatly. Everything came my way, of course, though'—he grinned—'I didn't do what I set out to do.'

'What was that?'

'Land the man who was threatening Jimson in jail. It's a mighty serious thing to try to kill a man—even a crook. But all this is away from the point. There's been nothing very miraculous about it. When Jimson came to me yesterday, I hadn't the faintest idea how things were going to turn out. I put men on to one or two possible lines of inquiry and handled what seemed to be the most likely myself. It looked to me uncommonly as if a woman was at the bottom of it. I drew all the most obvious places without much luck. Then I learned that Gabrielle Yatdown had been seen with Jimson, and an idea entered my mind that you might be concerned. I knew you had been seen with Jimson, and it required no remarkable acuteness to judge what was happening when a man like yourself associated with a man like him. I tried to bluff Gabrielle, but she saw I was fishing and just laughed at me. So there I was up a gumtree.

'You were still a reserve possibility in my mind this morning, but I saw Jimson first. He was in a blue funk over the dagger trick, and it was then I got my first line on the case. I must have been muzzy not to think of it before. The whole thing was a frame-up from the inside—the mysterious letters put in his pocket, the spilling of the poisoned milk, the dagger through the desk—it was as clear as noon. More than that, the melodrama of the dagger showed that the whole murder business was a bluff. Someone wanted to frighten Jimson out of the country—quick. That meant somebody he's got his hooks into, and just as I'd made up my mind the answer came pat. You called on Jimson—I don't know what pretext you made, but it was clear that you had come to see how he took it.'

'I don't quite see—' interrupted Sir Melton.

'No. I'm coming to the other points. For one thing all the time I was with you, although you knew I was a police officer, you never evinced any curiosity as to my business. You knew what I was on.

'I had a man on observation outside Jimson's flat and when we went out I passed him the knife. With a manufacturer's name on it, it was perfectly simple to find out the retailers who handled it, and then get descriptions of recent purchasers—and one fitted you. You bought a Colt at the same time. Incidentally, I passed word to find Jimson's servant—no very difficult matter.

'When you told me your story of blackmail, I 'phoned through to the Yard to collect Gabrielle and Lightning Fred and bring them along to the flat.' He paused to light his pipe. 'What happened there, you know. It wasn't perhaps my strict duty, but still . . .'

XV

FOUND—A PEARL

In a snarling, twisting heap the three men rolled into the gutter. The half-dozen spectators, who quickly grew into forty or fifty, lifted no finger to help. They seemed, with that curious lack of initiative which so often seizes London crowds, to regard the fight as an abstract spectacle in which it would be impertinent to interfere.

Quex, overmatched and fighting with dynamic energy, wasted no breath in appeals for aid. He jabbed his elbow under one man's jaw and tore away a thumb that was pressing relentlessly on his eyeball. With a quick twist he became for a moment uppermost in the tangle. He had struggled to his knees before they again pulled him down, and, snapping like a wild dog, he felt his teeth meet in one man's hand.

A wolfish ejaculation of pain punctuated the grunts of the struggle, and a kick that would have smashed an ordinary man's ribs caught him in the chest. He went numb and sick and the vigour of his resistance relaxed. Someone in the crowd gave an involuntary cry as a knife flickered in the dim lamplight. He shut his eyes in helpless anticipation of the blow he could not avert.

'Where is it?' demanded a voice. 'It's your last chance—quick.'

He opened his eyes and laughed defiantly. 'I'll see you burn first,' he said with an oath. 'You'll swing for this—'

'Here's the police,' said a sharp voice from the crowd, and Quex felt the weight that was pressing him to the ground relax. His two assailants had pushed their way through the crowd and the quick sound of their footsteps was dying away in the distance ere a big constable had reached the prostrate man.

'What's all this?' he asked.

Quex sat up slowly and tried mechanically to brush the mud from his light coat. Someone picked up his battered hat and passed it to him. He accepted the officer's helping hand and rose dizzily to his feet.

'It's all right, constable,' he said quietly. 'Just a little joke of some friends of mine. They were having a game.'

'Game!' It was the shrill voice of a woman in the crowd. 'They were going to murder. I see a knife. If the pleece 'adn't come—'

'That's right,' interpolated half a dozen other voices.

The constable wheeled swiftly. He had observed the ruffled evening dress under Quex's overcoat and he was puzzled. He jerked a note-book out of his breast pocket.

'Queer thing it looks to me,' he commented. 'If you say it was a lark, I can't do anything. However, I'd better have your name and address, and you and you.' He indicated the woman who had spoken and another person. 'Now, sir.'

Quex frowned. He stooped forward as though to brush his coat, in reality to hide his hesitation. 'All right,' he said at last. 'John Blake, Hotel Splendid, will find me. Good-night, officer.' He strode abruptly away.

But it was not to the Hotel Splendid that he made his way. Once clear of the throng he hailed a taxi and gave an address at. Balham. He let himself in with a latch-key and went up to the sitting room of the furnished apartments he rented on the second floor. There he stretched himself in an armchair and felt himself tenderly.

'A close thing, John, my boy,' he said aloud. 'I oughta have carried a gatt. I didn't think they'd be so close on to me. Never mind—they didn't get it.'

He put his fingers casually in his waistcoat pocket and an epithet sprang from his lips as they came away empty. With furious haste he searched the rest of his pockets knowing all the time that it was hopeless.

'Gone!' he swore. 'Those blighters have done it!'

His lips compressed in a wicked straight line. Going through to the adjoining bedroom he pulled a suit-case from under the bed and rummaged till he found an automatic. Pressing it open he slipped in a clip of cartridges and flung the weapon on the bed while he proceeded to change out of his stained evening dress.

John Quex could be an ugly man when he was roused.

Garton, divisional detective inspector of the 13th division, was looked upon at headquarters as a coming man. He had some of the qualities with which the traditional detective is endowed, and more than that he had a complete understanding of the possibilities and limitations of the machinery of the Criminal Investigation Department. Where other men succeeded by dour determination and a steady remorseless sifting of facts, he had a genius for swiftly discarding non-essentials and putting through an investigation at a gallop. A hard, tenacious man, who would not swerve a hair's breadth from what he conceived his duty, he yet had a natural geniality which made him not disliked even among those whose sphere of operations was liable to be curtailed by his activities.

Being a business man it was his habit to drop office affairs punctually at six each evening unless there were special reasons for staying on. Between nine and ten he would drop in again on the off-chance of anything having arisen that needed immediate attention. So it was that he hit with little loss of time on the matter of the pearl.

He had been to the local variety show and in an interval strolled casually over to the station. In the uniformed inspectors' room he nodded genially to the senior man on duty.

'Nothing doing my way?' he observed.

The other shook his head. 'Nothing doing, Mr Garton. Bit

of a row down near the Green Dragon.' He closed a heavy folio book in which he had been writing and came over to the counter. 'Funny thing rather. Couple of roughs tried to lay out a man in evening dress—a real rough house until the man on the beat turned up. Two of 'em did a bolt leaving the third on the ground. He told our man it was a joke. All the same he'd been pretty badly beaten up, and the people in the crowd said they'd tried to knife him.' He moved to his desk and took out something which he passed to Garton. 'After he'd gone someone found this on the ground. If it's the real thing it's worth something, but I guess it's a fake.'

The detective examined the object with curiosity and an alert light leapt into his face.

'Say, Greig, this is a pearl all right, all right. Send it round to the jeweller's on the corner for me, will you, to make sure. I'd like someone to go and rake out a couple of my men—Hewitt and Blackson will do. Where's the constable who first got on to this?'

'On his beat. I'll have him fetched. You on to something?'

Garton smashed his hand down on the counter. 'If I'm any guesser that pearl is worth something running into thousands. I smell something in this, Greig. I really do.'

For a while things began to stir at the police-station. Garton hustled himself and his subordinates with cold enthusiasm. A hurried telephone call to the Hotel Splendid made certain that no guest named Blake was there and the local jeweller confirmed the genuineness of the pearl while diffidently hesitating to express a value. Garton had little use for intuitions and deductions while he was 'getting organised'.

In two hundred police-stations tape machines ticked out a report and inquiries. Men pored over the files of 'Informations' for any description of a missing pearl. Persons who had witnessed the fight near the Green Dragon were sought out and gave the usual vague and conflicting descriptions of the men concerned.

At half an hour before midnight Hewitt, Garton's right-hand sergeant, stretched his arms above his head and yawned wearily. 'It's a dead trail,' he observed. 'Can't see that we can do anything more tonight, sir. It isn't as if we were sure a robbery had been committed. For all we know there may be some quite natural explanation of the whole thing.'

Garton looked up from the 'Special Release Notices' he was studying. 'Sure thing you're getting tired,' he said a trifle acidly. 'Now I'm just getting interested. I couldn't rest with this on my mind. I want to know. Let's go take a walk. That'll freshen you up.'

Hewitt reached stiffly for his hat and coat. 'I'm no slacker, sir,' he retorted. 'All the same, I'd like to know what we *are* looking for.'

'Why,' said Garton with simplicity, 'for the man who dropped the pearl, of course.'

It was one thing to hunt John Quex; it was another to be hunted by him. He was barely forty and looked less; yet for the school in which he had graduated that was a ripe old age. There were few of his fraternity left. Sudden death in one form or another had cut the majority of them off. Some few had had their lives prolonged by long terms in penitentiaries; some like Quex had had the foresight to drop out of New York. On the whole, the career of a gunman in New York is not conducive to longevity.

Many years and much experience had passed over Quex's head since the days when he had been a champion among the 'strong arms' of the East Side. He had long learnt that patience and subtlety in crime were of more avail that the fiercest and quickest revolver fusillade. Yet he retained still some of the old instinct for battle.

His way led citywards. Suburban passengers on the electric car never dreamed that the neatly dressed man, quietly absorbed in an evening paper, was bound upon a murder quest. Why should they? He had neither the low forehead nor the big jaw of the desperado. A man less likely to make trouble never travelled from Balham.

At Blackfriars he changed for the Underground and when at last he emerged at Aldgate Station both hands were plunged deeply in his overcoat pockets and he walked alertly. His eyes dodged to and fro among the foot passengers, as a man who is determined not to be taken unawares.

Half a dozen times he twisted in and out of mean streets bordering the Commercial Road and at last came to a pause before a shabby three-storeyed house. It was noticeable that he used his left hand to knock and ring in a peculiar combination. His right hand was still deep in his pocket.

The door swung back creakily and an unshaven man in jersey and belted trousers peered at the visitor doubtfully for an instant.

'Hello, Dick,' said Quex amiably. 'How'd she go?'

'It's you, is it? Come along in. There's a little faro school upstairs. Y' know the way?'

Quex waited as the other shut the door. 'Seen anything of Big Mike tonight?' he asked.

Dick twisted the stub of an anaemic cigarette with his tongue. 'Sure. 'E's bin 'ere some time. Come in with Jimmie Alford.'

Quex clicked his tongue against his cheek and followed the door-keeper up to the first floor to a room thick with tobacco smoke. At the top of a long table a squint-eyed man in shirt sleeves presided at a faro 'lay-out'. His eyes flickered momentarily to the newcomer and he nodded dispassionately. Then he turned a fresh card. No one else was interested enough in the visitor to raise a head.

Quex was smiling as he moved towards the table. He touched a stockily built man who was sitting by the operator on the shoulder.

'Well, Mike,' he said in a hard metallic voice. 'I've come after you, you see.'

The man he addressed swerved round, fists clenched, and

his chair toppled over with a crash. Quex had taken two paces backwards and his pistol showed in his hand. He was still smiling.

'Didn't expect me, didn't you?' he went on. 'Keep where you are, you lumbering stiff, or I'll bump you off just now. And you, Jimmie Alford, don't you move. I was an easy mark an hour or two ago, wasn't I? I fell for you, didn't I?'

There was something more than consternation in the faces of the two men to whom he spoke. Mike was a picture of surprise. His mouth gaped and his bleary eyes watched the muzzle of the weapon as though fascinated.

The keeper of the gambling house recovered his wits first. 'Here, that don't go here, Jack,' he remonstrated. 'Put that gun away. If you've got any difference with these gents you settle it somewhere else.'

'Don't you bat in on this, Soapy,' advised Quex sharply. 'I'm talking to my old partners there.' His eyes were glowing though his speech was soft enough. 'Now Mike, what about it?'

Mike made no answer. Like Quex he had been reared in a school where resource was everything. The why or how of Quex's appearance had little immediate concern for him. The gas, for reasons which every gambling house keeper will appreciate, was close to the dealer's hand. Mike's arm scarcely seemed to move and in an instant the place was in blackness. Almost in the same movement he dropped forward on hands and knees like a runner at a starting point.

Two vivid splashes of flame split the blackness and there was a cry from the panic-stricken punters. They were used to fists, to heavy tongued belts—even to knives on occasion—but gun-play was carrying a dispute too far. Mike leapt towards the flashes like a panther, a wicked sheath-knife in his hand. He struck viciously at emptiness and cautiously flattened himself out again. The tense breathing, the hurried shuffling of men's feet ceased.

Uncertain whether his adversary might still be waiting in the darkness with weapon poised, Mike lay still, every muscle tense. Heavy footsteps at last sounded on the stairs and someone within the room scraped a match. The gas flared up and Mike rose to his feet. Soapy dropped the match from between his fingers.

'Can you beat that?' he said helplessly. 'Can you beat it?'

At the table Alford was leaning forward, his hand pressed to his left shoulder. The groan he had repressed while there was a danger of a recurrence of the firing now broke from his lips.

'He got me, Mike,' he said. 'The dog got me.'

They were the only three left in the room. Without the formality of a knock the door was thrust open. A huge figure seemed to fill the room and behind loomed the form of a uniformed constable.

Soapy tried to smile ingratiatingly. 'It's all right, Mr O'Reilly,' he said with suave huskiness. 'There ain't nothin' wrong.'

O'Reilly had been too long a detective in the East End to waste words. 'So you say,' he agreed. 'That's why those other blokes ran out. Who's been doing the shooting up?' His eyes rested on the faro box. 'Anyway, we'll take you along. We'd been wondering where you'd pitched your faro joint for a long time, Soapy.'

There are lucky detectives as there are lucky generals, and Garton was usually kissed by the imp of fortune in any campaign he undertook. If his luck was analysed, however—a matter in which critics never took trouble—it would usually be found to have a background of brains and work. He had reflected that whether the men concerned in the affray were honest men or crooks there might be some significance in the proximity of the Green Dragon. So it was that with the reluctant Hewitt by his side he happened into the saloon of that hostelry ten minutes before closing time and leaning on the counter put the usual question to his aide.

'Mine's a Scotch,' said Hewitt.

'Why, here's Phyllis,' said Garton. He winked at the girl behind the bar. 'How are you, my dear? Do you still love me or have you trampled on another heart? Let's have two Scotches, Phyllis.'

The girl behind the bar giggled. 'Go on with you.'

'She gives me the boot,' lamented Garton. 'Hewitt, my life is ruined.' He caught her hand as she placed the drinks in front of him. 'Phyllis, did you ever have your fortune told?' He traced a line on her palm with his finger. 'Now listen. There's a fair man and a dark man—'

She tried to wrench her hand away. 'Don't be silly,' she protested. 'It'll be closing time in a minute and you'll have to go without your drinks.'

'Never mind the drinks,' persisted the inspector. 'If you don't believe I can read fortunes I'll prove it to you. Take tonight. At about nine o'clock there were two men here—or was it three?' He appeared to study the palm intently. 'I can't quite make it out. Anyway one of 'em was a particular pal of yours—a man in the jewellery line.' He was no longer watching her hand but her face. She had changed colour and suddenly wrenched her hand free.

'It's all nonsense,' she declared stiffly. 'And anyway it's closing time.'

'All right, Phyllis, we're going,' said Garton lightly. He lifted his hat. 'Good-night, my dear. See you again soon.'

Outside Hewitt shrugged his shoulders grimly. 'For a family man, sir, if I may say so, you made the going there,' he commented. 'I don't quite get the idea.'

'I'd hate to be without you sometimes,' said Garton evasively. 'Why, Hewitt, didn't you see the ring that girl was wearing? Look here, I'm afraid it's too late after all to push our luck tonight but bright and early tomorrow morning I want that girl's name, the post-mark of all the letters she gets, and the names and addresses on all the letters she sends out. Get me.

You can handle it yourself or put young Wren on it if you like, but it's got to be done.'

'Very good, sir,' said Hewitt formally.

By what means Garton's instructions were carried out he never knew nor did he trouble to inquire. It was wisest to take for granted that they were lawful. Anyway Hewitt had produced from somewhere a list of two letters which had gone out and of one that had been received. The out-going letters had been addressed—one to 'John Quex, Esq., 5 Spanish Grove, Balham', the other to 'Mrs Boswell, 33 Hodson's Lane, Leytonstone'.

'Girl's name's Boswell' observed Hewitt. 'There was only one letter for her by the first post. I left Wren there to pick up anything else.'

'John Quex!' repeated Garton thoughtfully. 'Know the name, Hewitt? I don't.'

'No, sir. There was a play or something with a name like it once.'

'If I'm right he should be a useful man to know more about. In this kind of case, Hewitt, where there's nothing tangible to go on, we can only jump to conclusions and be thankful for any fact that they lead us to. We'll have a man go down to Spanish Grove and I'll come along later myself if things seem all right.'

There is always a certain amount of routine work that has to be dealt with by a divisional chief of detectives whatever major investigation he has in hand, and for an hour Garton put the pearl case out of his mind. Though the report of the wounded man found at an East End gambling house, whose companions told a cock and bull story of an accident, came under his official notice, he failed to connect it with the pearl ease. What interested him more was a special communication from headquarters.

'The pearl you have sent on for expert examination corresponds to the description of one stolen by a trick from the establishment of a M. Rouget at Amsterdam three weeks ago, of which no report had hitherto been received. It is valued at £5,000. It was sent to an hotel in charge of an assistant to be viewed by a man calling himself Alfred Rockerbilt, who posed as an American millionaire. The assistant was stunned, gagged and left in a bedroom while his assailants decamped. Amsterdam authorities believed assistant's story a bogus one and have him under arrest. No descriptions of supposed robbers to hand yet. Have cabled for further particulars.'

Garton chuckled softly to himself. 'That puts that point in order. I think I can begin to see something like daylight.' He poked his head into the adjoining room used by his staff. 'Say, one of you boys cut down to the Green Dragon. There's a barmaid there named Boswell. I want her brought up here right away.'

It was an unwilling and somewhat frightened girl who presently entered Garton's dingy little office. She looked startled as she beheld in the divisional chief the man who, on the previous evening, she had thought to be a slightly fresh business man. His cold keen face was stern as he nodded towards a chair.

'Sit down, my girl. You didn't expect to see me again so soon.'

She gingerly took the edge of the chair. Her fingers fluttered nervously. 'No—no, sir.'

'Now don't get frightened. There's nothing at all to be alarmed about. I just want to ask you one or two questions. You know a gentleman named Mr Quex, don't you?'

'No, sir.' Her voice was bolder now though her eyes avoided his.

'You don't, eh? Then how was it you sent him a letter this morning? Come, my girl, don't play with me.'

She shrugged her shoulders a little impudently. Her self-possession was coming back to her. 'Very well. If you knew, what did you ask me for?'

'I know a great deal. You'll be wise if you believe me. He gave you that diamond ring you're wearing, didn't he?'

His manner dissipated any vague idea the girl might have formed of defying him. 'Yes, sir,' she agreed.

'I see. Now how long ago was it that you first met him?'

'About four months. He came into the saloon and—'

'He's told you what he is?'

'Oh, yes. Besides, you know. You said so last night. He's a jewel merchant and he's going to marry me when—in a month or two.'

'H'm. Had you arranged to meet him yesterday?'

She shook her head. 'No. He's away from home a lot and he drops in at the Dragon sometimes when he gets back.'

'You've got a photograph of him, of course?'

She hesitated. His fingers drummed impatiently on his desk. 'I—I'm not sure—that is, I believe I have,' she admitted unwillingly.

'Ah, good. Now Miss Boswell, I'll send someone with you and you'll let us have it.' He crossed over and dropped a hand gently on her shoulder. 'And see here, there's no reason for you to worry. If this man's what I think you've had a narrow escape. That'll do for now. I'll have another talk some other time.'

'So Mr Quex is a jewel merchant, eh?' he muttered aloud as she went out. 'Well, jewel merchants may fall in love with pretty barmaids and they may give 'em diamond rings that cost £200 if they cost a penny, but—' He ran a hand through his thick black hair. 'However, we'll wait till we see that photograph.'

Twenty minutes later he was surveying with elation the portrait in profile of a handsome man with iron-grey hair and a firm jaw. He carried it triumphantly to the outer office and laid it in front of Hewitt.

'Have I got to send that up to the Criminal Record Office or can you tell me who that is?'

Hewitt made a prolonged, steady scrutiny of the photograph. His memory had been trained to recall faces over long years. 'Why,' he said slowly, 'it reminds me uncommonly of that chap—it's five years since I saw him and I forget his right moniker—Slim Jack, isn't it?'

'If you say so,' grinned Garton. 'Only the name he's known by in respectable circles nowadays is—Mr John Quex. Now, Hewitt, we've got to get busy. You'll have to go down to the Yard.'

The simplicity with which the hatchety-faced detective hero of fiction is apt to lay the guilty person by the heels once he has been identified is quite a different thing to the care with which the most humdrum Scotland Yard man makes sure of his prey before springing a trap. Garton wanted not only Quex but his confederates. The methods by which they were to be disclosed involved a certain degree of co-operative work familiar to every detective bureau in the world but no special mental brilliance. He sent another man down to Balham to aid in keeping an eye on the main quarry, and Hewitt boarded a car for Scotland Yard.

There, in the Criminal Record Office, was a dossier that told all available facts, gained over many years in many quarters of the world, of Quex's activities. It was embellished by full and side face photographs and the key number to his finger-prints. In that record now lay the germ of the investigation, for upon it were based inquiries by word of mouth, by telephone, by letter. It would have been wonderful if among the hundred closely organised detectives of London, Quex and his associates had entirely escaped notice.

Then it was that a telephone call from Hewitt had sent Garton on a flying visit to Brixton Prison where three prisoners remanded that morning in connection with an East End gambling house case were due to arrive. Somewhere in the prison he spent two active hours—hours that would have caused John Quex considerable uneasiness if he had known of them.

But John Quex for all his experience did not know. He was

sitting in bed a mile or two away smoking a cigarette and reading the morning paper. He wasn't sure whether he had killed a man overnight but he hoped he had. He had all the philosophy of the veteran professional. Today was a new day. He had taught Mike Alford that he was a man not to be interfered with with impunity. If he had failed and they still held up the pearl he could still show them that he was a live wire.

So he read the paper placidly, his conscience easy, his nerves unwrung. It was midday and a savoury smell of cooking from below heralded breakfast. He slipped languidly out of bed, strolled to the window and raised the blind. His eyebrows contracted as he peered out.

'Hell!' he muttered viciously.

Yet the casual observer would have noticed nothing to warrant the expletive. It was an ordinary suburban street like thousands of other streets in London—that was why Quex had pitched his tent there. A baker's cart was ambling along the roadway, and a maid was cleaning the steps of one of the houses opposite. At an oblique angle to Quex some distance away on the far pavement two men were talking. These it was who interested the crook.

He drew back, his brow furrowed, and hurriedly began to dress. If those two idlers were really detectives—and he had small doubt of it—someone at the gambling house must—as he would have put it—have 'squealed'. Possibly he had after all killed Mike or Alford. There was that much satisfaction in the situation anyway.

As he adjusted his tie a sound caught his ear—a sound so trivial that at any other time with senses less alert he would have failed to hear it. He dropped into a chair, and placing something in his lap picked up the discarded newspaper.

He raised his eyes in mild astonishment as the door was pushed swiftly open. One hand grasped the thing under the paper.

'Well,' he demanded irritably. 'Who are you? What do you

mean by bursting in on a man like this?' And then his tone suddenly changed. 'Ah, keep off, will you.' The newspaper dropped and an automatic flew to a level.

Neither Garton nor Hewitt were novices in this kind of thing. They knew the type of man with whom they had to deal and wasted no time in parley. They had spread out to either side as they entered and it was with the recognition that they meant business that Quex's opening bluff had changed to defiance.

Garton stood stock still. The muzzle of the pistol was near enough to him to make sudden death a certainty should the crook's finger compress on the trigger. He was as brave as most men but he was not foolish. Besides, their tactics had carried Hewitt out of the line of fire.

Quex became aware of the sergeant's rush just half a second too late. He swerved in his chair and the pistol exploded harmlessly as Hewitt's muscular arms sought his throat. He was borne backwards and as he fell someone kicked the pistol out of his hand.

Three minutes later he was on his feet again with handcuffs encircling his wrists and Garton was dusting the knees of his trousers.

'You've got no sense, Jack,' complained Hewitt peevishly. 'You might have killed someone with that gun of yours.'

Quex grinned. Now that it was all over he was without malice. 'You guys would have stood a fat chance if I'd known you were after me earlier. I'd like to know what I'm pinched for anyway?'

'You will be charged with the attempted murder of a man named Alford,' said Garton.

'That all? I hoped I had croaked one of those ginks.'

'Also,' went on the inspector, 'there is an application from the Dutch police for your extradition for stealing a pearl.'

'No!' Quex's jaw dropped. 'I suppose Alford snitched on that too. Did he say that Mike and he have got that pearl laid up?'

Garton's face never changed. 'No,' he declared. 'It wouldn't be likely, would it? But what's the use of all this talk? You know anything you say may be used as evidence against you.'

'I reckon I can't do myself much more harm. If that little snipe can uncork so can I. Listen here.'

Over dinner that night with a colleague of the C.I.D. Garton talked with pardonable triumph. 'If some of those writer chaps put this in a yarn it mightn't sound much,' he confessed, 'but believe me, it's the longest shot I ever pulled off. You should have seen Jack's face when I told him that he had lost the pearl in the rough and tumble and that his pals hadn't had it at all.

'Of course it was a bad start when at first we couldn't tell where the thing had come from. I'd have bet my next six month's salary that the thing had been stolen but it looked like a dead end, especially as none of the descriptions we got of the three men who had been fighting corresponded. It was one of those off-chance ideas that took Hewitt and me to the Green Dragon where I surmised that one or the other of the men concerned might have been during the evening. When I noticed that the barmaid was wearing a ring that must have been worth a couple of hundred, I began to think things. That the pearl should have been picked up at hand and that she should have such costly trinkets and that neither of the events should be connected was too much of a coincidence to swallow.

'Still I didn't know and I didn't want to commit myself till I was dead sure that a robbery had taken place somewhere. She was a pretty girl and I played with her a bit on a theory I manufactured for the occasion. It was clear that she had a lover who could afford expensive presents—and I managed to get his name and address without her knowing. You don't want to ask me how I did it.

'From then on things were like clockwork. In the morning

came the news of this Dutch robbery which put me on safer ground. I dug a photograph out of the girl and of course recognised Slim Jack. It began to look like a clean-up. A little inquiry showed that he had been seen about with Big Mike and Jim Alford, and that the three of 'em were absent from London when the Amsterdam affair was pulled off. I don't need to tell you that that was no evidence against 'em in a court of law, but as a moral certainty it was good enough for us.

'Then it seems Mike and Jimmie were collared in a gambling joint where somebody had shot the little man up. That didn't need a Sherlock, did it? It was as plain as paint that there'd been a quarrel over the pearl. The other two knew that Jack was mushy on the barmaid and hung about to get a chance at him. They had a rough and tumble in the roadway and were interrupted. None of 'em was too anxious to stop and answer questions, and Jack, who spilled the pearl in the gutter somehow, thought the others had it. That was how he came to invite himself to a little shooting party—see!

'Of course I was on to Mike like a bird. Both he and Alford were sore with Jack but they were cautious. They didn't tell me very much that I didn't already know and I wasn't too sure that the Dutch police would be able to send over witnesses to identify them. But I had got an idea.

'When we went to get Jack we didn't take any chances with the rough stuff. He was ready to eat out of my hand by the time we'd got the handcuffs on. I flashed the extradition charge on him suddenly and he fell for it. He didn't know that we had the pearl and he dropped into the error of thinking his pals had talked. When a crook like that gets in that frame of mind practically everything is over.

'He told me how the job was pulled off on the other side and that the three made a getaway in different directions. To avoid risks in case they were suspected the pearl was posted to Jack's address. He had some idea of taking it over to the

States to get rid of it; the others wanted to sell it here. They didn't trust him too much. Well, it seems he told them that he'd got the thing and he was going to do as he darned well pleased. I suppose they thought that to leave it to him would make their chances of getting a bit mighty small in the end. That started the whole thing.'

'A good case, old man,' commented his friend.

'I believe you,' said Garton.

THE END

THE DETECTIVE STORY CLUB

FOR DETECTIVE CONNOISSEURS

recommends

"The Man with the Gun."

The Murder of Roger Ackroyd

By AGATHA CHRISTIE

THE *MURDER OF ROGER ACKROYD* is one of Mrs. Christie's most brilliant detective novels. As a play, under the title of *Alibi*, it enjoyed a long and successful run with Charles Laughton as the popular detective, Hercule Poirot. The novel has now been filmed, and its clever plot, skilful characterisation, and sparkling dialogue will make every one who sees the film want to read the book. M. Poirot, the hero of many brilliant pieces of detective deduction, comes out of his temporary retirement like a giant refreshed, to undertake the investigation of a peculiarly brutal and mysterious murder. Geniuses like Sherlock Holmes often find a use for faithful mediocrities like Dr. Watson, and by a coincidence it is the local doctor who follows Poirot round and himself tells the story. Furthermore, what seldom happens in these cases, he is instrumental in giving Poirot one of the most valuable clues to the mystery.

The Death of a Millionaire

By G. D. H. & M. COLE

THIS is one of the most baffling and ingenious detective novels in which G.D.H. and Margaret Cole have collaborated. Hugh Radlett was one of the richest men in the United States. After a breach with his wife he disappeared, and was heard nothing of for several years. Then he turned up again in London, coming from Russia, where, with his partner, John Pasquett, he had fixed up a great mining concession with the Soviet Government. The morning after his arrival his suite at the hotel is found in disorder, with all the signs of a violent struggle. An eyewitness, discovered under curious circumstances, deposes to having seen the murderer and Radlett's dead body. But the body cannot be found, and the man suspected of the crime, a Russian named Rosenbaum, has left before the discovery with a heavy trunk. How did Hugh Radlett die, and what has become of his body?

LOOK FOR THE MAN WITH THE GUN

THE DETECTIVE STORY CLUB

FOR DETECTIVE CONNOISSEURS

recommends

"The Man with the Gun."

AN ENTIRELY NEW

EDGAR WALLACE

The Terror

THE NOVEL OF THE MOST SUCCESSFUL DETECTIVE PLAY OF RECENT YEARS

EDGAR WALLACE, greatest of all detective writers, has given us, in *The Terror*, one of his most amazing thrillers, packed with dramatic incident and breathless suspense. A sensational success as a play, it has been made into as exciting a film, and now comes the book to provide hours of wonderful reading for all who enjoy a first-rate detective story in Edgar Wallace's characteristic style. Follow the unravelling of the mystery of the lonely house throughout whose dark corridors echoed the strange notes of an organ. Where did it come from and who played it? Whose was the hooded form which swept down in the night unseen upon its prey and dragged its victim to destruction? Follow the clues as suspicion moves from one inmate of that strange house to another. Experience a thrill on every page, until the biggest thrill of all comes with the solution of the mystery. *The Terror* proves, once again, that there are many imitators—but only *one* Edgar Wallace!

LOOK FOR THE MAN WITH THE GUN

THE DETECTIVE STORY CLUB

FOR DETECTIVE CONNOISSEURS

"The Man with the Gun."

recommends

THE PERFECT CRIME

THE FILM STORY OF

ISRAEL ZANGWILL'S famous detective thriller, THE BIG BOW MYSTERY

A MAN is murdered for no apparent reason. He has no enemies, and there seemed to be no motive for any one murdering him. No clues remained, and the instrument with which the murder was committed could not be traced. The door of the room in which the body was discovered was locked and bolted on the inside, both windows were latched, and there was no trace of any intruder. The greatest detectives in the land were puzzled. Here indeed was the perfect crime, the work of a master mind. Can you solve the problem which baffled Scotland Yard for so long, until at last the missing link in the chain of evidence was revealed?

LOOK OUT

FOR FURTHER SELECTIONS FROM THE DETECTIVE STORY CLUB—READY SHORTLY

LOOK FOR THE MAN WITH THE GUN